DEVIL'S BREAKFAST

Devil's Breakfast

By
Kevin Leicinger

DEVIL'S BREAKFAST

It had all been leading to this. The murders. My vengeance. The rejections and humiliations I had spent a lifetime enduring. In that moment, I finally understood. Well, not that first moment. At first I was really, really, confused. But then, after. After it all settled a bit and I had some time to think about everything. It was then when I realized how my entire existence was about that moment in the farm house. A moment I had always, somehow, sensed but never been able to make concrete. And there it was, clear as day. My time had come.

I watched as Karen removed a package surrounded by dry ice. It was a glass test tube. The way she and all her little terrorist buddies looked at it, I expected a tiny unicorn or hundreds of angels to be in it or something. This group of people that thought nothing of risking their lives and facing unimaginable pain at the hands of the government seemed astounded and frightened by the contents of the test tube. Terrified even. Which was all the more strange because she held it up directly in front of me and what I saw was this. Nothing. It was empty. A sealed empty test tube. No unicorns. No angels. Not even some sort of powder. I took it from Karen and looked at it even more closely. It was only after a second had passed that I realized that the act of passing me the test tube was as if I had been handed the Royal Scepter by Karen and her followers. Emperor Daniel L. Hastings.

They looked at me and waited for me to react. In all honesty, it was quite awkward. They clearly expected something. Some answer from me that I acknowledged the seriousness of the moment. Unfortunately, all I could get out of my mouth was a mumble. They didn't understand what I said. So, I repeated it more loudly and more clearly. "I said "thanks."" Karen seemed stunned. "Thanks?" she asked. "That's all you have to say is "thanks"? A different look came over her face. It was an expression I knew very, very well. I had been seeing it when others interacted with me since I was a small child. It was a look of pity and disappointment. This was not going as Karen and her comrades had planned.

"Don't you understand what you have in your hand?" she asked. It seemed like a ridiculous question. Clearly I didn't have a clue. "It is the end of history as we know it. The beginning of a new dawn. Everything will change after you release its contents. Everything..." She said the last "everything" with enough drama in her voice to win an acting award or two, totally milking every syllable of it for maximum effect. It was very impressive. The others all nodded and silently agreed that this empty test tube was a very big deal. Huge in fact. But I still wasn't getting it.

I finally came out and just asked. "I'm sorry, Karen. I'm really not following you. What, exactly is it? I mean, I'm totally for world changing and all. At least I think I am. But I'm not seeing how this empty test tube really does all that much. I mean..., there's nothing in here from..." I started to twist off the cap of the vile. I mean, I wasn't really going to open it. How dumb would that be? Alright, maybe I was. I wasn't exactly thinking straight at that moment. Either way, shouts and gasps and other expressions of panic erupted. Karen grabbed my arm. "What are you doing?!" Oops. She was pissed. "That took us years to produce and cost us the lives of dozens of people. We had agents undergo agony beyond your imagination protecting that. And you just want to open it up?!" She snatched the vile out of my hand. "Clearly, I misjudged you."

Once again I had proven true to form. I mean, what could I say to that? "Yes, yes I think you did. I have no idea what you are talking about and think you're all pretty nuts. But you're hot, Karen. Really, damn, amazingly hot. And nuts can be good in bed so..." No, I didn't say that. I didn't say much of anything. Either did Karen or anyone else.

It appeared my job was done. It was time to quietly try to slink away from the scene of the crime. Twelve feet from my chair to the door and away from all those horrible looks. Her horrible look. Never had twelve feet felt so long. Nobody tried to stop me. As I reached the door, I looked Karen in those big brown eyes of hers and actually had to turn away. Whatever I had done, or had not done, had clearly upset her. It was as if her cat had died or something. Tears for Fluffy. And I was the cat killer.

"I don't understand any of this" I mumbled. She responded angrily. "Don't understand what? Why, in spite of all the fear, panic and disruption it might cause, why this absolutely, positively, must happen? Or why you, Dan, out of all the people on the planet, were chosen for this task?" She was making this even worse. If I was confused before, I was pretty much as lost as I could get about then.

I turned to her and just blurted it out. "What the hell are you talking about? What task? Is there something in the vile that's microscopic and kills people? You want me to murder thousands of people for your cause? Is that what I'm not getting?" Oh crap. Now that I had said it, I realized that's what they were asking me to do. They wanted me to release some horrible poison into the air to kill everyone.

It was my turn to be disappointed. I think about killing people all the time. The guy that cut in front of me at the coffee place, for instance. But really doing it. Not my thing. Not my thing at all. I mean, I actually have killed one or two people. But that was different. It's not like a regular thing I do. How could Karen think that of me? "I don't kill innocent people" I said. Rather perfectly in tone, too, I might add. Serious. Stern. Weighty. But not too pretentious. I kind of rocked sometimes, if I did say so myself. "Not people" Karen replied with an almost equally impressive delivery. "God. We want you to kill God."

I need to backtrack a bit here. First of all, no matter what was said in this meeting it would have been a bit weird. You see, Karen was the leader of a group called "The Clear Thinkers." They were considered highly annoying by the government. Not threatening. Not dangerous. Just really irritating. Brief kidnapping incident aside, up until this point they were known mainly for doing things like going to the Central Church and hanging a placard under the crucifix that said...ready?, "His Name Was Bob." You wouldn't think that would offend people or set them off. Confuse them, maybe, but it's not exactly like swearing at someone now, is it? "His Name Was Bob." See, according to the press release. There was one, of course, written by Karen to explain this act of desecration, "Christ is nothing more than fiction. This fictional creation, the Lord and Savior of mankind, can therefore be anything we chose. And we, the Clear Thinkers, choose to name him Bob."

I'm still not sure I understand, honestly. But they were making fun of things that shouldn't be made fun of. The Committee did not find such mocking of the official faith appropriate. Whatever questions people had about faith and God and Christ and all that good stuff they kept to themselves. Those that did otherwise were sought out and imprisoned or re-educated until they saw the light. Most citizens just went with it. It really wasn't worth the effort to get into when more important matters like making the rent had to be taken care of.

The point is, this "His Name Was Bob" thing annoyed the government but was way too lofty and confusing to have much impact on the general population. They saw it on the news and wondered who Bob was and what he had to do with the Church. The Clear Thinkers' press release was largely buried by the government. And as far as the people that did get a hold of it, they just thought the whole thing was kind of silly.

There was one journalist who saw it and blogged about how brilliant it was. About how it questioned the very foundation of religion, government and the relationship between the two. I actually read it. I can't say I really understood what he was going on about. Which is a real shame if most people that read the blog reacted the way I did. Especially, because the aforementioned journalist was tracked down and killed shortly afterward.

The fact was that Karen and the Clear Thinkers had been known for this "Bob" thing and not a whole lot else. Well, that kidnapping. But other than that. How exactly they got from that to "Let's Kill God" is a bit of a story. What's even more of a story is exactly how I, Daniel L. Hastings, ever got involved with the whole thing.

It all started one night when I got a call about a homicide. Not as unusual an event as one might think in my nightly routine. You see, I was a Police Inspector. Not just an Inspector, but a Chief Inspector. A Chief Inspector for The

People's Protection Agency. The Feds. The Big Boys. People would see me arrive on the scene and quake in their boots. Yeah. I was "The Man" with a capital "M." The face of the law in all its confusing, random, violent, "you'd better watch your step" glory. I have to admit, I kind of liked that part of it. It was certainly a head trip knowing that a few words from me could land somebody in an interrogation camp for the rest of their lives. I'd be scared of me too, knowing I could do that.

Of course, the flip side was that, as a Chief Inspector, I could lose favor with certain people and end up in such a camp myself. Such things occurred fairly rarely but with just enough frequency to make sure we didn't step out of line ourselves. It was a reminder to us to do our jobs and do them well but to never, ever, let our personal viewpoints, personalities or reputations overshadow that of the Party or Church. Not really caring much about such things, I was perfect for the job. I reached my esteemed position at the relatively young age of forty-one.

But back to this homicide case I was referring to... It was about four A.M. when I got the call. The Ring Road was empty and I was able to make the drive out to Halmen Estates in about twenty-minutes. Since I was alone on the drive I put the radio on for the trip and found myself listening to Aretha Franklin's early gospel music. The lyrics were deemed somewhat offensive to the official doctrine and there were those that tried to get such music banned. However, more than one party official was an Aretha Franklin fan and decided to let the infraction slide. A man's got to get his groove on.

I was almost disappointed to arrive so quickly at the scene of the crime. I was really enjoying my music. But duty called and I slowly weaved my way through the squad cars with their lights flashing. The driveway was a long, winding affair up a large hill. There was a gate and a large lawn. Whoever lived here was somebody with a bit of money and a lot of connections. That whole part of St. Dons was reserved for party loyalists, government officials and young blond actresses. I won't even bother getting into how that particular mix came about. But it was an interesting section of the city, to say the least.

There were the usual looks and whispers as I drove up to the front of the mansion. The thing was huge but looked like it was made out of cardboard. It was easily ten thousand square feet and, believe it or not, had Cherubs attached to the roof. Fat, little, piggy-looking angels with bows and arrows that were hung like gargoyles. Personally, I'd have liked another one of a griffin eating one of those fat little suckers, but that's just me.

It started to rain. I tried to think of how impressive that made me look. "Chief Inspector Daniel L. Hastings walked from his sedan. The wet cement reflected the flashing lights of the squad cars as he made his way through the cold, pounding rain." It didn't work. It was nasty outside. Really foul. I covered my head and ran inside like a little school girl. I would have much preferred still being home, alone, in bed. For all the coolness and power trippy-ness that came with being a Chief Inspector, it could really be a pain in the ass.

I was let into the foyer by a uniformed officer. Overhead was a backlit, stained glass dome. The subject of this massive dome glasswork was none other than the same sort of fat looking cherubs that had adorned the exterior. It occurred to me that I might have just walked into a large and expensive brothel. But no such luck. The gold gilded furniture and white fur rugs were actually someone's personal taste. The taste of the person now slumped over their kitchen table with a gun in their hand and a good chunk of their head gone.

This was the problem. I mean, aside from the obvious one that a guy is sitting at the kitchen table dead. Whoever the dead man was, he was somebody big. If not, he wouldn't have lived in the horrible monstrosity of a house in an even more horrible part of town. The second part of the complication was that, officially speaking, it was not his life to take. He had done a big no no. Very big, in fact.

Church doctrine was pretty clear that if you committed suicide you went to hell and had all sorts of very bad things happen to you for eternity. Which was enough to keep a good chunk of the potentially suicidal populace afraid to actually do the deed. However, there was a significant amount of people that were so depressed and in such emotional pain they really couldn't grasp the idea of an afterlife being worse than anything that they were already experiencing. So, they went ahead and did it anyway. It was because of these, "fine, whatever, go ahead and send me to hell" people that a subsection was added to The Sanctity of Life laws. Not only would the person evil enough to kill themselves go to hell, all their assets would be forfeited to the State. Moreover (I can't believe I just used that word. Sorry.). Moreover, the relatives of the person who had killed themselves would also forfeit all their assets. In theory, they could even face murder charges for not intervening and preventing the heretical act.

In short, killing yourself was a big deal. Not only to you, the deceased, but to your parents, spouse and children. One unintended consequence of this was that many a gloomy teenager who were angry at their parents just loved the fact they could screw them over by offing themselves. So, for several years, teen suicide rates actually increased. It was only when the courts were allowed to disregard these acts of revenge and waive such penalties that the suicide rates returned to their normal, pre-Sanctity of Life levels.

The good news in this case was that the victim, or technically, perpetrator, was no Goth-loving teenager. He was a man well into his fifties. According to the briefing officer, the perp/victim's name was Robert San Sebastian. He had lived alone in this horrible house of his for three years. No record of a spouse. When I asked about any sort of work identification, the officer said he hadn't seen any but hadn't searched the house, yet. He wanted to make sure I was present and that he had my OK before doing so.

I thanked the officer for his good work and took a closer look at my friend missing a chunk of his head. It looked like he had held the gun up to his temple and pulled the trigger. I was thankful he had not been one of those morons who put the gun in his mouth and sent a bullet through his face or neck and then still managed to survive. Those idiots cost the State a lot of money between their special medical needs and the cost of their re-education.

The gun was new. Probably legally purchased at the Guns Express down on the Boulevard. I'd have the permit checked but it wouldn't have much information on it other than the man's name and address. Robert San Sebastian. What sort of name is that, anyway?

A quick walk down the personal quarters wing of the house led me to his bedroom. There had been an attempt to make the place feel more masculine by having animal heads mounted on the wall. The "macho, world-traveling hunter" look. And then I saw the photo on his dresser. It was of Robert San Sebastion with an attractive older woman. The most striking thing about her was how much she resembled him. She was around my age and had that sort of (fake) blond hair, sorority girl look that some men enjoyed. Her facial features and general physique were similar to his. If that was his sister,

Robert just ruined her life. Big time. She was going to be prosecuted by the State for not stopping her brother from killing himself.

There was a second photo of him kissing the woman. Like, romantic, tongue-involved, kind of kissing. If that was his sister, he had some other issues going on beyond the ones previously mentioned. So, assuming this woman was not his sibling from some mountain clan where such physical interactions between brother and sister were acceptable, I assumed that she was his girlfriend. But she still looked weirdly similar to him. What narcissists.

I called in the briefing officer and had him bag the photos for me. I needed to talk to this woman. Maybe she could shed some light on Robert San Sebastian's state of mind and what drove him to this awful cherub-loving state of self-loathing.

I then heard the Medical Examiner and his team arrive with all their gear. A voice I knew well yelled throughout the cardboard hallways. "Hastings? You here?" it asked. I exited the faux-haunting lodge and returned to the kitchen. Boratch was already causing problems. "Did you fools really walk into my crime scene?! How am I supposed to be able to learn anything from a scene already contaminated by you clods? Hmm? Tell me. How is this a good thing for anybody?" The poor uniform made the mistake of trying to answer. "Sir, we did not..." and that was as far as he got before Boratch raised the volume and intensity of his tirade and really went after the officer.

Boratch knew the poor kid had probably done everything right and that the crime scene was just fine. But he was not happy being called out at night in the rain and felt like yelling at somebody. This particular officer just happened to be there. It had happened so often, to so many of them, that many of the kid's colleagues were trying not to laugh. They didn't think it was so funny when it was them getting the verbal beat down. But it was actually something which had become a right of passage. Boratch was loud but harmless. In fact, on more than one occasion, he had actually covered for an officer, or two, who had not appropriately followed procedure. He yelled his head off at them. But when the reports were written, they made no mention of any mistakes made and fledgling careers were allowed to continue.

"Boratch, quit yelling at the kid and tell me something useful" I said. Boratch turned. He still had an angry glare in his eyes. Then his face became one huge smile and he hugged me. Yes, hugged me, right there at the crime scene with a corpse not two feet away from us. Such were the ways of Medical Examiner Boratch. "Chief Inspector Hastings! Such a site for sore eyes!" It had only been about two days since we saw each other last, but it was good to be missed, I suppose. "How are you?" he asked. "Just fine, Samuel. At least as fine as can be, given the circumstances."

He looked over to the body. "Who is he? Some party official?" he asked. "I don't know yet?" Boratch stepped closer to the corpse on the table. It had already started to smell. Not the process of decay and decomposition of the body kind of smelling. Mr. San Sebastian wasn't dead long enough for that, yet. But the degrading, humiliating ritual that all humans do as their final farewell to this life. They shit themselves.

As Boratch and his people did their thing in the kitchen, I returned to the bedroom. After a bit of looking around I found San Sebastian's wallet. Ostrich skin, of course. There was over three hundred dollars inside it. There were also more photos of his female companion. In addition, there were a lot of business cards inside, a party membership ID and discount cards to various fast food restaurants. Then I noticed the work ID badge. It was for Life Gen, one of the largest pharmaceutical companies in the country. His title was on it. "Senior Vice-President of Sales, Golden Years Division," Whatever that means.

I also found his cell phone. His contact list was huge. Hundreds, maybe even thousands, of numbers. I looked up a few of them. They were mostly hospitals and physicians networks. Pretty logical considering what he appeared to do for a living. Our two tiered medical system left room for a lot of people like San Sebastian to make a great deal of money. There was, in theory, medical care provided by the State for all. However, if you could afford private care you were encouraged to do so. State healthcare was, very intentionally, kept at a Third World quality level. This was for two reasons. One, a proper health care system would cost billions and the government didn't want to fund it. And two, they didn't want it to be so good people might actually want to use it instead of paying for their own. It was bad for the economy, or at least corporate profits, which many assumed was the same thing.

I was just starting to weed out the few phone numbers that were not clearly business related from the others when Boratch yelled for me to return to the kitchen. Before I had even entered the room, Boratch was coming at me. "Alright, I'm not sure what you expect me to do here but it's not going to be easy" he said. "What do you mean?" I asked. Boratch looked around the room at all the other people milling about and pulled me aside. He got so close to me I could smell the stale vodka on his breath. "What answer do you need?" he asked. "I don't know yet. I don't know enough about who he was" I said. "Alright, I'll put "Evidence Inconclusive," for now, but that's about as conclusive as I have ever seen." He laid it out very quickly. San Sebastian had a drink or two, put the pistol up to his forehead, and pulled the trigger. Nobody else was involved and it was definitely, positively, not an accident.

I asked Boratch to mark his report "inconclusive pending further investigation." I needed to make a call before I could do anything more. I walked down the other hallway and stepped into a large, open room. It was filled with fake Roman statues of naked people. I tried to ignore my surroundings and shut the door behind me. I dialed the number of Minister Kaposkov. It was five thirty in the morning. He was not going to be pleased to hear from me at this hour. His assistant answered. "This is Chief Inspector Hastings. I need to speak with the Minister." The assistant did not bother to ask if it was urgent or if it could wait for a few hours. Obviously, if I was calling now, I needed to speak with his boss.

An inaudible groan came over the line. "Minister Kapinskov? It's Chief Inspector Hastings." I explained the reason for my call. The conversation did not go well. I needed to know if he wanted this whole thing to go away or to be reported straight. "What did you say his name was again?" the Minister asked. "San Sebastian, Robert San Sebastian." "I've never heard of him." "So, what would you like me to do then?" I asked. His answer did not make me very happy. Basically, he said to keep the whole thing covered up until we could learn more about who he was. But the Minister wanted the option left open to tell the full truth or maybe even blow the crime up into something bigger. If San Sebastian was an ally of one of his political enemies, the damage a scandal would cause might be well worth the trouble.

The problem wasn't going to be covering it up. That was old hat. Routine. But what if San Sebastian was connected to someone huge? Someone of Minister Kapinskov's level or higher? Given San Sebastian's position and wealth it was highly possible. Such a person would want to make sure that the situation was handled in the way that they needed. Which might be very different from the way Minister Kapinskov needed. And yours truly would be caught between the two. I really didn't need that sort of complication in my life.

I didn't leave the crime scene until seven in the morning. I should have gone to the station immediately to file a report. But I needed eggs. Eggs and sausage. And coffee. A lot of coffee. I wasn't actually sleepy. Just that sort of tired that makes you a little light headed and makes thinking coherently a major chore. I had my choice of three fast food chain places or driving an extra twenty minutes out of my way to Kimmel's. I chose Kimmel's. The food there wasn't anything special. In fact, it tended to be on the overly greasy side. However, it was across from the University and I always found going there gave me a warm, nostalgic kind of feeling. The fact that young, college-aged women could always be found there had absolutely nothing to do with it.

I parked my car and walked into the diner. The place was packed. Luckily, being alone, I could usually find a place by the counter. I heard the voices of some of the young college girls of the type previously described from a booth behind me. Actually, it wasn't right behind me. It was well across the restaurant. These girls were being very, very loud. Their conversation seemed to be about a certain teaching assistant but seemed mostly of the words, "like" "I mean" and "and he goes." It made me wonder what sort of youths we were letting into our universities. In my day, there were actually some basic requirements and a certain level of intellect required to be allowed admission. Now-a-days, however, it seemed to come down to who your parents were and if you could pay the ever rising "Tuition Supplement."

Officially speaking, higher education was free to any worthy citizen in our country. However, much like the healthcare system, a dual track system was created. The free one was allowed to remain but was slowly starved financially. The other, private one, under the "Tuition Supplement" heading, required massive amounts of money. At one point, this money was borrowed by students from banks which charged them exorbitant interest rates. However, after a great number of our recent graduates defaulted on these massive loans and ended up in prison, the State came up with a much better solution. Students were required to pay back their loans in a timely manner or they would be, involuntarily, inducted into the Armed Forces for nine years. This applied to both men and women.

It was actually a brilliant bit of thinking. After several long-lasting and bloody wars around the world, the average soldier had gone from fairly intelligent young man, capable of handling advanced weaponry, to complete moron who had no other prospects in life. This was born out in statistics which showed a twenty-one point drop in the IQ levels of the average recruit over a ten year period. By making the best and the brightest, at least the best and the brightest without the right connections or cash, become part of the military, things were set right. We, once again, had a smart, educated military that could be counted on to kill people in an efficient manner.

"Oh my God!" a young shrill voice shrieked. "MY God too" another responded. "I hate when you do that!" the first shrill voice replied. It was all too much. I was not pleased to have to get up from my seat but I was less pleased at listening to our future leaders cackle on so loudly at that early hour in the morning. I made my way across the diner and over to their booth. "Can we help you?" shrill girl number one of four asked. I was so annoyed with her I hardly noticed her lovely, lithe, young body and the way her sweater was clinging to it. "Yes, please keep your voices down a little" I said. "Were we that loud? We're sorry" shrill girl number two said. The one who I might have noticed was an overweight, short, Asian girl with a very bad complexion if I had been paying attention to such things. "Yes, you were. Please keep it down" I said. "Sorry, we will" shrill girl number one promised. I nodded and walked away. No need to show my ID or play the "do you know who I am?" card at all. Another example of how if you are just nice to people they will be quite reasonable.

I had only gotten about twenty feet across the room when shrill girl number one then added a parting comment.

"Asshole." The malicious little youths erupted into a jarring, earth-shattering noise which put my teeth on edge. This, combined with the fact I saw my eggs and sausage getting cold on the counter during this whole time, did not make me a happy man. Not in the least.

I walked back over to the group of self-involved youngsters. My expression changed to one which has been known to make suspects confess at the mere sight of it. I pointed to shrill girl number one. "You, get up. You're coming with me" I said. "What for?" she asked. I just glared at her. "Shut your mouth and come with me." She thought about resisting. I pulled out my ID card. The shrill girl had that magic instance of recognition I had seen a lot as an Inspector. It is the look of a criminal who believed they would never be caught as they come to realize they are going off to jail. It's a sort of "oh, shit, that's not the way it was supposed to go" look that I enjoy watching a great deal. This little, well formed harpy did a very nice little version of it. "Come on, move" I commanded.

She got up from the booth. Every single person in the place was trying not to look like they were staring, yet, doing exactly that. I guided the young girl out. Shrill girl number four spoke up. She was shockingly polite for a young blond with beautiful eyes but not so great body. "Officer, may I ask where you are taking her?" I turned my death glare upon her. "No" I said. Shrill girl number one became completely silent as I led her out of the diner. I walked her over to my sedan and saw her eyes grow wide with terror as she saw the government issued plates on it. It confirmed what was happening to her.

My plain looking little sedan was associated with many things that caused fear in people. Far more than an average squad car, being taken away in one was not the sign of a happy future ahead. I opened the back door for my prisoner. "Get in." I didn't bother to cuff her. I didn't need to. She looked up at me with tears in her eyes. "I said get in" I repeated. She did as she was told and climbed into the back of the sedan.

When the door shut the tears really started to flow. Maximum terror achieved. I then returned to the diner, leaving the girl in the back of the sedan. I couldn't see her but I imagined my passenger was now as confused as she was scared. As I walked back into the restaurant, all eyes were upon me as I took my seat back at the counter. The place was silent. I turned and faced the "trying not to be caught looking but clearly looking" crowd. "Does anybody have a problem with me they would like to discuss?" I asked. Nothing but murmurs and lots of shuffling. More than a few patrons decided leaving would be a good idea.

My waitress came immediately. "Your food has gone cold, I'll order you another." I thanked her and drank my coffee. The whispers resumed behind me among the remaining patrons. Out of the corner of my eye I saw the other shrill girls leave money on the table and leave along with some of the others.

None of this was what I had planned. I really just wanted to have a good breakfast after being up most of the night dealing with Robert San Sebastian. And this had really put a dent in things. Although I kind of enjoyed being able to silence a whole restaurant full of people and shut shrill girl up, the trade-off just wasn't worth it. I was so self-conscious that people were looking at me, I didn't enjoy the meal at all.

I ate quickly but felt like I had to stay longer than I wanted to just to make a point. It was all very uncomfortable, which really pissed me off. In spite of being told the meal was on the house, I paid and even over-tipped as I returned to the parking lot. Shrill girl was still in the back weeping as her friends looked on from across the parking lot. She wasn't handcuffed and the door was unlocked. She could have run away at any point. However, the fear of further punishment was so great that I knew that she wouldn't dare.

I approached her three friends, my awesome, terrorizing presence now in full force. I think they even stepped back a few feet. "Go on. Get to class or wherever you need to be. This is no longer your concern unless you would like to join your friend in the back of the sedan." They took off so quickly that I barely had time to notice the rather well shaped ass of one of them. Then I got into the driver's seat of my car and looked back at my passenger in the rear-view mirror. She averted her eyes from mine and tried, unsuccessfully, to stifle her tears. "You need to be more careful who you antagonize" I said. She didn't answer. "Did you hear me?" I asked. "Yes, Sir." I turned my head around to face her. "Look at me." She did, bloodshot eyes all pink, but otherwise none the worse for wear. "Things have changed and are getting even worse. You need to be very, very careful about saying the wrong thing or making the wrong enemies. Does that make sense to you?" I asked. "Yes, Sir" she said. "Are you sure you understand?" She nodded. "Yes, Sir. I understand. I really do."

I stayed silent for a moment. I strongly doubted she would change her ways but at least I had tried. "Alright then, get out of my car." She didn't move. "Go on, you're free to go. Do you need a note or anything for being late to class?" She shook her head. "Then go. The door's not locked. Get out." She seemed to think it was a trick or something and it took her a moment to get her body to move. But she did. She got out of my car and was still standing in the parking lot staring at me as I drove off. I have to admit, she was rather pretty for being such a petulant brat.

As I was driving my way to the station I had no idea at the time that my little breakfast stop would have several unintended consequences. One I have already told you about. The large, greasy breakfast that I was so hoping to enjoy turned out to be completely unpleasant. I even got indigestion afterward and was farting and burping for hours afterward. If that weren't horrific enough, there was another depressing consequence later that night. I was home thinking I might indulge myself in some self-pleasure, priestly warnings be damned. I was hoping to capitalize on my recent interactions with the lovely young college girl I had taken for a time out in the back of my sedan. A fantasy maybe involving spankings and other punishments for her own good. However, much to my annoyance, instead of the hot young coed getting what she deserved, all I could think about was another certain moment of the interaction.

It was that brief second when I had looked at her in the rear view mirror right before turning around to face her. She looked so very, very young. Not hot and sexy, barely legal, young. Like a kid. A child. Someone that might have been my own daughter if I had gone that particular route in life. That image made it impossible to think of her as the sexual plaything I was trying to create in my fantasies. It completely ruined everything. I just went to bed and forgot about having any fun thoughts of debauchery. Mission unfulfilled. What was even worse was the other feeling I was left with. It just kind of lingered there and never left. I felt very, very old.

The next morning I went to see Father Mike before going into the office. I had known Father Mike for almost twenty years. We had gone to University together before he changed paths and left for the Priesthood. He had every intention in the world of being a fund manager for one of the major banks. However, back then, the Collapse was at full peak. There was talk of the banks being nationalized and the entire field of finance being overhauled. Those events had nothing to do with his decision to enter the Priesthood. Just as the timing had nothing to do with the fact that the Oligarchs and the Church were about to ascend hand-in-hand to take over the nation. Nor did it have to do with the fact that the Church desperately needed new blood that was highly educated and good at managing their vast wealth at that very same time. Or that the clergy would become more rich and powerful than they had been in six or seven centuries. Nope. None of it affected him making his decision at all. Not in the least.

The thing that made Father Mike my friend, then and now, is how open he was about it all. That is, after he got to know you a little bit. Over the fourth of fifth of many beers, he once talked about his reasoning to me. Joining the Church was an open invitation to a life far better than any finance guy's. He, flat out, admitted it. But Father Mike said the one thing he was worried about was the whole celibacy thing. He knew, or thought he knew at the time, that he was not the sort of man to let his healthy, physical urges go unfulfilled. However, even that problem also looked to be on its way to resolution.

In spite of trying very hard to ignore all the evidence, the Church had come to realize that a certain element attracted to minors might be a much larger part of their organization than they would have liked. One very popular plan at the time was to scrap the celibacy requirement and to encourage marriage.

Eventually though, it was deemed too politically unpopular to become official. But they still liked the idea. Pedophiles were bad business in every sense of the phrase. So, an unofficial policy was, in fact, put in place. Men who liked women sexually, like Father Mike, were told they could have physical relationships, as long as they kept it on the down low. However, there would still be no marriage allowed. Some traditions had to remain in place for the public eye.

The new policy had a rather interesting result. It was a well known fact the chicks dug priests. At least in our country. Just one of those things. Men had strippers, dominatrixes and college girls. Women had movie stars and priests. So, when this unofficial policy became almost, but not quite, official, it made priests the most sexually desirable men in the country. Even rock stars were jealous. And the "no marriage" rule made it perfect for guys that just wanted their fun without the whole nasty commitment thing. It really worked out well for many a horny man.

The saddest part of the story was this: Father Mike entered the Priesthood because he could have a lucrative career and because he thought it would help him get laid a lot. It did neither. Somewhere during his first year at the seminary he found God. Although in a position to attain key positions at major financial institutions handling the Church's billions, he declined every offer. Instead, Father Mike lived in a three-hundred square foot room which was also his office at the mission. The rest of the building was used to house the homeless and provide food to anyone who asked. His financial skills were used to solicit donations and to make those donations work well in the not-so-free market. He produced yields high enough to support the entire mission.

As for the women, he still admired them sexually. He hadn't started liking young boys or anything. But he described it this way to me. "They are something I appreciate like a great painting in a museum. The brief interaction I get just speaking with a beautiful woman is enough for me. I do not need to sleep with her any more than I need to own the painting and have it hanging in my living room to get value from it." It sounded a bit creepy to me. Keep in mind, I was drunk when he told all this to me. I told him he was full of shit. I think I even vaguely recall making some joke about wanting to own the beautiful woman AND the painting. I don't know for sure. Like I said, I was drunk at the time.

What I did know was Father Mike is a stand up guy. You could still talk to him like a normal Joe. But you could also see how much his faith had done for him. He had this peace about him I truly admire. Kind of like he knows that, no matter what, it's all going to be Ok. Oh, how I envied that in him. I wouldn't have the indigestion I do all the time if I had such certainty. Belief that the times we lived in were not going to turn out very, very badly for a whole lot of people, including myself. But Father Mike just seemed to know differently. He spent every waking hour, which was at least nineteen hours a day, making the world just a little bit better. Everyone who came into contact with him from the poor, drug-addicted bastard that needed a place to sleep, to the world weary Chief Inspector that needed his advice, just seemed better off after encountering him. Which is what brought me to him that afternoon.

I walked over to his mission and made my way through the bustling commissary. The staff was preparing for the dinner rush already. Father Mike was busy supervising various tasks and was far too busy to speak with me. But, him being him, he made it feel as if he had all the time in the world just to hear my woes. We went for a walk in the park behind the mission which had once been a place to dump garbage and to shoot up. He waited patiently for me to tell him why I was there.

"Did you ever just have a feeling something really, really terrible was going to happen?" I asked. He said he did, long ago, before he found his own form of peace. He quickly honed in on what I was getting at. "Are you talking about a general, free floating anxiety or something specific?" he asked. "I don't know" I said. And I didn't. Which was why such a stupid answer was the most honest. "I think it's a combination of seeing all these things lining up in a very damaging way and..." I didn't know how to finish the sentence. "And what?" he asked. "I don't know. Feeling like I'm just going with it. You know, like that old phrase. The light at the end of the tunnel is a train." He smiled. "I haven't heard that one in a while." We sat down and he once again tried to get me to be as specific as possible.

I told him about work and how it was going well enough. I told him about a woman I had gone out with a few times but just stopped calling for some reason. I told him all sorts of whining, poor me, my life isn't really fulfilling, middle-aged, regret filled stories. He listened to me in that way he does that people love him for. He is not just waiting for you to shut up so he can talk again. He is really and truly listening and hearing every word you say. It's really kind of scary how much you find yourself drawn to him when he does that. Hell, it even made me want to sleep with him and I don't go that way.

At the end of my self-indulgent rambling, he got right to the heart of the matter. "It sounds like you've convinced yourself you really don't believe in anything. That it's all just going through the motions and an unfulfilling waste of time" he said. Man, he was good. "Exactly!" I said. He looked at me and nodded. I actually hated when he did that. The nodding thing. But it did usually mark the moment before he said something really wise and useful. "You believe in plenty of things" he said. "But I just told you. Work. Relationships..." He smiled. "Listen, I've known you for a long time. You're one of the most committed, driven men I have ever known. Your problem is the constant questioning. Quit questioning and just do. You might not grasp things intellectually that your heart already knows."

I thought about what he said. Suddenly, I felt angry. "That's all you've got? Your heart knows the truth? Seriously Mike, I mean Father Mike? Really?" I asked. He wasn't offended. Alright, maybe he was. But he was pretty good about not letting it show too much. He spoke again. "Look, if this were the old days and I said that when we were both drunk, you would totally get what I was saying. You really would" he said. "So, I'm too sober to think straight, right now?" I asked. "Kind of." The anger wasn't leaving me. I was starting to really regret opening up to him. Maybe I had built him up into somebody more than he was. Maybe I had a secret sexual priest thing myself for all I knew. I just had one of those moments where I felt like I had just poured my heart out and gotten nothing in return. Kind of like telling a woman you are deeply, madly in love with her and her replying "That's nice. So, where are we going for dinner?"

My confidant and advisor continued. "Daniel, believe me. I'm not lying to you. I know this. I absolutely, positively know that you are not as lost as you feel. You already know your path and I think THAT is what is really scaring you. Not all the rest of this complaining you're doing about your life being so trivial and meaningless." I shook my head. I'm not sure he was aware how annoying it was to hear someone tell you that you're really not feeling what you are feeling. Just imagine someone telling you that you're not upset that your dog died. That you just THINK that you're upset. How irritating. But he kept at it.

He ended the ordeal by asking me about my plants. "Do you water them?"he asked. "Yes" I replied. "Why? If a plant dies does it cause you physical pain? Does it cost you your job? Does it in any way change your life in any noticeable way?" he asked. "No." "Exactly" he said. And then a look came into his eyes as if he had told me the biggest secret in the universe. I had no idea what the hell he was going on about. Maybe I'm just not spiritually equipped to understand such profound wisdom. I told him I had to go. "Keep watering the plants, Dan. Keep watering the plants" he said as I walked away. Whatever, Dude.

The workday did not make my life feel any easier. I had just gotten in when Boratch approached me. I hadn't even taken my coat off. "Comrade Hastings! Greetings!" And then the hug. The satisfying but somewhat painful hug. And the breath. Boratch's breakfast that morning seemed to have involved smoked fish of one sort or another. And coffee. Which didn't stop him from telling me that we needed to go get coffee. I had yet to finish my report on the San Sebastian thing and would catch a lot of flack unless it was on the boss's desk before ten. But Boratch insisted. So, coffee it was.

We walked outside and talked briefly about the weather. I wanted to ask him what this was really about but knew better than to do it anywhere near Headquarters. As we walked the eight blocks or so to his favorite coffee bar he started telling me about his daughter Anna. She was having problems with her husband. He had not only cheated on her but had done it very blatantly. Boratch was very upset about it. Not so much the cheating itself but about the embarrassment it caused Anna. There were rules to these things and Anna's husband had broken them.

"So, you want me to bring him in for questioning? Is that what this is all about?" I asked. Boratch looked at me. "What? No. I suppose, maybe. I really hadn't thought about it. You would do that for me?" he asked. "Of course! I've met Anna. She deserves better" I replied. "Like you, for instance?" "She could do worse" I said. The truth was I had no interest in Anna. None. She was old, nearly my age, and I did not find her physically appealing. She also sounded rather demanding from the stories Boratch told me about her. A big house in The Lake District. A vacation house in the South. The latest cars, dresses, furniture, etc. that her friend had. Honestly, she seemed like kind of a nightmare.

"Like I said, Anna is a great girl and deserves better" I repeated. Boratch looked at me as we approached the coffee bar. "I may take you up on your offer" he said. I was already regretting making it. On the one hand, Boratch was a great friend who had been part of my world for a long time. I liked the idea of helping him out. On the other, I had enough crap going on in my life without getting involved in the soap opera world of Anna Boratch. I was about to go into the coffee bar when Boratch stopped me. "It's too crowded. Let's go to the other one." I looked through the glass door into the coffee bar. It didn't seem any more crowded than usual. There was a line but it seemed to be moving fairly quickly. But Boratch insisted.

It was only when we walked another block or so that Boratch started talking again. "Let me think about your offer but that's not why I asked you to walk with me." "Ok" I said. "It's about the San Sebastian case." I stopped walking. "Ok." He looked down at his muddy shoes for a moment. If I didn't know better I would say he looked a little nervous. Boratch didn't get nervous. So, seeing him look nervous made me nervous. "Well?" I prompted. "I've declared it an Accidental Death" he said" I let that sink in for a moment.

"So, Robert San Sebastian mistakenly grabbed a pistol, held it to his temple and had a sudden convulsion of the finger that happened to be on the trigger?" I asked. Boratch let out a frustrated sigh. "You know how these things work. If Kapinskov had asked you to attain that finding, you would have. "But that's the problem. Not only did he say NOT to find that conclusion. He wanted the case left open for a while to determine if it could be used against one of his opponents."

Boratch seemed to be getting angrier. "Accidental Death, my report will be to you before noon. Please don't get in my way on this. Please" he said.

He started to walk away. "Samuel. I'll do it. I'll do as you ask but I need to know why. This is not going to go over well with Kapinskov" I said. Boratch looked at me. He was weighing his words carefully. "I understand. I know what I am asking you to do. But you know how these things work. I have been told in no uncertain terms what the report must say. So, it will say it. I would suggest you follow along and make sure the entire matter goes away as quickly as possible." I looked at him but didn't say anything. In all the years I had known Boratch we had traded many a favor. However, this was different. For one thing, his favors didn't usually involve directly contradicting what the higher ups had told me. For another, he usually explained why things needed to be done as a courtesy, if nothing else. But a friend was a friend. "Ok. Done" I said.

We walked the rest of the way in silence until we arrived at the second coffee place. It was far more crowded than the first. We gave up and returned to Headquarters with nothing. As I left Boratch to return to my desk, he thanked me. A very sincere, relieved thanks.He looked exhausted. Not just from working too many hours but from spending his nights churning things over in his head. The fact that he wouldn't tell me what those things were really bothered me. But, for now, I would just trust him. Our years together had earned him at least that.

Boratch's report was delivered by a clerk and received by another clerk. Both of those clerks had to sign for it before it was sent to a third clerk, then the office administrator and then to the office assistant, both of whom also had to sign it, before finally reaching my desk. Which, by that time, was already after four in the afternoon.

I looked over his findings. To say Boratch fudged the facts would be a serious understatement. The report was flat out lies. It concluded that San Sebastian was cleaning his weapon and that it had accidentally gone off. Aside from the particularly bad phrasing which reminded me of something I told my priest once, it was also a conclusion which simply made no sense. However, any contradictory photographs failed to be included and three new ones were added. The three new ones showed a gun cleaning kit on an examination bench and stated that the kit had been found on the kitchen table of the crime scene. It was all total crap. But it was Boratch's total crap. So I did as I had promised. My report corroborated his findings and backed him up to the hilt.

I thought about contacting Minster Kapinskov and giving him the heads up about the, soon to be released, reports but decided against it. I would just wait for Kapinskov to learn of it. Then I would wait for that horrible accusing, berating, humiliating phone call. Probably a bad decision. Waiting was only going to make things worse. But I just wasn't up for it. This way, I probably had about three days. Three days before a very powerful, well connected government Minister called me and demanded to know what the fuck I thought I was doing. I felt ill just imagining it. I would feign incompetence and stupidity which, insultingly, was often readily accepted by others. Far, too much so, if I thought about it. But in this case, it would be my saving grace. The more incompetent I could appear, the more my report would be seen as a mistake, not an act of direct defiance.

The remainder of the work day was the usual nonsense of domestic violence, random street crimes and violent assaults. All of which was far too trivial for someone in my position to be bothered with. I left the office by five thirty and stopped at a Chinese place to get dinner. I usually got it to go but disliked the idea of being home while it was still light out. It was just one of those things. At the end of my meal, I opened my fortune cookie hoping for some profound wisdom. Whatever it was couldn't be any worse than Father Mike's rant about getting into gardening. My fortune cookie said: "Next meal %10 off!" Which wasn't really a fortune. But at least I would save two dollars on my next Kung Pao Chicken.

By the time I got home, it had gotten dark. Something about being at home watching TV when it was dark out felt safe and cozy, whereas doing so in the light made me feel pathetic. Kind of like I should be out doing things and being with people and getting laid. It was a relatively new thing that had happened to me in the last year or two. Until then, like most people, I actually liked the fact that the days were warmer and longer when spring came. Now, darkness and me had become friends. It was all seriously lame. Something I knew and just accepted.

I wanted to call Boratch to let him know I had turned in my report. However, I couldn't. Our phones were being monitored. As one of the conditions to being hired both of us had to sign waivers that such monitoring was acceptable. We were assured it was only to protect us from any accusations of misconduct. By having recordings of our conversations, we could easily prove our innocence, should it prove necessary. I would tell Boratch soon enough. Probably in person, tomorrow. But it was really irritating that I couldn't somehow let him know until then. The act somehow felt incomplete without that final exchange.

As I sat back in my chair about to flip through the channels, I looked around my cluttered apartment. It was then that I realized something. Even if I wanted to follow Father Mike's advice, I couldn't. The only plant I owned was already looking quite dead.

The next morning did not start off well. The traffic on the way to work was extraordinarily bad. So much so that I turned my official warning lights on and made the annoying people in my way pull to the side of the road. When I first started, it was the privilege of all those that worked for the Agency to clear traffic in this way. However, it soon became a point of real contention between various government agencies which had the authority to use warning lights and which did not. At one point, so many government and church employees were doing it that traffic accidents occurred on a regular basis between officials. It was after a particular incident when the President of the Energy Resources Department had his Mercedes totaled by a lowly employee of The Parks Department that the rules were abruptly changed. Only the highest officials could now clear crowded roads at their whim. And, of course, law enforcement officials while on duty. Although technically not on duty yet, I was going to be late for duty. Which seemed close enough. So, warning lights, it was.

Even with that, I still arrived at Headquarters about fifteen minutes later than usual. Normally, no one would have noticed. However, that morning, one that I have already mentioned did not start off very well, was truly cursed. Before I even had the chance to take my coat off and get my first cup of work coffee, I was summoned. What made it even more painful is that I was summoned by my boss, Superintendent Kim, to be told that I had been summoned by someone else. An executive at Energex wanted to speak with me. He was waiting for me in the conference room. When I asked for further explanation,

Superintendent Kim smiled that evil smile of his and just said "You'll find out soon enough, Chief Inspector."

As curious as I was, I was actually really annoyed that I didn't have time to go through my usual morning ritual. Normally, I get into the office, use the bathroom, talk with a few of my co-workers about sports events, get some coffee down the street, have more discussions about sports, check my emails and don't actually start "working," as such, until about an hour after my arrival. Yet, here was some executive with enough clout to keep me from my much needed Americano with three shots to discuss heaven knows what.

I walked into the conference room and almost froze when I saw who was in it. It was the shrill college girl I had made sit in my car while I had my breakfast ruined. A man in his late forties wearing a very, very expensive looking suit was sitting next to her. These people clearly had no respect for the importance of breakfast and morning rituals. The man got up and walked toward me with an extended hand. "Chief Inspector Hastings, I believe" he said. "I'm Mike Laughton." It all came out of his mouth in such a way intended to make me feel we had been friends for decades. "And I believe you have already met my daughter, Isabella." The shrill girl stood up and also shook my hand. She didn't say a word. The whole thing felt so strange I was about to ask, flat out, why they were there. I didn't get the chance. This was clearly Mr. Laughton's show.

"Please have a seat" he said. I did so, even though it seemed remarkable that this man was acting as if Headquarters were his home and I was the visitor. "I wanted to stop in today so that we could have a little discussion" he said. I finally got a sentence out "What would you like to discuss, Mr. Laughton?" "Mike, please" he said. In that brief moment before he explained his presence, I was struck with a terrible fear. In spite of the friendly, let's have a chat façade, I was about to get my teeth kicked in for how I treated his little brat princess. Just my luck the stupid little nitwit would have a daddy connected to the big wigs. He was here to make sure that I paid the price for my insolence.

"Isabella has something she would like to say to you. Don't you Isabella?" he said. And then, in an instance, it all became clear. The exact opposite of what I had feared. Mr. Laughton had a healthy respect for authority and was teaching his dirty little minx of a daughter to do the same. There was a long, pregnant pause as Isabella looked at me with those lovely green eyes of hers. I imagined finding all sorts of ways for her to make it up to me which I'm sure her father would have been abhorred by. Isabella said what she had come there to say. "You're an asshole."

The words just hung there. Her words. Did she really just say that? She continued. "You're an asshole but I understand how, in your own egotistical, dirty old man, way, you actually meant to do something good. So, I forgive you." I looked over to the father. Mr. Laughton was brimming over with pride. "You forgive me?" I asked. "Yes, I do. You can't help who you are or the fact that you have such a limited capacity to understand the world." My head was exploding. Exactly what I had feared before deciding I didn't need to fear it was happening. "What?! Now, look here you little...!" I yelled. "I would watch your tone, Chief Inspector" Mr. Laughton said. "After hearing about what you did to my daughter and your abuse of power, I was fully prepared to make a few phone calls and to have you fired." I turned to him. Sized him up. Could this faux-friendly fake really have the juice to get a Chief Inspector of the People's Protection Agency fired like that? I saw his smile and relaxed posture and knew the answer. Yes. Yes he could. God damn it!

Laughton continued. "It was only after Isabella pleaded with me to be more understanding that we agreed to let you off with a simple apology" he said. Apology? An apology to this annoying brat and her fake friendly father? I thought. "Did you have anything that you wanted to add, Isabella?" Mr. Laughton asked. Isabella just smiled at me with a look so superior I wanted to push her face in mud. Or better yet, shit. I wanted to find the world's most used, least cleaned, outhouse, grab her legs and plunge her into it, head first, over and over and over again. That would teach her to smile like that at me. A voice cried out in my head. I'm a Chief Inspector, damn it! I have authority! I am someone!

The shrill little bitch and her gloating father looked at me and waited. My cue. My cue to verbally demean myself and make it clear to everyone in the room that I was a spineless, groveling peon who had no pride. And I did. I said the horrible words about how very wrong I was and blamed some of it on the fatigue and stress of the crime scene I had just come from. And I said both the "s" and "a" words. In fact, I heard the words "sorry" and "I apologize" come out of my mouth multiple times. If Isabella could have looked any more pleased with herself she would burst into a blazing explosion of smug rays brighter than a thousand suns. Oh, how I hated her. And her father. Death. Death by fire ants and flesh eating termites would not have been justice enough.

And it got even worse. I know. I know. It's hard to image how my humiliation and degradation at having to apologize to this nasty child could have gotten worse. But it did. First of all Mr. Laughton acted all, "now that wasn't too bad, was it Chief Inspector?" He didn't exactly say it but it was clear that he thought he was a super-great guy for sparing my job and handling things the way he had. I could see where little Isabella got her smug ray gene. But it was her, that sadistic harpy, that really knew how to twist the knife in. As she left, she said "It's really just pathetic the way you leer at young girls. Sad really. Have a nice day, Inspector."

Finally, they were gone. It was over. I sat in the conference room for a few moments trying to recover. I had done my share of shit eating over the years but this was top of the list. There was a time when I would have just refused. Or quit. Or let them have it with both guns. When did all that go out the window? It's not like I had kids to feed or a family depending on me. What had I become?

I called Boratch and asked him if we could meet for lunch. He said "yes" very quickly and named a time. Then he hung up. I realized, after the fact, that he probably assumed I was asking him to meet so we could discuss the San Sebastian case. Honestly, I had forgotten about our friend with his missing chunk of skull. I was far too engulfed in my own world of humiliation and pain to really care, right then. I thought about calling Samuel back and telling him it wasn't a request for one of "those" kind of lunches. But I really needed to bitch to someone and decided to just let him believe what he believed. Better than having my lunch rescheduled for some later day. My venting could not wait.

By one o' clock my mood had changed from an energetic, I want to kill things, anger to more of a depression. I was hating my life. A beer or two and some good conversation with a friend would do wonders to make existence feel bearable again. I walked down the staircase and was hit by the familiar scent of chemicals used to inspect and preserve the dead. The Medical Examiner's office was quiet except for the sound of a power saw cutting through some body part. Most of the staff were already on their lunch.

I followed the sound of the saw and found Boratch buzzing away energetically at the corpse of a very, very obese man. He was slicing him open and about to fold his skin down to do an autopsy. Then he saw me and stopped. "Is it one already? I had no idea" he said. The man loved his work. How else could you explain how someone got into the zone playing with dead people? "Let me wash up and then we'll go" he said. Once again, I thought about clarifying my request for our lunch meeting and downgrading its urgency. I could tell that Boratch would much rather have been left alone with his obese friend than going out with me. But I had my needs.

A few minutes later, Boratch returned smelling of harsh soap on top of a layer of sweat and chemicals. It was the cologne of his trade. As usual, we just made small talk about the weather and various sporting events as we drove to a fish place in the Hollows section of town. Then Boratch cut to the chase. Or, should I say, he thought he was. "So, let me guess, Friend. You are going to tell me that you've thought about my request regarding the San Sebastian case and, for various reasons, simply cannot do it. Before you say anything, just let me say I understand and completely sympathize with your position." For some reason I actually enjoyed him going on about things the way he was and was really reluctant to stop him. So, I let him continue. "It was a horrible position to put you in and, as difficult as it will be, I will inform those that wanted the outcome as I asked that it will not be so and just deal with the consequences" he said. I really was enjoying how serious and dramatic he was being.

"I did it last night. The report reads "Accidental Death" just like you said. Already turned it in yesterday. Done." He looked at me for a moment. "So, do you expect some sort of complication? Why the big lunch meeting then?" he asked. "No, it should be fine. Another false report. Big deal. Whatever. No, the reason I needed to see you has nothing to do with that. It has to do with something that happened this morning."

I started to tell him the details of my ordeal in slightly embellished fashion to make a better story out of it. I had just gotten to the part where I was describing the overly friendly manner of Mr. Laughton when Samuel interjected. "You bastard. You let me worry all morning about that report and then let me think there was a problem with it on purpose, didn't you?" he asked. "You got your report finding. Quit your complaining. Now, do you want to hear about this little college twit and her father or not?"

After a fine meal of fried Pollack fresh from the river, I actually apologized to Boratch about not being more aware of how anxious the San Sebastian thing was making him. I didn't go as far as to admit how much I enjoyed hearing him be all dramatic about something that was already taken care of and done. But I did say that I was sorry. Between Boratch, the fish and the beer I was almost able to forget how miserable my life was for a few hours.

Three days later, Kapinskov still hadn't called. It was just the usual agitators, bank robbers, protestors, abortionists and so on. All painfully normal. It was only when coming home on that next Thursday that anything remotely interesting took place. I was driving by Saint Anthony's Square when I noticed people running. Most were running from the square, trying to get away from something. But a few hearty souls were actually running towards it. All with their cell phones, of course. I really didn't care much about it either way and would have kept driving but traffic had come to a standstill.

As I was sitting in my car debating whether I should use my warning lights or not, I saw a woman covered in something. Foam. She was covered, head to toe, in white foam. It was the sort washing machines create. And then I saw a second person and a third also covered in foam.

A call came over my radio. "Terrorist Incident at St. Anthony's Square. Any available units, please report." As a Chief Inspector I did not have to answer such general calls the way regular officers did. However, it would probably make me look good with Superintendent Kim if I did. And it was pretty odd the way these people were all covered in foam for some reason.

I radioed in that I had already arrived at the crime scene and would be investigating. I made sure my immediate response was noted in order to get the credit I fully deserved. I then pulled my car to the side of the road and got out.

I had barely walked five feet when a swarm of more foam covered people ran right towards me. I tried to stop one or two of them but they just kept going. Finally, I saw an old woman hobbling as fast as she could to try to get past me. A crippled old person I could probably catch. So, I did. I grabbed her by both foamy shoulders and asked her what was going on. "The church" she said. "It's the church." And then she wriggled free and slipped away.

I made my way toward the square. The amount of people running from it had dwindled to near nothing. Now, it was far more about over-excited passers by hoping to see something interesting. I saw an attractive woman in a foamy, wet, white shirt and decided to approach her. I put on my most impressive, Chief Inspectorly, airs and started her way. How could she not be impressed by my commanding presence and aura of authority and power? Just as I was getting close enough to determine her eye color, and other physical details, she turned and looked right at me. At which point my leather shoes slid across something very slick and I promptly landed on my ass.

It hurt. A lot. For a moment I stared up at the sky wondering what had happened. It took me a second to realize I had slipped on some foam and was lying on my back in the middle of St. Anthony's Square. And then those eyes were upon me. Big, beautiful, brown eyes. The face that those eyes were a part of was lovely. A bit older than I would have preferred, easily in her late thirties. But, wow, what a face.

The mouth on the face then asked me "Are you Ok?" I sat up. "Yes, thanks" I said. I got to my feet as soon as possible. I was hoping to chat up this fine looking Good Samaritan. But somewhere during the act of raising my rugged frame from the wet cement, she had moved on. I turned and caught a glimpse of her older, but holding up very impressively, ass, as she turned the corner and disappeared. I had no idea at the time that I had just met Karen. The woman who would turn me into the history altering, everything changing, more famous than anyone in existence, figure I was destined to become.

I resumed my way to the source of all this foamy madness. I tried to be as dignified as possible but it was next to impossible. The seat of my pants was soaking wet and clinging to me in a most unflattering way. Trying to pry them off of my skin only made me appear more worthy of ridicule. It was so degrading and uncomfortable I considered turning back to the safety of my car. I could possibly claim physical injury from my fall as an explanation. However, without any actual injury, that might not seem very credible. I sucked it up and continued my walk of humiliation, soaking wet pants and all. For all I knew, the women in the gathering crowd might have found the look very stimulating. If females with wet t-shirts are enticing, why not this?

A crowd had gathered around St. Anthony's Cathedral. It was not a cathedral in the great architectural tradition of such things. No soaring arches. No grand statues. No balustrades. It was more a large concrete box with a smaller concrete box attached to it, that had been built in the nineteen-eighties. It was a completely bland and unremarkable building on most days. However, today it was a spectacle to be sure. For one thing, there were forty foot high piles of foam pouring out of it. For another, there was a giant banner strung from the cheesy-looking attempt at creating a faux bell tower. The banner said the following: "FREE BRAINWASHING HERE." The Clear Thinkers had struck again.

There was, of course, another press release put out about an hour later. This one was on video and uploaded to the internet. It was delivered by a woman in a burka. You couldn't see much of her but I knew those eyes. They were the ones that had looked at me lying flat on my back in the square. Those big, brown, beautiful eyes that were so concerned with my well-being.

The female figure explained how the soap referred to the cleansing, not of the soul, but of the mind. And how the government worked hand in hand with the church to brainwash the populace into following a political and economic agenda against their own self-interests. There was also something in her speech that I think hurt their cause a great deal. She quoted Marx. That's all the News Agency needed to tie the whole incident to a terrorist group that worshiped Stalin and his mass murdering ways.

It was all really kind of a shame because I think the whole incident would have been much more effective if had just been left to stand on its own. Soap. Church. Brainwashing. I think even your average citizen might have figured out that on their own. Unlike the whole "Bob" thing, this one actually made sense right away. It was honestly quite clever until they started talking about it and kind of ruined it. I suppose being a law enforcement official, I should be thankful that terrorists like to hear themselves talk so much. If they didn't have that incredibly egotistical personality trait, they would be much, much more difficult to apprehend.

It became clear how the foam incident had been done once I flashed my ID a few times and gained access to the actual crime scene. The Clear Thinkers had driven a tanker truck right up to church, I mean cathedral, and hooked a giant hose up to a second floor window. This was done in broad daylight. They had pretended that they were putting in additional noise retardant, as per Health and Safety Department orders. The lowly church workers present of the time were far too fearful of challenging a government issued order that they spent all their time trying to bump the issue up the chain of command. Someone had just reached the office of Cardinal Rooney when the valves were turned on the tanker truck and white foam started to flood the interior of the church, I mean cathedral. The banner was unfurled sometime during the confusion that ensued.

The interior of the cathedral was quite a site. The foam was piled high and everything was wet. A group of energetic, young, uniformed officers almost didn't see me as they ran through. The officers had been ordered to take the banner down as quickly as possible. One of those simple orders that proved harder than it sounded between the foam, water and confusion about which stairway led to where. I looked up at the giant, abstract version of a crucifix made of steel as it rose above the fluffy, foamy white. A tear came to my eye. It was not due to the beauty of it all. Nor was it due to some profound understanding of the nature of Christ. Nothing of the sort. It was because the soap had gotten into my eyes and it stung like a mother fucker.

Chief Windsor, of the dreaded Anti-Terror Division, showed up at the crime scene. He held an impromptu press conference and vowed to personally bring the perpetrators to justice. He referred to the foam incident as, and I quote, "A brazen act of terrorism by those that wish to strip us of our freedom." It's normally a very safe thing to assume, I suppose. What do terrorists want?! To take our freedom! It had been a line of thinking that had worked for centuries. There was one problem, however. One that Chief Windsor could not have seen coming. After consulting with his advisors, the President of our great nation decided that the foamy church event wasn't an act of terrorism at all. It was simply "an unfortunate accident which triggered a fire extinguishing system and caused a modest amount of property damage to the church."

The people at the top of the food chain might be lacking in morals and completely hateful in many ways. They were not, however, dumb. The consensus was that the very accessible and clear symbolism of the foam/brainwashing stunt was great propaganda. This was before Karen's video statement, which muddled the whole thing up quite a bit, had been released. Anyway, the government advisors realized the best thing that they could do was to downplay the entire thing. After all, the way to kill good advertising is to just not let it reach the public in the first place.

Shortly after this decision was made, the News Agency instructed all media outlets to report the incident as an accident. Details were invented to explain how the foam system was there because the church was dealing with some highly flammable chemical materials as they restored a ceiling painting. Its activation was triggered by a faulty sensor. As messy and dramatic as the incident superficially appeared, nobody was hurt and the damage to the church was minor. As for the banner and Clear Thinkers press release, great effort was put into making sure as few people saw them as possible.

None of which was good news for Chief Windsor. He had to go on the air for the next several weeks admitting he had screwed up very badly. He had made an erroneous conclusion by declaring the incident a terrorist event. A conclusion which might have caused public panic for no good reason. He blamed such faulty reasoning on lack of sleep and cold medication which clouded his judgment. It was an accident triggered by a faulty sensor just as the government said. Having done the best he could to repair the damage done, Chief Windsor was offered, and accepted, early retirement shortly afterward. Not right away. That would be too obvious. But soon. He should have never been so anxious to get in front of those cameras.

Which should prove to you just how smart and clever yours truly, really is. You see, I had the opportunity to make myself a hero the afternoon of the incident. It was about two hours after leaving my stinging, soapy torment, changing out of my very wet and uncomfortable pants and returning to the office that I actually saw it. The Clear Thinkers press release. That's when I saw those eyes. And knew. If I were ambitious I would have made a huge deal about it. I would have yelled across the office so that everyone could have heard "I spoke with that woman!" But I was far too wise for that. As Chief Windsor had learned the hard way, trying to grab the brass ring can sometimes cause you to fall off your horse. It is far more likely that you will have a long, if not exceptional, career and live a longer, healthier life if you do not rush to conclusions. I kept my information to myself to see how things would play out.

I woke up the next morning still thinking of Karen. Not that way. Ok, maybe a little that way. But more along the lines of I would tell Superintendent Kim that I might have had visual contact with one of the terrorists. The conversation did not go as well as I had hoped. "Her eyes?" Superintendent Kim asked. "You think you might be able to identify the terrorist's spokesperson just by her eyes?" he asked. When he put it that way, it did sound a bit far fetched. There was no easy way to explain to him that they weren't just any old eyes. They were big, beautiful, magnetic orbs that had peered into my very soul. Or at least checked me out a little bit, which was almost as good. "And why didn't you mention this yesterday?" he asked. That one I had prepared for. "It took me a while to understand why the person on the video press release seemed so familiar" I said. "I see."

This was followed by a silence which was there partially because neither one of us had anything to say and partially so that Superintendent Kim could make me feel stupid. Which I did. Horribly so. I kept charging in, all the same. "With your permission, I'd like to pursue my own leads on who this woman might be." Superintendent Kim looked at me like I was a talking Panda Bear or something. But not nearly that cute. Like a very ugly, repulsive, talking Panda Bear that had just said something nasty about his mother. "Do you realize that across the street at 2100 they have a squad of forty-three people already investigating this event?" he asked. "What, exactly, do you think you can bring to the case that our colleagues over in Anti-Terror cannot? My answer was succinct but brilliant. Really and truly brilliant. I said one word. "Confusion."

That got his attention. I proceeded to lay out my theory that Karen (who's name I didn't know yet and just referred to as "the terrorist leader") was very proud of her events for the Clear Thinkers. She probably considered herself highly gifted at being able to think up clever things like the "Bob" stunt and this foam thing. You could hear it in her voice when she did the video. She loved talking about her little happenings and explaining them with all sorts of references and symbolic meanings which often made them so confusing that they lost any impact that they might have had. But she could not stop herself from talking about such things. It was an addiction of self-aggrandizement and pretension that she just couldn't control.

"And where do you come into play on that, Chief Inspector?" I was filled with self-confidence and pride in my plan. "I'm going to rewrite her press releases. Well, actually, I'm going to do my own and then release them as the official statements from The Clear Thinkers." I waited for him to understand the beauty and intellectual heft of this idea. He just kept staring at me waiting for me to spell it out for him. Some people really don't understand the elegance of understatement.

"And what, exactly, is that going to do?" The Chief Superintendent asked. "Annoy her" I responded. "Annoy her a very great deal" I added with glee. The Superintendent's face scrunched up like he had just eaten something very sour. It was not a good look. He still wasn't seeing it. "You plan to annoy the terrorists into submission?" he asked. I remained confident. "Exactly." He shook his head back and forth and started to rummage around the papers on his desk. "Please get out of my office, Chief Inspector. And don't come back for a while. Ok?" he said. If I had one bit of common sense regarding my professional well being, I would have slunk away as quietly as possible and stayed out of the way. But no. No, for some reason I cannot understand to this day, I kept going. I kept trying to make my case, fully aware that every word was pushing me one step closer to demotion or dismissal.

"Hear me out, Sir" I pleaded. "The terrorists are very proud of the symbolic nature of their attacks. I'm going to do my own press releases, which will do two things. It will muddle the meaning of the act so much that nobody will be much affected or influenced by it. Two, it will so irritate the terrorists that they will become increasingly rattled and make a mistake." I waited for a change in his expression. I wasn't seeing one. "The only mistake was letting you into my office, Chief Superintendent. I have work to do. So do you. There are reports of an active abortionist in your section. Please look into it."

And then I got the glare. The "don't say another word, You Idiot" glare that meant I was to leave without saying another word. I left his office feeling totally defeated. My plan was brilliant and I knew it. If only others could appreciate the genius that was me. In spite of knowing there was absolutely no upside to it, I started to consider going ahead and testing out my plan anyway. Such a move could get me into serious trouble with the Agency. But it could also prove to them what a great officer I was. It might be a risk worth taking.

At lunch, I mentioned my plan to Boratch. His advice was wise and profound. "Don't be a moron. Do as you are told and not a thing more. Sometimes, I wonder how you haven't already ended up at a re-education center. What were you thinking?" I told him how much I thought the foam thing was really effective until the terrorists started explaining it. I knew that such egos couldn't take someone questioning their conceptual theories. "And then what happens?" he asked. "They get rattled and make a mistake." Boratch looked down at his sandwich of soggy bread and processed turkey. It was what he had eaten for lunch every Tuesday for at least seven years straight. "What sort of mistake?" he asked. "I don't know. A big one, hopefully."

He then asked me a pretty important question. "If they get really annoyed, as you say, don't you think there's a chance they might want to kill you?" Believe it or not, I hadn't thought of that. My expression must have betrayed my sudden doubt. "That's what I thought" Boratch said. He kept going. "Just leave it alone, keep your career intact and don't anger people that might have the means to murder you." When he put it like that, it did sound pretty wise to just let the whole thing slide and move on.

He quickly changed the subject. Anna. He wanted to talk about his daughter Anna and all her woes with her husband again. Listening to Boratch vent was the least I could do. He certainly listened to a lot of my whining. Although, honestly, he could have been a little bit more sympathetic about my plan to nail The Clear Thinkers. I guess I shouldn't expect someone who's not a crime fighting professional, like myself, to fully appreciate and grasp such things. "Are you even listening to me?" he challenged. "Yes, go on. Anna's husband is embarrassing her. I understand." Boratch looked almost as annoyed with me as Superintendent Kim had. "You're not hearing a word I'm saying. Why do I waste my breath?" he asked.

I apologized and attributed my lack of concentration to severe hunger. It wasn't. It was actually too early for me to be eating lunch. Then again, I did have a very light breakfast. Boratch put half of his sandwich in front of me. "Eat it so you are at least approaching someone capable of having a conversation" he said. "Fine. Whatever. I was listening." I grabbed the soggy breaded thing and shoved it into my mouth. I guess I was hungry after all. "So, will you come?" he asked. What? I thought. But stopped myself from uttering aloud. Boratch's eyes flared with anger. He knew I hadn't been listening to him. "Of course" I answered. Boratch sized me up a second. It was as if he was daring me to ask what I had just agreed to attend. I didn't. Which made it worse. Boratch smiled an evil, malicious smile. He had tricked me. He had played upon my inattentiveness to get me to commit to some horrible, tedious, unpleasant event and I had fallen for it. Best friend or not, sometimes I really hated him for such things.

Boratch changed the subject, yet again, before I could delve into the details of the event I had just promised him that I would attend. "What happened with Minister Kapinskov?" he asked. "Last time we spoke you were very worried how he would react to closing the case, as we did." As soon as he said it, I realized that a full week had gone by and I hadn't heard from Kapinskov. I could only assume that there were other matters of state more pressing than some heathen that had killed himself. I told Boratch that I hadn't heard from him. He looked relieved. He apologized for putting me in such a difficult position. I told him not to worry about it.

Remembering the favor I had done him seemed to make up for my attention lapse in the earlier part of our conversation. Boratch was all smiles and jokes again. As hard as I tried to focus on his every word, my mind drifted back to other things. My press release plan was brilliant. Why didn't other people see that? It was only Boratch's words as we parted company and returned to our respective offices that shook me out of my own thoughts. "Anna will be so pleased to see you. Until Saturday." He waved and turned his back to me.

I got home that night and, just as an experiment, found some video footage of the church and foam event at Saint Anthony's. A few stations were running it as a humor piece. "Fire Hoax Gets Foamy" one writer had come up with. It was probably written by one of the staff writers at the Ministry of Information. Some of those guys were good. Really good. Their talents were once used to sell cars and software services. Now they were all about the spin. I could totally do that. I mean, maybe not the same way they did. But I knew I had it in me to be just as creative and clever as they were. I searched the internet for some footage of the event without words superimposed over it. Cute headlines were all well and good but I had something much more effective in mind. I watched the footage and got to work.

My first attempt read as follows: "The work represents the power of God's love as it washes over us and cleanses us of evil, anxiety, and the frailties of being human. It's white purity..." Shit. I forgot about the banner. The one that read "Free Brainwash Here." How would I explain that? I could try to re-appropriate the term "brainwash." Something like: "The tendency of mankind to follow intellect, science and logic has led to thousands of years of pain and suffering. By cleansing the brain of these tendencies, washing them away, if you will, man can attain a higher form of being. One of love, faith and devotion which will..." Yeah, that was pretty good. Or...Or I could just blame the bad guys. The terrorists. I could get rid of the whole twisting of the brainwash thing by just saying it was a frame up.

My new piece became something a bit different. The first part was all about the cleansing and so on, just like I had written previously. But the very next part was this: "It was because of the power of this simple message that a terrorist group needed to try to undermine the work with this feeble, handmade banner." That would work. But then I remembered that I was the terrorist. I mean, in theory. This was supposed to be from their point of view. So, how would that work? I was getting myself so confused.

I was thrilled when I saw a new email come in. It was something to distract me from the circular reasoning I was falling into. I knew that I was on to something. I was just having trouble defining it well enough to use it. The email was from Boratch. It was an invite with details of an event taking place on Saturday. Formal attire required. It was an awards ceremony for Citizen Achievement. I had trouble believing that this was the social engagement Boratch had tricked me into attending. It sounded so painful I couldn't imagine even he would have the endurance for it. Then I saw the names of those being honored. Anna Boratch was among them. If the whole evening didn't sound unappealing enough, there was another bit of information at the bottom of the invite. "Suggested donation, $100." I would get Boratch for this.

It was three days later when life would throw me another curve ball. It had been a fairly productive week. The abortionist had been caught and confessed after a few hours in the Interrogation Center. The Clear Thinkers didn't pull off any new pranks, I mean, terrorist activities. The weather was even nice. Low sixties and sunny. Perfect. All of which I should have known were just signs of my own personal apocalypse about to arrive.

It was on a Thursday evening when it all started to go wrong. I was in the middle of some personal recreational activity involving a fantasy about twenty-three year olds when there was a knock on my door. It was a horrible moment. I was just about...and then the knock. Like I said, a horrible moment. Highly unnerving and awkward. And this was before I even got up to answer the door.

There was a second knock on my door. Not only wasn't I expecting anyone but this person should have, in theory, had to have called me or buzzed up to my apartment before being allowed in. The knock repeated, this time even louder. "Chief

Inspector Hastings. Please open the door." It was a good voice. A male voice. Loud and authoritative. But one I didn't recognize. I looked through the peephole and saw a very large man in a black topcoat and suit. Behind him were two similarly dressed men. They had that look to them. That, "don't mess with us or we will kill you" look. It was hard to tell if they were private or governmental thugs. But they were thugs, one way or another. I quickly looked around my apartment for any embarrassing or incriminating evidence. Not seeing any, I slowly opened the door.

The thug closest to my door spoke. "Chief Inspector Hastings?" he asked. "Yes." "We need you to come with us." I looked at him and his two buddies. "And who might you be? You do realize I am a Chief Inspector, right?" I said, hoping to intimidate him a little with my official title. The thug seemed confused by the question. "Yes, we just confirmed that fact, I believe. Please come with us Chief Inspector. All will be explained on the way." "On the way, where?" I asked. "Sir, please." He gave me that look that thugs are so good at. That way of asking you to do something that's not a question at all but a fact. You are going to do what they asked, whether you liked it or not, and everyone knows it. The "Sir" is just window dressing that makes you feel even more powerless.

I asked for a moment to get my jacket. As I walked across the room, I took one last glance to see if I had left anything embarrassing out. If they come to investigate my disappearance, the last thing I wanted them to find was my "Confessions of a Slave Girl" video on the screen. The whole time I was doing this, the head thug was watching me. I exited my apartment and locked up. The thugs guided me to a black SUV waiting in front of my building. There was yet another thug driving. I thought about asking more questions but decided to let this happy gang of suited intimidators go first. The head thug sat next to me. He closed the door and we silently drove off into the darkness. Finally, he had the courtesy to introduce himself.

"Chief Inspector, I am Special Agent Wussle of the Department of DBBD. He stuck out a hand. I tried not to think too much about where my own hand had just been. I hadn't had the chance to wash it. I shook anyway and waited for him to say more. Nothing. Just an introduction. Which seemed kind of rude. Shouldn't an explanation or something come after?

I decided to ask again. "So, where are we going, Agent Wussle? What does DBBD want with me?" I asked. He smiled. "Your questions will be answered shortly. Please just relax and enjoy the ride." Enjoy the ride? Right. This whole thing was not going to sit well with Superintendent Kim. It made his whole Agency seem weak and like we could just be bossed around by anyone. We were the People's Protection Agency after all. Didn't that mean anything to anyone, anymore? How dare they cart me off like this? Don't they know who I am?

I got more worried as I realized the route the car was taking. We were not headed across town to the Government Center or DBBD Headquarters near Martyrs Square. We were headed out of town. It was all incredibly disconcerting and not at all what I had hoped my evening was going to be like. I considered asking Agent Wussle, yet again, for some answers. Maybe just a hint. The whole not knowing thing was really grating. Which, of course, was the point.

Twenty, very long, minutes later we arrived at a long, dirt road leading into the woods. I should have been struck with panic that I was about to be executed and buried near some bushes. But I wasn't. All I could think about was how very annoying the whole thing was. I was pissed. I'm a Chief Inspector! This just isn't right! Whoever was behind this whole show better have a very, very good explanation for it or there was going to be trouble. Big trouble.

The car pulled in front of a wood cabin. Cabin is a bit inaccurate. It was more like a massive hunting lodge or one of those grand hotels built in the nineteen-twenties out of logs. There were more thugs standing just outside of it. "We're here" the head thug next to me said. He opened the door for me and I got out. The front door to the lodge was opened for me and I was shown inside.

"Hello" a far more friendly voice said. A female voice. It came from a thirty something Asian woman in a red dress. Much more appealing than my steroid-addled companions in every conceivable way. She was a little small for my taste, probably only about five foot three. But she had a nice looking face and a truly great looking body. Nice and taut in all the right places. In spite of all that, I was much more concerned about what I was doing out there and who it was that wanted to see me. I decided to ask. "Can you please..." My little Asian friend put a slender finger up to her lips. I guess I still wasn't allowed to ask questions. "Now, look here. I am a Chief Inspector of the People's Protection Agency. I will not be treated this way!" I declared. Not one, not two, but three different thugs seemed to instantly appear. They didn't say anything but looked at my friend for instructions. She shook her head very subtly. The thugs all receded as quickly as they had arrived. I decided that my questions could wait a little longer.

A few minutes later, things became much clearer. My Asian friend opened a large wooden door for me. It led to a very dark den. Inside was a large stone fireplace with fire blazing and lots of heavy leather furniture. Then I saw a rotund figure stand up from a chair and face me. A rotund figure that I recognized. I breathed a sigh of relief as I heard the door shut behind me. Minister Kapinskov stepped forward.

"Welcome Chief Inspector" he said. "Minister." I turned and took a better look at my Asian guide. She really did have a lovely face. She smiled at me. It was a look that could have even been an invitation. Hopefully, we could talk more later.

After me and my old friend the Minister had our chat. Just as I was starting to feel back in control of things, my Asian friend rammed her elbow right into my balls. I kid you not. A full-force, violent jab which crushed them and sent them swinging about in searing pain. I bent over in agony with tears running down my face. I heard the Minister say "Thank you Miki, that will be all" and saw her leave. What the fuck? I thought. "That was for disobeying me" the Minister said. I felt nauseous and was trying too hard not to throw up to say much in response. "Please have a seat so that we can straighten this matter out."

The idea of moving did not sound appealing to me. Somehow, I forced myself to walk the few steps required to land in a high-backed leather chair facing the Minister. "I would apologize for all the intrigue involved in bringing you out here but I wanted to remind you of what can happen if you cross the wrong people" he said. His words were still barely getting through. I was far too consumed with the throbbing agony of my testicles to really care very much. "Do you like the lodge? It belongs to a friend of mine. He uses it primarily for visits to his mistress but recently had to cut back on those activities. Prostate cancer. So sad." The Minister poured me a shot of Scotch which I downed quickly. Anything to numb the pain.

"So, why did you ignore my request and close the San Sebastian case?" the Minister asked. I wasn't sure how to answer. "Daniel, there's no need to make this difficult. Just answer my question. Why did you close the Robert San Sebastian case?" The Scotch burned my throat and made me feel even more nauseous. For a second, I thought that I was going to puke all over the place. Getting words of any sort out took an incredible amount of effort. But I mumbled a response.

"I screwed up" I said. "Yes, that's obvious. But what do you mean by that?" My brain was scrambling to come up with a plausible lie that wouldn't implicate Boratch. I invented a fairly good story, considering the situation. "I came into the office in pretty sad shape one morning and the Chief Superintendent asked if the case was closed. I said "yes" and then couldn't find a reason to change my answer." The Minister nodded as he pondered over my explanation. He looked right into my eyes. I wondered if he bought it. "I see" he said. I suddenly regretted not coming up with a better excuse. Saying, "I got confused" was probably not going to cut it. But at least it sounded honest.

The Minister stood and picked up a phone. "Yes, Miki. Please ask Agent Wussle and his men to take the Chief Inspector home." That's it? I thought. Then I saw the look on the Minister's face. It was an expression of disappointment. "That's it?" I asked aloud. The thugs all returned to the room. "Yes, that's it. Good-bye Chief Inspector." The thugs started to come for me. Wherever they were taking me, it wasn't going to be home. At the time, I was far too unnerved to think of much else but trying to save my life. It was only much later that I got really insulted by all of this. I'm a Chief Inspector, damn it, and nobody seemed to care. But, like I said, that was later when I was in the safety of my own bed instead of facing a short drive to a shallow grave.

"Wait" I said. The Minister held up his hand to the thugs. "Yes?" I made my play. "It wasn't a mistake. I was asked by someone" I said. "You were asked by someone to ignore my request and to close the case." "Yes" I said. "Who?" I looked around at all the thugs. "Not with them here" I said. I was just buying time. The idea of informing on Boratch was too unbearable. It was possible, however, that whoever had asked him to ask me to close the case outranked the Minister. Then again, I couldn't count on it. And, for that matter, that powerful person would think nothing of sacrificing Boratch and me if it made their own world better. The thugs left the room. I had seconds to come up with an answer that would satisfy Kapinskov and save my life.

The Minister took his chair again and waited. And waited some more. I had no idea what to tell him. I could feel the heat of the fire. The entire room felt so hot and stuffy that I could barely breathe. I thought that I was going to faint. "Well?" the Minister prompted. I had no choice. The name came from my lips. The name of the person who had asked me to close the case. But it wasn't Boratch's name that I uttered. It was Laughton's. Mike Laughton's, the big shot businessman and father of the shrill college girl, Isabella. I could have just as easily blamed the grocery store clerk or a fellow agent. But it was the Laughtons in all their smug glory that made me name them. I had no idea whether the story would fly. I hadn't exactly had time to think it through and work it out.

"Mike Laughton?" Kapinskov asked. "Yes, He came to the station and told me he would make it worth my while. I needed the money to clear up some debts. So, I did it. I'm sorry Minister. It was stupid of me but I was desperate." "Mike Laughton of Energex?" he asked. The question was as much to himself as to me. Actually, totally to himself and not to me. Which let me be quiet for a moment which I much appreciated. I could see Kapinskov going through all the angles, motivations and possible power plays for various government, church and business interests. He slowly started to move his head. It was not a shake. A "there's no fucking way" shake. No, not all. Much to my amazement it was a nod. An agreement. Mike Laughton was behind this whole thing. And then he even said it. "Mike Laughton. Of course. That makes so much sense. I should have seen it. I so should have seen it." I just kept quiet.

"I don't suppose he elaborated" he asked. "No." "No, of course he didn't. Why would he bother? How much?" he asked. "How much what?" "How much money did he give you?" I thought about saying he had promised to pay me but never did. Instead a number came out. "fifty grand" I said. The Minister nodded again. I was praying he wouldn't ask me to turn it over to him which would have been a real problem since I only had eighteen-hundred-dollars to my name.

The Minister was lost in his own thoughts again for a few moments. And then Kapinskov was all smiles. For a man ready to have me disappeared five minutes earlier, he was downright cuddly. "I'll tell you what, Chief Inspector. You keep the fifty thousand dollars that Mr. Laughton already gave you and I will add another fifty thousand to it." "OK" I said, not really knowing what else I could have possibly said to that. "A hundred thousand dollars" he said. "All you have to do is to re-open the case" he added. I didn't even hesitate. "Alright" I said. I had no idea how I was going to pull that off but I figured getting home alive and making some money to boot were a higher priority at that moment. I even thought about asking how and when I would get my cash but decided it might be a little inappropriate.

"Mike Laughton" Kapinskov repeated to himself. And then he smiled again like it was the best joke he had ever heard. "How are your balls, Inspector?" he asked. The answer, especially in hindsight, is that they were bigger than he would ever know. Ginormous even.

It was only when I was safely deposited back home that I had time to think about what I had done. After checking to see that my testicles were not permanently damaged, I sat in my chair. Knowing the Minister's ways, Mr. Laughton might already be on his way to the Interrogation Center or worse. What if he had an alibi? I could always say that the meeting took place that time he came to Headquarters. That time that he was such an ass to me. Or maybe even say there were two meetings and that his impertinent little daughter was the messenger between us. The more I thought about it, the more odd it seemed that the Minister hadn't asked me for all those sorts of details when he had me in front of him. I guess Laughton was such an interesting adversary to him that he forgot. Or it was so obvious to him that he didn't feel the need to ask. And then it struck me that I knew almost nothing about this man I had probably sent to days of unimaginable torture and eventual death. I mean, other than he was kind of a prick. I decided to look up some information on Mike Laughton.

I was able to access quite a bit of information very quickly. Laughton was a City University graduate who had become a major executive at Dynamic, the energy company. He had made his name quite early in his career. He did this by taking a new technology which made oil drilling cheaper and changing the way people thought about it. The technique, "Forced Extraction" actually produced less oil than traditional methods but was one tenth the cost. It also had a nasty drawback of poisoning the water table and making vast areas around the drill sites barren wastelands. Because of that, for many years, the method was considered politically untenable and never used. It was Laughton who realized that if he could change the perception of the technique, he might be able to win its acceptance.

It was his use of genetically modified grass which changed everything. The grass grew in sheets and wasn't really grass at all. It was more akin to Astroturf. It didn't need nutrients from the soil, just a bit of sunlight. Laughton had giant grass sheets rolled over the barren, dry ground that appeared after Forced Extraction was used. From a distance, and more importantly, on camera, the areas looked amazingly lush and beautiful. It was only when one actually walked across the new grass product that you would notice that it wasn't real grass. At least not the sort of grass most of us remember from our childhoods.

It looked like grass and smelled like grass. But there was a feel to it that wasn't quite right. It could actually cause cuts deep enough to require stitches if you caught it at the wrong angle. It also caused cancer should you be exposed to it for too long. But it was close, kind-of-grass. Close enough that, under Laughton's supervision, hundreds of millions of dollars were spent on advertising promoting the new combination of F.E. and genetically engineered grass as "Green Made Greener." And it worked brilliantly.

There was an internal argument that the real message should have been about cheaper prices at the pump but Laughton completely nixed that. He didn't see why the ninety percent savings in production costs should be passed on to the consumer when it could be used to boost corporate profits. In fact, the efficiency of the techniques was kept secret for years for fear that the people would demand a reduction in gas and oil prices. By the time such information was made public, nobody seemed too angry about it. Oil profits were good for the economy. Anybody who was against the idea of companies making money was clearly a terrorist sympathizer, hell bent on destroying our way of life. So, there was little protest.

In any case, the whole thing made Laughton's career. At the age of thirty-eight he was named the President of Dynamic. Then, at forty-three, he was offered a part ownership stake in Energex, along with a massive salary and bonus package, to switch teams. He did so and became CEO. A title he has now held for four years. No wonder he was such an arrogant asshole when he came to castigate me.

It was later in the evening that I understood why the Minister had reacted the way he had. There was a reason Laughton's name would have been so familiar to him. Dynamic was an oil company largely owned by current, and former, government officials. The Minister probably had a healthy financial stake in the company. When their golden boy, Laughton, left for the competition, it was not only seen as disloyal, it torpedoed their stock price. The value of the company was down to about half of what it was just two years ago. I'm sure the Minister, and others with inside knowledge of Laughton's impending move, sold before that huge devaluation. However, they couldn't have been happy their biggest cash cow had been slaughtered.

All of which made me wonder about Energex. Who owned it? It must be somebody very powerful, in their own right, to stand up to the people that had an interest in Dynamic. It was a privately held company, all seven-hundred billion dollars of it. There was virtually no public information about it. It was only after using my very high level security clearance that I got an answer. Dynamic was a hundred percent owned by the State Church. God bless us, every one.

There was no way the Minister was just going to arrest Laughton. Doing so would be an open declaration of political warfare on the Church. Nobody could afford that. Literally. Which made me wonder what they would do about Laughton and his interest in the San Sebastian case. An interest he didn't really have but I made up for him. Oh, Man, this was going to be ugly.

And then there was possibly the most pressing problem of all. I mean, aside from Mike Laughton and the entire State Church leadership wanting to know who implicated him and why. Who had asked Boratch to close the San Sebastian case in the first place? San Sebastian was a drug salesman and, as far as I knew, had no connection to the oil industry at all. It was all so damn confusing.

I called Boratch. It was after midnight but he would still pick up. The good news was that he answered his phone. But there were some problems. One, I really couldn't take the chance of saying much over the phone. Two, Boratch picked up but was very, very drunk. He told me to find someone else to deal with the body. I didn't know what he meant at first until I realized that he had assumed it was a normal work call. A command performance to appear at a crime scene and inspect a corpse or two. When I told him the call wasn't about that, he got very confused. I just said I would be coming over right away and left it at that.

I drove across town to Boratch's apartment. What should have been a short, traffic-free drive turned into a tedious ordeal. The road was being repaired again, for the second time in three years. It was down to one lane. Almost an hour later, I arrived at the large complex Boratch lived in. He was in one of ten massive towers called "Gilman Center." So named because the Mayor behind the project was Peter Gilman, a former actor turned politician. I parked my car and made my way to Tower Three where Boratch lived. I buzzed up and got no response. I buzzed again. Nothing. He was probably passed out. I called him on the phone again. Still no answer. I was getting quite annoyed.

I picked apartment number 101 and buzzed. I was hoping it would be the super. An old lady answered. I told her I was with People's Protection and demanded that she let me in. She did as instructed. At least some people still had proper respect for the position. I arrived on the twelfth floor and pounded on

Boratch's door. Nothing. I did it again, even louder. This time I heard a stirring inside. Boratch opened the door with groggy eyes and hair that was all over the place. "Daniel" he said with a grin. He gave me a bear hug before I could duck out of the way. His breath stank of Vodka.

Finally, after I was released from his grip, we went into his apartment. Before I had even sat down, Boratch was back on his sofa and closing his eyes again. "Samuel! Wake up! I need to ask you something." He opened his eyes and made an effort to become more alert. "Of course. What is it? Is it about Anna?" he asked. I had no idea why he thought I was there to discuss his daughter. "No" I said. "Good. Because she is an ungrateful little bitch." I had never heard him talk that way about Anna before. He always praised her and spoke proudly of her. He mumbled on. "I don't mean that. I don't mean that at all. She's a lovely girl. Spoiled, perhaps. But she is a fine woman. She does justice to the Boratch name!" I wondered what had set Samuel off about Anna to provoke the initial outburst. But I would have to ask later.

I was just about to ask Boratch about San Sebastian when his eyes closed again. I walked over and shook him. "Boratch, wake up. I need to know about San Sebastian" I said. "He's dead" Boratch said. "I know he's dead. But who was it that asked you to make sure the case was ruled an accident?" Boratch just smiled. He shook his head "no." "Boratch, I was almost taken to the woods and shot tonight by Minister

Kipinskov because of this San Sebastian thing. You have to tell me." Boratch looked concerned. "You don't want to know. It will only make things worse." He started to fall asleep again. I was getting very frustrated. I shook him awake, yet again. "Boratch, who told you to make sure we found San Sebastian's death an accident?" His response was not what I expected.

He grinned and then pointed. He pointed straight up to the sky. "God? God told you to?" I asked. I was not happy with his reply. "Oh, come on!" I said. Drunk or not, that was an asinine answer. "Not God. But close" he explained. I waited for him to elaborate on his own. He didn't.

"Well, who then?" "You really don't want to know. I'm telling you. You don't." He was really starting to piss me off. Of course I wanted to know. I had my balls elbowed and had been threatened with death over this whole thing. Getting some answers was pretty high on my "to do" list. "Yes, I do. Please tell me" I said. Boratch sighed. "Alright, if you insist." "I do." He paused dramatically. Way, way too dramatically. Finally, he spoke.

"Rooney" he said. "Rooney?" "That's right, Cardinal Thomas Michael Rooney. I told you that you didn't want to know." And in many ways, Boratch was correct. It was about the worst name that could have come out of his mouth. Cardinal Rooney was the second most powerful man in the entire State Church. Actually, scratch that. He was the single most powerful man in the State Church. He even had more power than the Pope when it came down to it. He was the power behind who got named to what positions. Where the billions in investments went. Who got elected to public office. What laws were passed. He was not so much Cardinal as King, in all except the title. His interest in San Sebastian was odd enough. How a Medical Examiner like Boratch was even on his radar was truly mysterious.

"Alright. I've told you. Now, please let me sleep. You can stay here if you like. Or go. I don't really care. I just need to sleep" Boratch said. How Boratch expected me to just let it go after he dropped that little bomb is beyond me. "Please" he pleaded. "I know you have a lot of questions but not now. In the morning. Over coffee. We will talk then. Ok?" he asked. There was something in his voice that sounded desperate. A need to just be left alone so intense that it sounded like grilling him more would kill him. So, I nodded. It would have to wait until morning.

"Thank you, Daniel. You are a good friend." He carefully made his way down the hall and to his bedroom. I didn't move from my chair. My brain was far too filled with thoughts to sleep.

Actually, I guess my brain wasn't that active after all. I woke up in the chair sometime the next morning. Boratch was already awake. In spite of having so much to discuss, neither of us said a word as we drank our coffee. Boratch looked slightly worse for wear and I probably didn't look much better. I don't think either one of us really had the energy and concentration required to delve into things. Horrible, complicated things we had no business being a part of. But we did delve. Eventually.

Boratch sat at the table explaining how he had known Cardinal Rooney for almost forty years. His wife, Doris, had been very close to him. Too close. She had been in a relationship with the Cardinal before she was married to Boratch. Rather than harbor ill will at Doris after the relationship with her ended, Rooney and Doris remained friends. He often used his influence to make sure she was kept clear of whatever political cleansings were going on and to make sure that Samuel's career remained unfettered. Samuel made it clear, although offered, he never allowed Rooney to do anything more than to make sure Doris and he were just left alone. His career would have been very different if he had allowed the Cardinal to use his influence in such things.

When I asked him why he didn't take more advantage of the connection, Boratch's response was "The man fucked my wife. I know it was before she met me. But still. There's something very off-putting about that." Which then made me ask why he did Rooney favors then, if that was the way he felt. His answer was a single word. "Anna."

He told me that Rooney had been instrumental in making sure that Anna got into the Central University and got the appropriate job offers upon graduation. To this day, Anna is unaware of the powerful people paving the way for her. She, like most of us, assumes that if good things are happening for her, she must have earned them. In fact, Anna's opinion of herself as a genius in her field, and true talent, far exceeds her actual abilities. But that's another story.

It was because of what the Cardinal had done for Anna that Boratch felt obligated to come through when Rooney requested anything. The first time was some nineteen years ago. Boratch fudged some evidence that would have led to the conviction of one of the Cardinal's staff. The second was just about some information regarding a Priest's apparent drug overdose. And the third was the San Sebastian case. Boratch did not ask Rooney any questions. The Cardinal had asked for a favor and Boratch complied. Since I was the lead investigator on the case, Boratch didn't think it would be much of a problem. Why would he?

"So, you don't know why the Cardinal has an interest in this drug salesmen guy?" I asked. "No clue. I learned long ago not to ask such things." Although I had told him last night, I repeated to Boratch what had taken place between the Minister and I. Samuel graciously enquired about the comfort of my balls. Still sore but not overwhelmingly so. Then we tried to figure out what to do next. Between Cardinal Rooney, The Minister and Mike Laughton there were some very powerful and, possibly, very angry, people looking over my shoulder.

My next move would be critical. It had to be perfect or I would piss one of the three off enough to end up dead. For that matter, if Laughton found out it was me that informed on him, my death was a real possibility anyway. Which sucked. Really and truly sucked. I just wanted to go to work, arrest a few people and then go home and watch TV. I couldn't believe how complicated the whole thing had become.

"We should go to Cardinal Rooney" I suggested. My thinking was that since Boratch had done as he had asked, we were on his team. This would mean we would be protected accordingly. Between that and Boratch's existing relationship with him, we should be fine. Boratch begged to differ. "Except for one thing, My Friend. I told you about him. He's a man who expects total confidentiality regarding such issues. That puts you and I both on his shit list."

I then suggested that Boratch go alone to ask for my protection. Again, Boratch pointed out the downside. There was a very real possibility that Rooney would just decide it was better to tie up loose ends and have Boratch and I both disappear. "Fine. So what then? What do you think the best way to handle this is?" I asked. His answer was simply "Whatever you do, don't go against the Cardinal. You cannot win." "And Kapinskov?" I asked. "You will figure something out. You always do" he said. "So, we are agreed you will still close that case file, right. My Friend." I didn't answer. Bortach asked again. "Kapinskov is nothing compared to the Cardinal.

You know that. He is nothing." Easy for him to say. He's not the one facing a shallow grave if things aren't sorted out pretty quickly.

"You're being promoted" he said. I sat there staring at Superintendent Kim making sure that I heard correctly. "It's not official yet but it's already been informally discussed and you're the man" he said. Either the Superintendent forgot to mention some important details, or my mind was so preoccupied with not getting executed I was hearing things. "Chief Windsor is stepping down as the head of Anti-Terror and I will be replacing him in March. Again, none of this is official yet but, trust me, those that decide these things have already decided them." My mind went back to the unfortunate press conference Chief Windsor gave after the foaming of the church. The one where he referred to it as a terrorist act only to have that story completely undermined later. Decades of service down the drain for telling the truth. What an idiot.

Superintendent Kim was pacing around proudly with his hands behind his back as he looked out his window. There wasn't much of a view. Just the windows of an adjacent office building. But I guess he liked walking around a bit during his moment of glory. Being promoted to Chief of Anti-Terror was a big deal for him. It would put his career on a whole new level. Instead of just being another anonymous law-enforcement official, he would constantly be in the public eye.

I wanted to remind the Superintendent how that had turned out to be a very bad thing for several former Chiefs of Anti-Terror. Windsor was just the latest of several that had said the wrong thing in front of the cameras and paid the price for it. But Kim only saw the successes. The current favorite for next Party Chairman had made his name at Anti-Terror and was the personification of a law and order candidate. There were also two less prominent cabinet members that had served in the post briefly. There was even one who had been named to, the now largely ceremonial position, of Chief Justice. This, in spite of his lack of apparent qualifications including the fact that he never attended law school. Any way you sliced it, being Chief of Anti-Terror was a big deal.

Kim was already imagining himself as one of the top echelon. Well, not the top, top. Those were people like Cardinal Rooney. But top in terms of a lot of power and tremendous public visibility. It was all pretty remarkable for a man like Kim who had a very nondescript career. There was nothing exceptional about him or his professional record in the least.

Speaking of which, the conversation finally turned back to me. "And you will be taking my seat behind the desk, here. How do you feel about that?" he asked. I knew he wanted me to be excited. It was a major thing, in his eyes. My salary would more than double and I would have access to private clubs and parties that I would not be invited to as a lowly field officer. All good stuff.

"Sounds great" I said. From Superintendent Kim's response, it clearly wasn't enthusiastic enough of a reply. "I thought you would be a little more excited, Chief Inspector. I hope I haven't gone out on a limb backing the wrong horse" he said. "No, you haven't. I assure you that I am the right horse" I said. "Excellent! Of course, we both have to keep this under wraps until the official announcement. Chief Windsor has already handed in his resignation but it would be inappropriate to let people know I am his replacement before the Committee announces it." "Of course" I said. "And you will be named as my official replacement shortly afterward" he said. I nodded. "I do wish you looked a little bit more excited, Hastings. This is a very big break for both of us. Enjoy it!" he said.

"I'm just trying not to count on anything until it happens. You know how it is. Life has been filled with too many opportunities that have disappeared into thin air for one reason or another" I said. Kim nodded. He was still standing behind his desk as if he was already being photographed constantly by the press. "I knew you were the right man. An answer like that just goes to prove it." I thought about asking more details about my new salary and perks and so on but decided it would be wiser to throw things back to Superintendent Kim. He was just bursting to talk about his impending promotion. So I did. He went on for forty-minutes about his career and what he hoped to do in the future, etc. All without letting me get a word in.

It was over an hour later when I got out of the office and had time to really think about everything. In the scheme of things, the promotion really didn't seem to matter very much. Staying alive was a much bigger priority. In fact, news of my promotion would only remind people about me. Not like being put in the media glare of being the Chief of Anti-Terror would. But not exactly helpful in just quietly receding into the bureaucracy the way I had become so good at. It was just not good timing to have people suddenly paying attention to me. For one thing, I needed to investigate this whole thing with San Sebastian and fix the mess I had created. Which raised another issue. A very minor one compared to my getting tortured to death, for sure. But it was still on my mind. I actually liked my current job.

As a Chief Inspector, I still worked on individual cases. I was out on the crime scene talking with Boratch and other techs. I was interviewing witnesses. I was piecing together clues and interrogating suspects. Sometimes I was a little too tired to appreciate it the way I once had. But I still enjoyed it. I had long ago given up on the illusion that what I did made a lick of difference in the world. But being an investigator was active and interesting. And, dare I say it, even kind of glamorous.

Being a Superintendent was none of those things. It was office work. It was budgets. It was "man management." It was dull as dirt. I never did understand how those in charge thought being a good field detective equated to being a good manager. The two seem entirely unrelated to me. Then again, I wasn't being picked for the position because I had the highest clearance rate or had solved the most high-profile cases. There were one or two others who had me on those counts. I knew full well why they thought mine would be the best butt in the chair behind the desk. I didn't make waves. At least, I didn't used to.

The more I thought about it, the more anxious I got. How was I supposed to deal with Mike Laughton and what I had done to him when I panicked? Yes, I admit it. It was a total, "please, for the love of God, don't kill me" panic. A panic which I will never forgive them for creating. And it had solved the problem short term. I was still alive. But, long term, it had the potential to cause me all sorts of grief. Especially, knowing what I knew now about Boratch and his protectors. And now there would be people actually paying attention to me. This was terrible.

I called Boratch and told him I needed to meet him for lunch. He declined. I told him I really, really wanted to meet him for lunch. He said, yet again, that he couldn't. I hung up wondering if things were already in play against Boratch and/

or me. I really wanted to tell him about the promotion news. Not to mention, the plan I had yet to figure out on how to deal with all the rest of it. I had promised Kapinskov that I would reopen the San Sebastian case. Yet, Boratch had closed it at the request of someone even more powerful. This was going to be tricky. It was just then that I heard a voice from the not all that distant past. A shrill voice. A shrill, annoying voice that, in many ways, could be blamed for this entire thing. It was the voice of Isabella Laughton.

"How did you do it Inspector?" she asked. She was standing directly in front of me wearing a nicely fitting, blue shirt and jeans. "It's Chief Inspector. And do what, exactly?" I asked. "My father has disappeared. He left for work this morning with his bodyguards but never arrived at his office." Oh, shit. Kapinskov acted quickly. "I know nothing about it" I said. She wasn't about to let it go. "How did you do it? You're nobody. How could a lowly cop arrange something like that to get back at my father?" she asked. I tried to understand what she was implying. There was no possible way she could have known I tossed her high-powered, ass of a father, to the wolves to save my own hide.

"Where are you keeping him?" she demanded. This was getting better and better. "Wait a minute. You think I arranged to have your father arrested this morning? And I'm holding him in a cell somewhere?" I asked. Just hearing the words come out of my mouth made them seem even more ridiculous.

"How else would you explain it? He goes into your office to rip you a new one and the next thing we know, he disappears." I thought about what she was accusing me of. Oh, if only I really had that sort of power. I mean, I do with regular folks. Common, not connected to anyone, just going about their dreary, daily lives folks. But people like Mike Laughton. No way. Untouchable to a mere Chief Inspector like me. Unless, of course, you inadvertently accuse them of something in a moment of terror. But aside from that.

"Well?" she demanded, green eyes blazing with anger. Being angry suited her. "I didn't even realize he was missing. Did you report it?" I asked. "Of course, I reported it. A lot of good it will do. I know how you people work. The way you just take people away and they are never seen again. I'm not going to let you get away with this!" I was really kind of flattered by how much power she thought I had. Was she really that naïve about who her father was and how things worked in this country?

"Which department?" I asked. "What?" "Which department did you report it to?" She stammered a second. "Actually, I didn't report it, his co-workers did. They called me afterward." I asked for more details. I got the name of the co-worker, some VP, and learned that he reported it to his local Police station. I couldn't imagine calls weren't also made to some more powerful people in the government or in the Church hierarchy. But she didn't seem to know about those.

When I asked for details on his disappearance, I expected some dramatic tale of cars blocking the road and men armed with automatic weapons wearing balaclavas. She said, as far as she knew, there was nothing like that. Her father had just left for work and never shown up at the office. It's still possible it was more of an armed kidnapping but that was neither here nor there.

Mike Laughton was missing and I was being blamed. I wasn't being blamed in any realistic, plausible way. But I was still being blamed. And those connections would be made. The connections between me, Laughton, Kapinskov and all the rest. Crap. I needed to get on this.

I reiterated to Isabella Laughton that I had nothing to do with her father's disappearance. I also promised that I would look into it further for her. Her response to the last statement was interesting. "Why would you do that? To clear your name?" she asked. "I just want to help" I said. "Right." She wasn't buying it. I needed to give her a more plausible reason. So, I did.

"Alright, fine. The truth is I think you're a stunningly attractive young woman. I'm hoping if I can be your hero on this, maybe you would feel a little indebted to me." I made sure that she interpreted the last words as slimily as possible. "Like I'm gonna sleep with you? No way! Not gonna happen. Ever. The thought of sleeping with an old man like you makes me sick" she said. Ouch. What a bitch. But I kept up the act.

"Even if it's the difference between saving your father or not?" She didn't have an answer for that one. She left without saying another word. Take that, Bitch.

I had no intention of sleeping with Isabella Laughton. Long, lovely, young Isabella Laughton. Unless she asked nicely. But aside from that. Anyway, I contacted Central Records and looked up the Missing Persons Report. Mike Laughton had left his house at six-forty-six AM in his armored Mercedes. He was accompanied by the driver and one body guard. Both were trained security personnel and ex-military. The car could be tracked on CCTV along its normal route for the first ten minutes. Then all trace of it vanished. Not only wasn't it on the CCTV of the route normally taken by Laughton to work, all electronic signals had stopped. The internet connection from the car had been cut off. The GPS locator in the car and on the cell phones of all three men, also went quiet. A total communications black out.

Such a black out could have easily occurred if the car and its occupants were destroyed. Not shot. But obliterated. Like from an armor piercing missile. One would think such a thing might have been noticed though. It's not everyday you see a Mercedes get blown sky high by a rocket in our city. The other answer was that Laughton had gotten tipped off that he was a target and had shut everything off himself. Strictly speaking, it was illegal to turn off personal GPS devices because it made it harder for law enforcement officials and marketing companies to track people. However, Mike Laughton was no average citizen and may have done exactly that. It all sounded a little more plausible than the rocket idea.

Whether it was because he was blown up or because he had voluntarily disappeared, I found the whole thing very disturbing. Within days of me uttering his name to Minister Kapinskov, Mike Laughton had mysteriously disappeared. I'd love to say that my main concern was for the safety of a, more or less, innocent man. But it wasn't. It was for me. And a little for Boratch. But mostly for me. I knew that forces well beyond my control were now in play.

Thank the Lord for bureaucratic delays. Although almost a week had passed, the San Sebastian file had not been processed. Due to a computer incompatibility issue between the Agency's computers and The Department of Citizen Justice, there was a five to ten day delay. Assuming the worst, I had feared that it would have been five and the file would have moved forward. That would have caused me untold complications. Getting something undone that has been officially processed is like trying to uncook a burnt steak. More or less impossible. But, thanks to the differences in the various multi-million dollar computer systems, the file was still listed as "pending" when I found it. "Pending." "Pending" was downright great. It meant I could take the file out of the cue with very little effort.

Which raised the next question. Who did I want to piss off the least? I had gone back and forth on the issue a ridiculous amount of times in my head. Cardinal Rooney was far and away the most powerful player in the mix. And Bortach was directly involved. However, Minister Kapinskov had bruised my balls and threatened to have me executed and dumped in a muddy grave. In my book, that one won. If Cardinal Rooney asked Boratch why the file wasn't closed as he demanded, there was a plausible answer. It was marked "Closed: Accidental Death" but hadn't been officially processed yet. The Cardinal would easily believe that a file could get hung up for weeks due to the usual government inefficiencies. All Boratch had to do was re-assure him that it was done and was just being processed. How much trouble could that cause? Done and done.

With the stroke of a few keys, I had managed to buy myself at least three weeks. After that, my guess was that Cardinal Rooney would start to get suspicious that the file had not been formally closed. But three weeks? He would buy that. I had meant to explain to Boratch why this was the best course of action before I did all this. But then I would have had to listen to him complain and protest about how defying Rooney was a mistake, blah, blah, blah, powerful man, blah, blah re-education camp, torture, blah, blah, blah, and so on. He wasn't the one almost disappeared the other night. I was. So, I'd tell him afterward, when it was a done deal. That way he would have to cooperate for his own self-preservation.

Now, the obvious thing at this point would have been to find out more about Mike Laughton's disappearance. But that is not the way that I, a seasoned investigator and soon to be named Superintendent, went about things. For one thing, it would have raised a lot of red flags poking around too much. No, my brilliant and experienced mind knew that the real answers were still in that tacky house in the hills. The home of Robert San Sebastian. If I could determine why so many powerful people were interested in him, then the rest would become clear. At least, that was my hope at the time.

So, filled with renewed confidence, not to mention, having a convenient excuse to avoid Boratch for a while, I returned to the San Sebastian residence. When I arrived, there was a "For Sale" sign posted in the front. I wondered how many millions they would get for such a place. With any luck, someone would buy it for its location and just tear it down. It was hard to imagine anyone would have the cherub fetish that San Sebastian seemed to. Not to mention, the place was just horribly built. The quality of construction rivaled that of government projects in short cuts and shoddiness. As I entered the kitchen, I was finally snapped out of my hatred for the house and reminded why I had come there. A man had killed himself and a lot of important people seemed to care for reasons I had yet to understand.

I was hoping the surroundings might tell me something new. They didn't really. At least not directly. After pacing around the ghastly residence for a while I sat down at the kitchen table with San Sebastian's file. Yes, THAT, table. The one they had found him at with a chunk of his head missing. It had been cleaned up very thoroughly. Not a chunk of skull or brain matter anywhere. Amazing, really, considering how much blood and mess was there. It looked just like any other tacky kitchen now.

I opened the file. Crime scene photos. The "before" to the existing "after." Not a lot of new information there. Boratch had told me it was a suicide. It looked like a suicide. I had every indication that it was, in fact, exactly what it appeared as. A suicide. So, why did the Cardinal want it ruled an accident? The most likely answer was embarrassment. A criminal charge of suicide impacted a lot of people. Maybe someone in San Sebastian's family had some pull. Maybe they had asked the Cardinal to do them a favor and save their family from disgrace and civil and criminal charges. I made a note to look into the San Sebastian clan further. It was then that I remembered a photo. The woman San Sebastian had been with. I seemed to recall that it was in the bedroom.

I walked into the hunting lodge themed bordello of a room and over to San Sebastian's dresser. There was an empty picture frame. Then I remembered that I had asked the tech to bag the photo. It was back at HQ in an evidence locker somewhere. Maybe there were more of them. I walked around the house looking for more photos and found none. There were probably quite a few stored on San Sebastian's computer. But, that too, was back at HQ. I was getting increasingly annoyed that I came out to the house instead of just staying at the office. My hope was that the place would jar me into some great insight. So far, the only insight I was having was that it would have been much more productive to just review the evidence I already had back at Agency Headquarters.

Then I had a thought. The sort of Chief Inspectorly thought that had made my career. I needed to find his sock drawer. Every man has a place where he hides things. The classic location used to be a sock drawer. But it could be anything. A box in a closet. A bag under the bed. If San Sebastian had a girlfriend then he would have had someplace to stash the stuff he didn't want her to know about. I tore the place apart looking for said stash.

As it happened, it, quite literally, turned out to be his sock drawer. How unimaginative. But I found what I was looking for in there. There was a small box of memory sticks. Several had large, commercial type on them with such titles as "Ass Bangers: The Complete Series." Porn had once been easily accessible online and the business almost went bankrupt because so much of it had become free. But then the government got involved in the name of morality and saving society from itself. A number of decency laws were passed with heavy pressure from the church. Pornography was once again driven underground. Still widely available, of course. But more expensive and less convenient. The business was also more profitable than it had ever been before. Shocking, I know. The most popular format for smut was memory sticks which could contain a lot of videos and photos but were easily hidden. It wasn't porn, however, that I was looking for.

I was thinking he might have some other items in there that he wanted to remain secret. So, I searched further in the sock drawer and found something else. The owner's manual for an electronic safe with the combination written on it. Safe? I hadn't seen any safe. It made sense a custom built mansion like this would have one, I supposed. But where?

I left the bedroom and looked for an office or den of some sort. There were a number of sitting rooms, game rooms, a wrapping room for gifts, storage rooms, etc. But I didn't see a room that looked like an office. I knew that didn't make any sense. If San Sebastian had an entire room dedicated to his collection of antique toys, he certainly would have had one as an office. For appearances sake, if nothing else. Then I remembered the Cherub dome. It was there. Or off of there, at least. I had been so distracted by the hideousness of it all that I had walked right by an elevator door and, more or less, forgotten about it.

I walked back and got into the elevator. I expected to go up to the second story. But there was only one button. It went down. I pushed it and the elevator slowly took me below the main house. It stopped and the doors opened. It was an office. Not, like, a home office. Like a corporate office. There was a waiting room and a greeting desk. There were hallways to several small rooms and bigger ones filled with cubicles. And not a soul was there. In fact, nothing was there. The place had been stripped of almost everything. No computers. No phones. No sign of human existence. All in all, I'm guessing the place could have held about a hundred and fifty people. A hundred and fifty doing what, exactly, I had no clue, yet. But it was clear the home of Robert San Sebastian wasn't just a home but a secret business operation of some sort.

I got to the end of the hall and reached what appeared to be the largest office. I saw the safe on the wall. It was the one I had found the manual for. I typed in the combination and opened it. Predictably, there was nothing at all inside of it. After spending thirty minutes looking for any sort of clues, I gave up. The space had either never been occupied or had been cleared so thoroughly that it was spotless. Either way, it was a very strange location for a corporate office.

As much as I wanted to call an army full of techs in to go over the entire place, I decided against it. I couldn't afford to draw attention to actively investigating the case. I took some quick photos on my cell phone and made some more notes. Just before leaving, I returned to the sock drawer. Used or not, some of San Sebastian's collection had some things I wanted to see in it. Why let it go to waste?

"What are you doing!?" Boratch said. It was one of those whispers that was really a yell. Thankfully, this conversation occurred at All Saints Market and Bortach didn't want to make too much of a scene. "I'm buying kumquats. And some bread" I said. "You know what I mean!" he whispered/yelled again. I had finally gotten him to meet with me. We both took an hour out of our day to go to the market. Normally, it was a very peaceful routine. The freshest of everything from all around the region. All organic. All very expensive but worth it if you could afford it. "Look at the Sea Bass. Amazing" I said. "I didn't come here to talk about Sea Bass." Which I knew. Which is why I was torturing him a little. I was really annoyed Bortach hadn't made time to talk with me when I had asked. He expected me to fit my life around his schedule. I am a Chief Inspector, damn it! And nobody seems to respect that.

I brought Boratch up to speed on everything. I told him about San Sebastian's downstairs office. He didn't seem to care. All he kept going on about was how I hadn't closed the case. I told him, given the circumstance, I couldn't do that. He repeated, yet again, that Kapsinkov was nothing compared to Cardinal Rooney and that I had made a huge mess of things. The fish merchant took a live fish out of the tank. The fish flopped frantically as it suffocated. It wasn't an image I really needed to see at that moment. Luckily, the knife came down and put the thing out of its misery.

With fish now in hand, I explained to Bortach how we had a small window of time where everybody was happy. Kapinskov had gotten his case reopened. Cardinal Rooney would think it was closed and done with. At least for a while. Bortach looked at me as if I was nuts. "And then what? What happens when the Cardinal finds out the case is still open? We flee the country? We kill ourselves to avoid torture? What, my Friend? You clearly haven't thought this through!" Boratch was whispering/yelling again. He was actually annoying me. I had already gone over everything he was saying a hundred times in my head. There were no good answers. Out of the very bad choice of angering one powerful person over another, I picked the one I had the direct relationship with and the one that would have been harder to stall. I kept telling Bortach, again and again, that it would be a while before the Cardinal even realized what was happening.

"How long?" Boratch asked. "A file like that could easily get caught up for four or five weeks in the system" I replied. "And then what?" "Tell him there was a problem and the file had to be resubmitted which will buy us another five weeks" I said. Boratch shook his head. I was really not enjoying the conversation at all. "Look, Boratch. I bought us ten weeks to figure out something else. Given the choices we were facing that's the best I could do." "You mean the choices YOU were facing." The lack of understanding and sympathy from Boratch was too much. I thought he was my friend. I guess I was wrong. I asked him what he would do if he had been threatened directly with death. He didn't want to hear it. He, very dramatically, just said, "we're both dead, now, anyway."

That was it. I lost it. His narrow minded, self-serving drama was just too much for me. I exploded. I yelled at him. Not whisper/yelled but yelled, yelled. I told him his whining wasn't helping anything and that it was a bad situation for both of us. A situation that we would find a way out of. Somehow. Maybe. But, regardless. A situation that sucked for both of us and whining and complaining about the past wasn't going to do much of anything for anyone. All the stress and anger over everything seemed to boil up and it all came out in a torrent of words aimed at Boratch. I was so furious that I almost threw my fish at him. And just when I was about to ratchet it up another gear, Boratch did something even more annoying. Just when I was starting to really enjoy the release of all my pent up stuff, Boratch said he was sorry. I could have killed him. I wanted to be pissed and just go until I was exhausted. Instead he told me that he was sorry and understood why I made the decision I had made. He even told me that I was right. That my choice made the best sense given the situation we were in.

It was then that I noticed far too many people looking at us. People that should have been focused on which type of apple to buy but were enjoying the little live drama playing out in front of them. I felt like shooting them all. They want drama? How about a few bullets to the chest? I'll give them drama. But Boratch was still doing his understanding, old man, routine. He kept saying it over and over again. "You're right. What can I say? You made the best choice you could. "You're right." It was all so annoying.

Boratch wanted to go to a bar and get a drink. I wasn't that thrilled with carrying a fish around with me for too long, but I agreed. It was in the bar that Boratch asked me what my plan was. I knew it had to center on San Sebastian. I told him that I could do some things quietly, but anything involving official procedures could be easily checked. If someone with connections wanted to see what I was up to, all they had to do was check. They could get a list of what I had searched for on the computer, GPS records of where I had been, any requests for official documents, etc. etc. Every Detective in the Agency was watched and monitored at all times. As Superintendent Kim liked to say "transparency breeds honesty."

Of course, some things were much more transparent than others. But still. We worked in the shadows as far as the public was concerned but, in reality, we had far less privacy and independence than the average citizen. Which means, hardly any at all. We would have to act exactly as we always had. We had to keep to our usual routines. Neither Boratch or me could afford a sudden change in behavior that would arouse suspicion. Boratch not only understood, he used it against me.

He held me to my promise to attend Anna's award ceremony on Saturday. As unfortunate as it would be for a lot of people, I was hoping a multiple homicide or something similarly violent and pressing might still get me out of it. But no such luck.

The awards ceremony was held in the auditorium of the Science Center. I saw Bortach and Anna waiting for me by a display explaining the creation of man. From a distance, Anna actually looked almost attractive. She had lost some weight since I had seen her last and was looking quite fit. Almost too much so in the way certain older women overcompensate for aging and become over-muscular and toned. Her hair, however, was still that nasty fake blonde color which she swore was her natural hue. My objection wasn't to it being dyed. It was the choice of cheap, bleach-blond look that never worked for me. I'm sure if she knew my thoughts on the issue that she would shed tears. Her opinion of me was about as high as my opinion as her.

I made my way over and said hello. Anna put her face out for a fake kiss. I half, kind of, gave her one, smelling her, far too strong, perfume as I did. "Good to see you again Anna. You're looking well" I said. "Thanks, enabler" she said. "Anna, Stop It!" Boratch snapped. I let the accusation slide. Anna had decided that her father was an alcoholic and I was part of the problem. She may have been right on both counts but I really didn't need to be accused of it all the time. What did she want me to do? Lock Boratch up in rehab for his own protection?

"So, Anna. Your father tried to explain what the award you're getting is about but I'm still a little confused. Could you explain it to me?" She smiled. "Teaching." "Oh, that makes sense" I said. "Yes, I was elected by my peers as Teacher of the Year. Why did you find that confusing?" The truth was, I just didn't pay attention when Boratch told me. Which she knew. Which was why she was giving me a hard time. Which is why, in part, Anna really annoyed me. "And what grade do you teach again?" I asked. "Third Grade." "Excellent" I said with false but somewhat convincing enthusiasm.

Attendants opened the doors to the auditorium. Anna was directed to one of the front rows. Boratch gave her a big hug before we took our own seats farther back. As Anna walked away, I grudgingly admired how nice her ass looked in the dress she was wearing. Maybe working out and training so hard wasn't such a bad thing for her. "Daniel!" Boratch yelled. "That is my daughter you are leering at!" he said. I told him I wasn't leering. I was just admiring her choice of dress. Boratch didn't buy it. "In spite of their problems, she is still a married woman. Don't forget that" he said. I assured Samuel I had no interest in his daughter. Far too old and far too nasty a person for me to ever want anything to do with. Not to mention, that whole married with two kids issue. Besides, if I ever got within two feet of her, she was likely to stab me in the stomach and laugh at me as I slowly bled to death. Such was the nature of our relationship.

The awards ceremony was dull, amateurish and interminably long just as all awards ceremonies are. There was one part where someone tripped coming off of the stage. But that was about as exciting as it got. I didn't mind. It let my mind drift to matters far more important than which of the three women on stage I would most like to see naked. It allowed me to let the events of the last week or so settle. San Sebastian, Laughton, Rooney, Kapinskov, my promotion. I hadn't even mentioned my promotion to Boratch yet. Between my belief that it might still not happen and my fear of impending death and torture, it seemed to have slipped my mind.

In spite of knowing there was absolutely, positively, no way to do it without arousing suspicion, I needed to talk to people at the drug company. People that knew San Sebastian and what he did, professionally and personally. It was basic investigative procedure. Which was exactly the problem. Once people got wind of my conducting of interviews with drug company employees, they would know I was still investigating the, supposedly, closed case. It was going to be tricky.

I was pulled out of my, fairly useful, thoughts by a nudge from Boratch. Anna's name had just been called. She took the stage and had a plaque of some sort handed to her. Thank Heavens there were no individual thank you speeches. She shook some hands and smiled. I could see her looking over at us. I looked at Boratch. There was a huge grin on his face as if she had one the Nobel Prize instead of some lame teaching award. I just went with it. It might be the last time he has something to smile about for quite a while. Even if I pulled this off, things were going to get worse before they got better.

After the ceremony, Boratch insisted that the three of us all go to dinner together. I tried to make excuses and say I had work to do. Anna, actually backed me, not wanting me there any more than I wanted to be there. But Boratch insisted. "How often can I have two of the most important people in my life together, like this. Tonight we celebrate for tomorrow we may die!" Although it was a phrase he used often, I didn't feel his timing was very good. In any case, I ended up at dinner with them. More seafood.

Everything was fine until Boratch got a little too drunk. Somewhere between the main course and dessert he brought up Anna's marriage. He insisted that no matter what, she had to stay with her husband, Steve. Not only was it a promise before God, there were children involved. Those children, Boratch's grandkids, had every right in the world to a normal, healthy, stable family life. When Anna protested that her husband was a philandering scumbag who slept with every woman he met, Boratch said exactly the wrong thing. He explained to her that that's the way men were. It was nature. It had been going on for thousands of years and saw no sign of stopping in the next thousand.

Anna was aghast. "It's nature?" she asked. "It's NATURE?!!" she asked again, very, very loudly. "How can you say that?" And so it began. A terrible argument between Boratch and Anna in the middle of a good, if not great, seafood place on the East Side that caused us all a great deal of embarrassment. Well, me anyway. I think the other two were so busy arguing that they didn't get embarrassed at all. I knew better than to try to reason either one of them down and did the next best thing. I left. I excused myself to the bathroom and slipped away as quickly as I could. The waiter gave me a look as I walked by. A kind of "please fix this" look. I kept walking.

I stalled as long as I could in the men's room. Unfortunately, it was not a huge room. So, once one or other patrons walked in, it started to feel a little uncomfortable. Lurking around the men's room was not something I did on a regular basis. With dread, I returned to the main dining room. The yelling had stopped. Which is good. But Anna was in tears. Which is not great but honestly better than the yelling. Then again, from the amount of eyes on her from other tables, maybe not. The sight of a woman crying, even if Anna was that woman, was clearly an attention getter.

Boratch angrily paid the bill. The waiter mumbled "Thank you, Sir" as he brought the check. He clearly dreaded being there and tried to go about his business as quickly as possible.

I wasn't having the best of times myself. "You just don't understand" Anna said. Boratch begged to differ. "I DO understand and we are done having this discussion. There will be NO divorce. Do you understand? I will not provide you with any of the financial assistance you need. You will have nothing. Nothing but a sullied reputation and a broken home to raise your children in." I so wanted to leave. Eventually, the bill was sorted and we left the restaurant to a chorus of whispers and glares.

Anna left Boratch and I without saying a word. Boratch turned to me incredulously. "Can you believe that? She just walked off without saying anything. No "thank you" for dinner. No "good night." Nothing" he said. "You were pretty hard on her, Samuel." I prepared for an angry response. Instead what I got was sorrow. In spite of his bluster, Boratch was really a marshmallow and this sort of thing really got to him. "I just want what's best for her. A divorce is not the answer to her problems" he said. "So, what is?" I asked. "She needs to accept that fact that a marriage is for life. Instead of wishing there was some way out of it just needs to focus on making what she has work." I thought about arguing with him but I knew better. He was drunk and stubborn. It would do more harm than good. I just nodded.

Shortly afterward, I put him in a cab and drove myself home. I had an urge which I still can't explain to this day. I felt like I should call Anna to ask if she was alright. Thankfully, wisdom prevailed and I left the issue alone. The last thing I needed was to get between Boratch and his daughter.

For a corporation worth hundreds of billions of dollars, the Life Gen office complex was incredibly underwhelming. It was about forty-five minutes out of town. The "campus" consisted of row after row of identical looking, mirrored towers. Not tall, impressive looking towers. More the sort you would expect to find off of the highway near the mall. The only thing that gave passer-bys a clue as to what this mirrored festival of blandness was all about was a logo on the upper right hand corner of one of the towers. Giant letters spelled out the company name and there was an abstract symbol next to it. A hand? A duck? I really couldn't figure out what, if anything, the symbol was supposed to be.

I drove to the entrance gate and told the security officer my business. I announced myself, with authority, as Chief Inspector Daniel Hastings of the People's Protection Agency. And that I was there to speak with Ammanda Ridgecrumb. According to Human Talent, she was San Sebastian's boss. The security guard thoroughly checked over my ID and confirmed my meeting. He then handed me a print out. A map. After some very confusing instructions about a left, then straight, then two rights at the junction, I drove off. Twenty-two minutes later, I found Tower D.

I passed through, not one, but two, additional security points. I wasn't worried about getting through them. I was worried how extensive a record there now was of my visit. People would not only know I had been there but who I had spoken with and for how long. It was that sort of place.

An elevator took me up to the thirty-third floor. A lobby. And a beautiful young person to greet me. Unfortunately, this one was male. The male, Justin, was his name, I think, made a phone call and then hung up. He looked at me and explained that Miss Ridgecrumb was in a meeting and would be with me when she could. He asked me to have a seat. I didn't move. I was being too subtle, it seemed. He explained to me, again, how I would have to wait. I repeated that I was Chief Inspector Daniel Hastings of the People's Protection Agency and that it was very important that I speak with Miss Ridgecrumb. He said that he understood. Then he asked me, again, to take a seat and wait. I hated these people.

Given that I wanted the visit to be as low-key and matter of fact as possible, I did not make a fuss. I could have. I was a Chief Inspector, after all. But, I let it go. I sat there for forty-five minutes in the lobby thinking of how lucky Justin was. If I wanted him to, he could have gone to prison in a heartbeat. How dare they treat me like that?! But I let it go. I sat there calmly focused on San Sebastian and not remotely distracted by the incredible disrespect I was being shown.

Finally, a young, but disappointingly average looking, woman came to get me. She introduced herself and led me to a large office down the hall. A woman in her sixties sat behind a large glass desk. Her black dress and pulled back grey hair made her look more like a military officer than someone that worked at a drug company. She got up and put out a gaunt hand for me to shake. I did so, trying not to think about the feel of her lizard-like skin. "I am so sorry for keeping you waiting, Inspector…" "Chief Inspector" I corrected. "Right, Chief Inspector…I only have a few minutes. What can I do for you?" I tried to let the words go by. "A few minutes," these people were really pushing their luck. How would she like to spend "a few minutes" being interrogated by some guys I know in the basement? But I let it go. I remained thoroughly professional and undistracted by the humiliating treatment an officer of my stature was receiving.

We finally got to the matter at hand; Robert San Sebastian. I wanted to ask about his weird thing for Cherubs but skipped over it. I was glad I did. The first thing I learned was that San Sebastian hadn't actually worked for her in over two years. When I asked her to explain, she said that he had been put on some super special assignment and that was the last she had heard of him. When I pressed her for who put him on this assignment her answer was "The CEO, I presume. When somebody says Special Assignment in our company that would not refer to some little homework project. It would refer to some task personally given you by our Chief Executive Innovator, Rasheed Jones." "Does that happen often in your company?" I asked. "No, I've only seen it once or twice in the nine years I have been with Life Gen. Of course, one of those was the development of Sensoral which I'm sure you're familiar with."

I jogged my brain for some memory of Sensoral. Then it clicked. It was a drug that made post-menopausal women horny. For decades the problem of declining sexual appetite in older women was ignored. In fact, it wasn't considered a problem. Then older men started to complain that if they were to remain loyal and faithful to their marriage partners, that such partners had various obligations. The issue was brought to a head when the Church weighed in and agreed with the argument. Women had to provide certain marital services or they were letting God down. A scramble began as a search for a drug to remedy the problem was fast-tracked at all the pharmaceutical companies. Life Gen won the horse race and made record profits. Not to mention, that old geezers everywhere where getting oral sex again from their tired and aging wives. All part of God's plan.

"Do you have any idea what San Sebastian's special assignment was?" I asked. I was met with a look of disbelief. Ridgecrumb, the old bitty, then talked down to me as if I had a mental defect. "No. I do not. The whole point of putting someone on Special Assignment is to provide strict confidentiality. The only people that know the specifics are those directly involved and our Chief Executive Innovator." "And what if I wanted to speak to him?" I asked. "Rasheed Jones? Our CEI? You're kidding right? He's in China at the moment but, even if he weren't, getting an appointment to meet with him directly would require the influence of somebody with a much higher standing in government than you, I'm afraid." Like I didn't see that coming. Kapinskov or the Cardinal could get me in, I bet. Well, at least the Cardinal. Too bad that if he knew about what I was doing I would be shipped off and killed within minutes.

Ridgecrumb tried to be rid of me. I resisted long enough to get a slightly better picture of San Sebastian in my head. Before being put on this super top secret, picked by the head innovator guy assignment, he ran a department which developed drugs that dealt with Alzheimer's. His division created steady but unsurprising profits in an area glutted with competition. Although worded far more delicately, it sounded as if San Sebastian had a very stable but not exceptional career. Which is why it came to such a surprise to Ridgecrumb when he was selected for the Special Assignment. It was hard to tell how much of this information was fact, though, and how much pure jealousy and resentment that she had not been so fortunate.

I asked one more question before getting the bum's rush out the door. I asked why San Sebastian was the head of these departments that did mainly research when he was a sales guy. Ridgecrumb just smiled smugly and resumed her tone of total condescension. She ever so slowly explained that I clearly did not understand the pharmaceutical business. Then she made it clear I was leaving whether I wanted to or not. She had far more important things to deal with than some low ranking law enforcement officer asking idiotic questions.

As I left, I noticed the garish wedding ring on her boney finger. I took another look at Old Bitty Ridgewell. The idea of her on Sensoral almost made me nauseous.

I stopped for lunch at a burger place on my way home. It tasted fine but was so chewy, I really didn't enjoy it. I was sure there was some sort of metaphor or symbolism in that but, for the life of me, I couldn't figure out what it would be. I checked my phone and saw a message from Boratch. When I listened, it was a long, rambling apology. He hoped that he hadn't embarrassed me too much at dinner and thanked me again and again for coming. It was the Boratch I dealt with every day and had known for years. Not the blustering, angry, old man yelling at his daughter the way he had last night.

I called him back and got his voicemail. I said that I appreciated the apology. I also said I hoped that he had worked things out with Anna. Which I did. Not so much for her sake. She was a bitch and deserved all the misery she could get. But for his. If she ever got angry or vindictive enough to cut him out of her life, it would kill him. In spite of all the yelling and disapproval, she was about the only thing in his life that he was actually proud of.

I got back to the office and was greeted by a number of strange looks from my colleagues. Something was up. Something very not good was up. It was that "dead man walking" look. Crap. They found out about my visit to Life Gen. The Cardinal worked fast. Superintendent Kim approached me in the hallway. "Daniel, could you follow me, please?" He called me by my first name. That was bad. That was really, really, really bad. How could it have gone so bad, so quick?

I followed the Superintendent down the hall and past his office. He was leading me to one of the interrogation rooms. Hopefully, not the ones in the basement. But...Oh, Man, I didn't want to go down there. People had very, very nasty things happen to them down there. I don't want to be one of them. Honestly, I hated going down there even as one of the interrogators. I had to act all menacing and tough but watching my co-workers do what they did was not pleasant. Not my idea of a good time.

The Chief Inspector opened one of the small rooms on our floor. I guess the basement could wait. Inside were two guys in really unattractive blue blazers. Everything about them read BSACT. Business Security and Counter Terrorism. Not to be confused with Anti-Terror, these guys were all about protecting big business from threat. Honestly, nobody took them all that seriously. They spent a lot of time dealing with corporate espionage. Preventing one company from hacking into another's computer to get the blueprints for special prototype 40 Alpha Bravo. That sort of thing. So, why the whole drama walking in?

One of the BSACT geeks talked. "Chief Inspector, please take a seat." I looked over to Superintendent Kim. He nodded. He clearly wanted me to co-operate with these Bozos. The geek continued. "I'm Investigator Daily. This is my partner, Investigator Mutton." Mutton? I decided to let it slide. "We're here investigating the disappearance of Michael Laughton." And then it all made sense. At least I thought it did. "We'd like to talk to you about your discussion with him and his daughter..." He looked down at his notes. "Isabella" I said, doing my bit to be cooperative. "Right, Isabella. We understand they were here on the afternoon of the nineteenth. Is that correct?" Mutton asked. "Yes, I believe it is." "Can you tell us about the nature of that discussion?" I looked over to Kim. "It was Agency business. So, I'm not sure I am at liberty to discuss it" I said. Kim cut in. "You can. I already told them what it was about but they wanted to hear it from you." To which I responded, "Ok" and left it at that.

So, I explained, lied rather, that the meeting was about Laughton thanking me for teaching his daughter a very valuable life lesson without doing any damage to her reputation. Geek Daily chimed in. "So, you would characterize it as a very friendly, positive meeting?" he asked. "Yes, yes I would. I was quite honored actually that such an important and busy man like Mr. Laughton took the time to come down here and thank me, personally, like that. He seemed like a good man." Geek Daily nodded to Geek Mutton. Mutton got up from the table and left the room for a second. It was an interaction that made me a little nervous. What were they up to?

"You do understand, Chief Inspector, that we are here investigating the disappearance and possible kidnapping of Mr. Laughton. Your full cooperation, and honesty, is expected. Anything less than that might be cause for more serious actions" Daily said. Did he just threaten me? I actually said it out loud before I could stop myself. "Did you just threaten me?" I asked. I was not going to take shit from some little BSACT weasel. No way. No how. Even Superintendent Kim was appalled and reminded them that they were actually in HQ as a courtesy. The People's Protection Agency out trumped BSACT any day of the week. We mattered, damn it.

Just as I was about to lay into Geek Daily, a video monitor in the room came on. It was surveillance camera footage of Mr. Laughton, Isabella and myself in the very same room we were currently in. Oh crap. I thought I had deactivated the recording system. I guess I forgot. It goes on automatically unless you remember to shut it off. Which I swear I did. Or thought I did. The conversation started to play over the monitor. Geek Mutton returned with a shit eating grin on his face. This was going to be ugly.

Clearly, the BSACT guys had seen it before but Kim had not. He kept looking at me with a confused look on his face. He couldn't believe what he was watching. He had taken Laughton at his word when he told him that the visit was to thank me. Why wouldn't he? But what he was watching was one of his top officers and, lest we forget, heir apparent, getting his ass chewed off. Geek Mutton seemed to enjoy the whole thing way, way, way too much. It made me want to hit him.

Investigator Daily chimed in. "Do we need to watch the entire thing together or would you like to make some corrections to your story?" he asked. "Alright, it wasn't a good meeting. It sucked. What do you want from me?" I asked. "We want you to tell us the truth" Mutton said. Kim was shaking his head back and forth. Being blindsided like this made the Agency look bad and made him look even worse as the man, theoretically, in charge of it. There was going to be a high price paid for all this. "Well?" Mutton prompted.

I told them the truth. All of it. My original encounter with Isabella Laughton at the diner. The way I had made her think I was going to take her in for questioning. The way the meeting on tape actually went down. The conversation we had just had about her missing father. Superintendent Kim said "I can't believe I'm hearing all this" only to be silenced by a look from Investigator Daily. "So, why did you lie to us, Chief Inspector?" Mutton asked. "Because I was embarrassed. I thought the whole issue was done with. Mr. Laughton seemed satisfied he had gotten his pound of flesh. I really didn't see the point in keeping the issue alive." Agent Daily got a very serious look on his face. "The point is that, shortly following your meeting, a very important individual that you had words with mysteriously disappeared." "And you've been lying during an official investigation" Mutton added. "I was embarrassed. What do you want from me?" I protested. "We want the truth. All of it. You're in enough trouble already, Chief Inspector. If you don't cooperate fully, things are just going to get worse" Daily said. He was enjoying this way too much.

I promised to tell the whole truth, in its entirety, and apologized over and over again. Of course, I lied my ass off. I had to. At least about the one piece of information that really would have helped them. There was no way I could afford to implicate Minister Kapinskov in any of this. Whatever these guys thought they could do to me, what Kapinskov could bring to the table was ten times worse. So, I focused just on the events at the diner and the conversation at HQ. And, when it came to those, I told the truth. Fully. And embarrassingly so.

It all seemed to go fine until they tried to connect it to Laughton's disappearance. My defense was this....Even if I wanted revenge, there was no way someone like me could ever get to someone was powerful as Laughton. The idea was laughable. What hurt is how quickly and easily everyone agreed. Especially Mutton. "Of course that's ridiculous. Nobody is actually accusing you of arranging the kidnapping of one of the most powerful executives in the country. Maybe in your dreams but that's about it." He was being such a dick about my powerlessness I almost wanted to yell "Oh, yeah. Well, that's exactly what I did! Kind of. I have connections you don't know about. Important, powerful people. Very important, very powerful. You don't know, Mutton. You just don't know!" But I didn't. I kept quiet and let them gloat.

And then it was over. At least the part with the BSACT guys. Mutton and Daily, left and thanked the Superintendent for his co-operation. Mutton also got one last dig in on me. "As for you, Chief Inspector, it doesn't look like your disagreement has anything to do with Mr. Laughton's disappearance. So, you're cleared unless something new comes to light. As for lying to us, we'll just leave it up to your C.O. to deal with. Have a nice day." I wanted to kill him. But I had other problems to deal with. Superintendent Kim asked that I remain in the interrogation room after the BSACT guys left. He showed them out and returned a few minutes later.

"I don't know what to say" Kim said. "You have embarrassed me, the Agency and most of all, yourself" he added. I nodded. "The original act against Isabella Laughton is questionable enough. However, the fact that you lied to me about Mr. Laughton's visit..." I cut him off. "With all due respect, Sir, I didn't lie about it, Mr. Laughton did. And the reason he did so was that there was no need for any of it to become a major issue. He lied to you. I didn't" I repeated. Superintendent Kim got a look on his face I had only seen a few times before. He was a man of amazing calm. Zen-like calm. But this look indicated a murderous rage going on somewhere deep inside of him. I can tell you first hand, it was not a good look to be on the other end of.

"Are you saying you didn't lie today?" Kim asked. "No, I admit I lied. To them. Not to you. I mean, I guess to you too but mainly to them" I stammered. "So, I was just collateral damage?" he asked. "Yes. I mean. No. I don't know, Sir. I am very confused as to how all of this became such an issue" "This was bad, Daniel. Very bad" he said. "I know." "I think you should take some time off for the next week or two while I figure out what to do about all this" he said. Which meant, kiss your promotion goodbye and hope I don't decide to fire you too. I just nodded. Kim continued.

"Alright, then. I'll see you in two weeks. Until then, you might want to think about making some changes to your life." I wasn't sure what the last part meant, exactly. But it wasn't good. I got up and started to leave. "At least you weren't connected to Laughton's disappearance. If you were, no powerful connection in the world could save you. Not after this." I tried not to react to those parting words until I was out the door and out of sight. I wanted to puke. He was right. Kim was totally right. After BSACT busting me for lying and knowing about the run-in with Laughton, I was a major liability. Kapinskov might not want to take the chance that it would come back on him. It's probably not what Kim meant. Or wait, is it what Kim meant? Did that clever fuck know more than he was letting on? No. He couldn't. No way. He meant the words to provide some perspective. Instead, the Superintendent had just reminded me that too many people would be quite comforted by my death.

It was a strange feeling walking around the city at ten in the morning realizing I had nowhere I was required to be. What was worse is that I felt like I had a thousand different places to go and puzzles to solve but wasn't sure how to deal with any of it. I sat in a coffee bar summarizing events to date. I wrote a few notes on a napkin. Drug executive kills himself. Church wants closed. Government wants open. Oil executive is falsely accused. Oil executive disappears. Career over.

Right. It didn't make any more sense on a coffee stained napkin that it did in my head. It might have just as well have said; fish, rabbit, war, soap. Random words that had nothing to do with each other unless you really forced it. Animals taking a bath after a battle?. Suicide, drugs, oil, fired. It was a bit more logical, I guess. But not really. WTF? It was just then I saw something of interest on the TV in the corner. The sound was down but it was the state news channel. On it was an image of none other than Mike Laughton, himself, bound and blindfolded. He was surrounded by two masked figures with machetes. One was male, the other female. I asked the guy behind the coffee bar to turn it up. To my annoyance, he refused. "Sorry, we have a policy of no sound on the TV. It destroys the atmosphere." "I'll destroy your atmosphere" I said. And I reached over to turn the volume up. The coffee guy said something unintelligible but loud enough to annoy me. "Shut up" I told him and watched the TV. The female figure in a baklava faced the camera. It was her. Brown eyes. The leader of the Clear Thinkers.

"We will no longer tolerate the money-hungry alliance of church, government and big oil. If you ever want to see Mr. Laughton alive again, you will deliver..." And then the picture cut away to a skiing competition. What the? I flipped around to find the Clear Thinkers and Laughton. A game show. A soap opera. A show about losing weight. Where was the rest of the Laughton thing? "Oh, Man. Somebody is going to get fired for that one" the coffee guy said. I kept flipping around the channels in vain. "What? Why?" I asked. "Come on, really?" he asked. I just looked at him. "The government doesn't negotiate with terrorists. They're not going to let those people broadcast their demands, like that" he said. Oh, right. I knew that. Of course, I knew that. I was just so used to seeing such things as part of my Agency duties, I forgot how sheltered the general public was from such material. I needed to get back to the office.

When I returned to HQ, people were gathered in groups talking about the Laughton thing. They all looked at me oddly. Superintendent Kim came out of his office. "I thought I told you to take some time off" he said. "You did. I will. But I just saw part of the Laughton tape. Can I see the full thing?" "No." What did he mean "no?" I was more involved and knowledgeable of the facts in this case that almost anyone in the city. Anyone but the Clear Thinkers, probably. "I think I might be helpful on it, given my earlier contact with Laughton." Kim gave me that Zen, death look. "Your earlier contact with Laughton is exactly why you need to go home for a while and stay out of this. Go home, Chief Inspector. Go home before you cause even more damage to your career and this agency."

It wasn't worth arguing about. I looked at him and knew I was shut out and there wasn't a damn thing I could do about it. I left the office empty handed. I stood on the street for a moment just staring at HQ. The place where I once had a bright and promising future as the future Superintendent of the St. Anthony's office of the People's Protection Agency. Was that really all done with just because of that little thing with Laughton and his daughter?

I saw two uniformed officers that I vaguely recognized walk out of the building. They were talking animatedly to each other about something. Then I heard the words "video...nuts...watermelon" in their conversation. It made about as much sense as the animals showering after the war. One of them saw me standing there. "Hello, Chief Inspector" he said. It was the uniform Boratch had balled out at the suicide crime scene. "Hey there, officer. What are you guys talking about?" I asked. "The ransom video. You didn't see it?" They had no idea I wasn't at HQ in my role as fully empowered Chief Inspector. "No, I was out on a case. What video?" I asked innocently. "Those nut jobs, The Clear Thinkers, kidnapped some CEO and want ten million dollars for his release. To make the point that they were serious, they took a machete to a watermelon at the end of the video." "A watermelon?" I asked. "Can you believe it?" the other uniform asked. I could believe it, actually. The Clear Thinkers were not, exactly, traditional terrorists. In fact, kidnapping was a huge, huge leap for them. Almost too huge.

"It was hilarious, if you ask me" the uniform that I vaguely knew said. "Hilarious?" I asked. "Come on, a piece of fruit being chopped up is supposed to be threatening?" He had a point. But that wasn't the point. I assumed my full Chief Inspectorly airs. "There is nothing hilarious about a man being kidnapped and threatened with death" I said. "No, Sir." I glared at the other uniform. "No, Sir. Of course not, Sir" he said. Fear and respect. There's nothing like it. I told them to get back to their business and to quit gossiping. They ran away like little rats.

I had to admit, the watermelon destruction did seem a bit silly. But everything the Clear Thinkers did seemed silly to me. His name was Bob. The soap foam in the church. Fruit mutilation seemed par for the course. Kidnapping, however, did not. I wondered what had made them cross that line. Maybe they got tired of not being taken seriously. In any case, it looked like maybe it wasn't Minister Kapinskov who had disappeared Laughton after all. I was off the hook. I was mercifully, beautifully, off the hook for the torture and horrible death of a, more or less, innocent man. I breathed a little easier.

You would think by now being over such things would have happened just as part of doing my job. The Agency put a lot of people through a lot of very, very unpleasant things who may not have fully deserved them. But I would never go as far as to say those people were innocent. Well, most of them anyway. The people the Agency rounded up all had track records, of one sort or another, of causing trouble. Even if they hadn't committed the crimes they were punished for they certainly committed some sort of egregious acts or they wouldn't have been there. And, they probably would have committed quite a few more in the future. It was fair and it was reasonable. Preventative justice, as it were. But Laughton, would have been different. As far as I knew, his only crime against the state was having a spoiled little bitch of a daughter. But the same could be said of Boratch, on that count. Laughton was, as I keep repeating, more or less, innocent. Which made his kidnapping quite disturbing. But at least now I knew that I had nothing to do with it. Too bad that didn't solve the rest of my problems.

I contacted Boratch and told him that we needed to talk. He agreed. Insisted would be a better word. When I suggested dinner at an Italian place (I was craving Chicken Parmesan for some reason) he said no. I thought he was going to push me to go to that Mexican place he liked which I always found lacking. But it was neither. He said the only place he felt free talking was his apartment. And soon. Something had just happened which we needed to discuss. I had a bad feeling it was something about Anna. So, I asked. "Is this a personal thing or professional?" He reacted angrily. "Does it matter? I thought you were my friend" he said. "I am. I was just wondering if this was about Anna or..." "No, it's not. Just be at my apartment in twenty minutes. I'll see you then." And then he hung up. Rudely. Boratch was pretty polite and usually said "goodbye" or "I'll see you soon" or something. Not this time. Just click, and off the line he went.

I drove over to Boratch's tower complex and arrived early. Boratch wasn't there yet. I waited in my car trying to find additional news on the radio about Laughton. The Ministry of

Information had come up with a great spin. They always do. According to the official press release, Mike Laughton's kidnapping was a part of a performance art piece by a group of MFA students from Central University. The hoaxsters were now facing criminal charges for their misguided acts. However, according to high ranking state officials, CEO Mike Laughton is not, and has never been, in any actual danger. It was all just good fun gone wrong. I felt sorry for the poor schmoe at the state news channel who had broadcast the tape without that spin adhered to. His life was over. Possibly, literally. Another victim of trying to get the first scoop in the age of the internet. Just ask Chief Windsor how being first out of the gate tends to work out.

I saw Boratch drive up in the luxo-barge sedan he was so proud of. It was a badly designed, badly manufactured piece of trash. But back in Boratch's day, owning a car of that brand was a sign to the world that you had made it. Whatever made him happy. He parked his car in the assigned space and I got out to greet him. He had his briefcase with him. "Hello" I said. He barely bothered to answer as he rushed me upstairs. In the elevator he managed to ask how my day was. I told him I had probably lost my promotion and had been put on leave. He was sympathetic but didn't seem all that bothered by it. But I could understand that. It wasn't like he was the one who had been disgraced and thrown his career down the toilet over one insignificant act.

As we walked down the hall to his apartment, I realized his lack of sympathy for my plight had more to do with whatever pressing issue was on his mind. He opened the door to his apartment and let me in. As soon as the door shut he said "we have a problem" he said. "Yeah." I'd been under the impression we had a problem for a while by then. Was this news to him? "Look at these." Boratch sat on his sofa and opened his briefcase. He took out a folder. Then he took out what was in the folder. Photographs. Disgusting. Nasty. Highly unappetizing photographs. They were of a corpse charred black. Thin and crispy just the way they get when they get really fried. "Who is he?" I asked. "Not he, she" he said. Then he said "Deborah Marky" with drama and gravity. I recognized the name but couldn't remember where from. I kept looking at him. "Who?" I asked. "Deborah Marky" he repeated. He might as well have been speaking Spanish.

"Is that name supposed to mean something to me?" Boratch looked completely flustered. "Is that, or is that not, the name you mentioned the other night to me when we were out?" he asked. I had to admit that it did sound familiar. I just couldn't remember why. "You told me at dinner before the whole debacle with Anna." It was slowly coming back to me. Deborah Marky.

Then the little light bulb went off. It was a name I had gotten off of San Sebastian's phone. The one he had dialed most often. The one that was probably..."Oh, the one that was possibly San Sebastian's girlfriend" I said. "Exactly. Now look at her" he said. I did. It wasn't very attractive. "Do you know what this means?" I didn't say anything. "He knows" Boratch said. "Who knows?" I asked. "The Cardinal. Cardinal Rooney knows about the San Sebastian case being left open and is covering his tracks." Boratch was being mighty dramatic for something which seemed quite a stretch to me. But he made his case.

The body of Deborah Marky had been discovered all burnt and crispy just that morning. About the same time that I would have been out at Life Gen. She had been burned the night before. Not just burned but murdered in a very specific way. She had been burned at the stake. No, for real. It was something that had come back into fashion among certain far-right groups when they wanted to make a point. It didn't mean the victim was a witch, necessarily. But it meant that they were considered some form of devil worshipping, Godless heretic. Hence, fire was used to cleanse their evil souls and send them to the afterlife in better shape. All pretty nasty, medieval stuff, but I still wasn't seeing a connection to Cardinal Rooney or San Sebastian. So, I said so.

"I'm still not seeing a connection to Rooney or San Sebastian" I said. "The Cardinal has very, very tight ties with several of the more fringe elements of the Church. Especially H.O.G." "Hog?" I asked. "H.O.G., Hand of God. He came up through their ranks when he was still a nobody." "He did?" I asked. "Nobody talks about it much now but he told my wife. Before he was who he is now. This is his doing. I'm sure of it." I still wasn't convinced. I thought the Cardinal was a bit uptight but I'd never figured him for a witch burner. More importantly I didn't see how it had anything to do with us.

According to Bortach's theory, the Cardinal had needed to make San Sebastian's death and everything connected with it go away. Hence, the request that was not really a request for him to make sure the file was marked "Accidental Death" and officially closed. Since Deborah Marky was, in theory, San Sebastian's lover and confident, her death had been to tie up any loose ends. None of which, being the seasoned investigator I was, made one bit of sense to me. "Samuel, I'm sorry. But I think you're panicking here" I said. "How am I panicking? Look what they did to her? Just look!" He held up one of the gruesome photos for me. "Listen, even if you're right about Cardinal Rooney wanting to tie up loose ends, this wouldn't be the way he would do it?" I said. I went on to explain, very calmly and logically, I might add, that normally under such circumstances, discrete was good. The quieter someone disappears, the better. Not really all that different from the way the Agency thought about things, when it came down to it.

The expression on Boratch's face changed. "That makes sense" he muttered. I went on to explain that whoever murdered Deborah Marky was going for the exact opposite effect. They wanted the world to know that they had killed her and that she deserved it. It wasn't about covering up. It was about showing off. Boratch nodded. I have to say, I really did sound impressive and knowledgeable in these things. Even to me. I guess maybe I had learned something from all my years in law enforcement.

But Boratch still had his doubts. "You have to admit though, it's a strange coincidence that she was murdered so soon after San Sebastian took his own life. How do you explain the timing? Do you really think the murder of San Sebastian's girlfriend, shortly after his own death, is completely coincidental?" I admitted that I didn't know. I just knew that jumping to the conclusion that Cardinal Rooney was involved was as big of a mistake as assuming there was no correlation. We just had another couple random words on a napkin. More things which may, or may not, be connected. "I'll look into it" I promised. "How are you going to do that?" Boratch asked. "What do you mean?" "Didn't you tell me in the elevator that you were suspended?" he asked. Yeah, that would be a problem. But, honestly, given all the rest of the shit storm starting to brew, it was the least of my worries.

I thought about going back to HQ to beg to be reinstated. What's a little groveling and pleading when so much is at stake? But the thought of it did not sit well. Maybe being on leave would work to my advantage and make it easier to stay off the radar. At least that way I wouldn't be distracted from dealing with my situation with requests to arrest anti-government activists and abortionists and what not.

Boratch had not been in the mood for going out for a meal. I ended up just going back to my apartment with not very good take-out Indian. I turned on my own computer and logged in. I then did something I only did when I was searching for the most bizarre, degrading and embarrassing porn. I went to a sight which obscured my computer's ID address. In theory, it made me anonymous. As many a child rapist had learned, it wasn't. If any of the law enforcement agencies put some effort into it, they could still trace the source. However, for recreational purposes, it was just fine. What made me nervous is that what I was about to do was far from recreational. I was looking up information on Debra Marky.

She had been San Sebastian's secretary. And looked just like him. That was her. She had been at Gen Life for fourteen years. That's a ridiculously long time to stay with one company. Normally between the layoffs, turnover and taking advantage of other opportunities, workers stayed an average of only two and a half years with a single company. Admittedly, Gen Life was massive enough that you could stay there your entire career and do completely different things every year or two. But Deborah hadn't done that. She had started as a secretary and stayed a secretary for fourteen years. The only change in her life was who her boss was.

She jumped desks, and possibly beds, with the first three men very quickly. Her bosses started to become bigger and bigger. I can only assume that there was some prestige attached to who she assisted. Being the CEO's assistant obviously ranked higher than being some mid-level nobody's. Which is why it was really interesting when she took a step down to work with San Sebastian.

She had been secretary to the Regional Head of Sales when San Sebastian was still out in the field pushing drugs to doctors and hospitals. Yet, she left that desk to work with San Sebastian. Had she seen such talent in him she knew he was the right horse to hitch a ride with? Was she in love with him? There must have been some reason. In any case, she remained with San Sebastian for the next eight years. Every time San Sebastian got a promotion, she went with him.

Other than that, there wasn't much interesting information on Marky. She belonged to the right church and all the right social organizations. She was active in God's Love and other charitable organizations. She liked skiing, sailing and volleyball. Her parents were both alive and living in Rickets, three hours north of the city.

I took a different track. Past crimes that involved burning at the stake. Turns out that there were far too many to comb through. It was something which seemed all the rage for certain types of right wing, vigilante groups twenty years ago or so. Since then, it has been replaced by more normal methods of execution like guns and knives and so on. But still, it was quite the fad for a while. I paid special attention to any of them tied to the group that Boratch had said the Cardinal had been associated with, Hand of God. H.O.G. were credited with making the burning at the stake method a thing again. Which, from the records I was looking at anyway, didn't seem quite fair. There were other groups that had done it first and plenty that had done it more. I guess the H.O.G. folks just did it bigger and better.

There was one case, in particular, that got them a lot of press. Their victim had been a priest who had molested children. It made H.O.G. heroes and probably helped Rooney gain a lot of influence and power. Within three months of that incident, he went from being just another priest to being assigned to the Grand Cathedral in Longview. A post considered a major stepping stone to higher rank within the Church.

I decided to do one more bit of research on Deborah before calling it a night. I still had San Sebastian's porn sticks. I looked for the ones that were unlabeled. The non-professional looking ones. I was hoping that San Sebastian and Deborah may have made some home movies of interest. Just a hunch. But hunches had paid off well for me in my career. Well, actually, they hadn't and I was usually mistaken. But that was beside the point.

I put the first unlabeled stick into my video monitor. I sat back preparing for the worst. Maybe I would find out that Deborah was into more than sailing in terms of water sports. What I got instead was nothing. There was not a single video or image on the stick. I guess San Sebastian never got around to filling it with the smut of his choosing. I pulled out the memory stick and put in the second, unlabeled one. Nothing. Also blank. So much for my night of homemade porn.

Determined not to let the evening be a total waste, I went through the other porn sticks and found one, a professional one, called "Three On a Dick." I figured with a title like that, there had to be something interesting to it. I had just put the stick in when there was a knock at my door. A knock. A knock at eleven forty-five in the evening. Who the hell could that be? I made a half-hearted effort to put the lid on the box of porn sticks and went to see who it was. It was Boratch's daughter, Anna. She was crying and looked like hell. I was not happy to see her. She knocked again. Samuel owed me for this. Against all my instincts, I opened the door and let her in.

"Anna, why are you here?" I asked. She didn't answer and sat down on the sofa right in my spot. "Anna, what's wrong?" I asked. "He's a pig. A totally unreasonable, selfish, deluded, pig" she said. "Who is? Your husband, Alex?" I asked. "Alex? My husband's name is Steve. How did you get Alex?" By not really giving a shit and never listening to you when you started whining about it. I didn't actually say that, of course. Instead I looked concerned and sympathetic. "My mistake. Sorry. But why are you here?" I asked again. "Not Steve" she said. I was totally confused. "My father. My father is the one being totally unreasonable." "I'm sure you'll work it out. Now, if you don't mind..." Anna saw a bottle of Scotch on the counter. I hadn't touched it in months. She grabbed it. "Got any ice?" she asked. It was then that I realized she was drunk. She was one of those good drinkers that hid it perfectly well but every now and again her alcohol-infused body would betray her. I got her a glass and ice. Which was odd. I should have kicked her out and been done with it. But I got her a drink and she thanked me. Then she downed a good swig and put the glass out for another.

I didn't give it to her. "Not until you tell me why you are here" I said. She held the empty glass out insistently. I, reluctantly, poured her another one. "I asked him for money" she said. "Who, Steve?" I asked. She glared at me. "No, my father." I was getting incredibly annoyed. I had enough problems without this. And like hell I was going to get entangled in something between Boratch and his drunk, bitchy daughter. "You need to go" I said. I grabbed her by the shoulders and physically moved her toward the door. I wasn't going to get involved in this. No way. I expected her to yell or call me names or something. She didn't, which worried me. She just let herself be shown out the door.

"You're right. I'm sorry. I never should have come here" she said. And then she reached into her pocket. Or tried to. She missed. And then she fumbled a bit and pulled her keys out. "Good night, Inspector" she said. Thank heavens that was over. She staggered away. The quick shots of Scotch must have already been hitting. She had gone from being a good drunk to a "we need to cut that woman off" drunk. Which left me in a bad spot. I really just wanted her to be gone and to get back to my evening. But letting Boratch's daughter kill herself driving home drunk like that wasn't right. Tempting. But not right. Not to her. She could crash into a brick wall for all I cared. But to Boratch. He was my friend and this was his daughter. The least I could do was call her a cab.

"Wait a second" I said. And guided her back into my apartment. I called a cab for her. Or started to. "Were you watching porn?" she said. She looked at me with a smile on her face. An "Oh, I just busted you so bad" smile. She staggered over to the memory stick plugged into the TV. "Three on a Dick? Catchy" she said. I hung up the phone. Why was she so annoying? "It's for a case" I said. "Sure it is" she said. "Sit down!" I said, losing my temper a bit. "I love it when you're commanding" she joked. What was the deal with her? I had never, ever seen her like this. "I asked my father to lend me ten thousand dollars so I could rent a new apartment and take the kids." "I don't want to hear it. That's between you and your father and Alex" I said. I misdialed the phone number and hung up. I started dialing again. "Steve. But you can just call him Asshole. I do." I got the cab company and was put on hold. Anna helped herself to some more Scotch. Finally, I got through to the taxi dispatcher and gave her my address. I was then asked for the destination address and realized I didn't know it. "Anna, where do you live?" I asked. I'm not going to tell you." Jesus. "Fine, I'll give them your father's." That got her. She gave me her address in the unpleasant little yuppie suburb that she lived in.

"Can't you please talk to him for me?" she asked. "You are the only person in the entire world my father listens to since my mother died. He trusts you." I tried not to let the words flatter me but they did. And it was probably true. Boratch and I trusted each other in a way few people dared to, given the age in which we lived. Of course, we could both end up dead soon because of that trust. But whatever. "Anna, I really don't want to get involved in any issues between you and your father." "But he trusts you" she said again.

I refused to take the bait. She got visibly annoyed. She grabbed something next to her on the sofa. Just as I realized what it was, she hit the play button. She had turned on the TV and its debaucherous contents. "Turn that off!" I yelled. She left it on and just looked at me. I walked over to her to try to grab the control. She put it behind her back. "What are you, five years old or something?" I asked. "You won't let me leave, you won't let me talk to you about what I came to talk about, the least you could do is let me watch some TV" "That's not TV. Turn it off!" I yelled. A naked woman appeared on the screen. She was using a cucumber to pleasure herself. "Interesting use of produce" Anna snickered. "Fine, you win. Turn it off and we'll talk about your father." She gloated for a second and then turned off the TV.

"Anna, I don't get this. We barely know each other and you come over drunk and act like this. I really don't understand." She got a more serious expression on her face. "I told you, I need help with my father. You're the only one he listens to." "I really don't want to get involved" I said, yet again. "My husband is a cheating, drug addicted asshole who terrorizes me and the children. I don't want him anywhere near any of us anymore." I refused to comment. "And my father just keeps insisting that marriage is a promise before God and I have to honor and obey my husband." I wasn't buying it. "Obey? Your father would not tell you that" I said. "He did. He used that exact word. I had to obey Steve because he was the man." When she put it that way, it actually sounded like a good thing. "He's unstable. He takes drugs and just flips out on us." "Does he hit you?" I asked. She didn't answer. "Anna, does he hit you or your children?" She looked frustrated. "No, but he yells and throws things and calls me all sorts of horrible names in front of the kids." Her husband was sounding like quite the jerk but it was hard to tell. All couples argued. How was this any different?

Anna just shook her head and sulked. "You're not going to help me, I can tell. This was a mistake" she said. I had to agree. Yes, it was. "I should go." Anna stood up and started to head toward the door. "Wait for your cab" I said. "I'll wait outside." "It's cold and it could be a while. The dispatcher said they were backed up." She stood there and didn't move as she thought about it. "Fine. But only if you let me watch more of the lady with the cucumber. I've never seen one of those kinds of movies." "You're not missing anything" I replied. "Apparently I am. These girls seem very inventive" she said. I didn't answer, which she must have taken as a yes. She sat down and turned the movie back on. How would I ever explain this to Boratch? His drunken daughter was in my apartment at midnight watching illegal pornography.

"Sit down. You're making me nervous" she said. I couldn't deal with this. I walked over to her just as the woman on the screen started to get more audible. "Please turn that off" I said. "You're blocking my view." "Anna!" "Daniel!" And then she put her hand on my crotch. I was too shocked to do anything. Her hand was just resting there on my pants. Over my cock. And she was looking at me. Looking at me and grinning. I pulled back.

"What do you think you're doing?!" I said. "Just checking to see how much you were enjoying the movie." She stood up and moved closer to me. "It's work. I wasn't enjoying it" I said. And then she got this really evil look in her eye. "Maybe you weren't but you liked my hand there. I could feel it" she said. "You felt no such thing!" I said. She smiled. "Yes, you did." And then she leaned in and kissed me. Before I fully even realized what was happening, I was kissing Boratch's bitchy, self-centered, not really all that attractive, daughter and it felt really, really nice. Her hand returned to its previous position. I wasn't going to be able to lie my way out of my reaction, this time.

Her hand slowly toyed and teased me as we stood there making out. The woman on the screen reached orgasm. Loudly. I was trying to make sure I didn't get there too soon myself. I grabbed Anna's ass as we kept kissing. And then something happened. It took a second to figure out what it was. The porn had cut off and the screen had gotten quiet. Anna didn't seem to notice. Or maybe she just didn't care. I had to agree. It was all feeling really good. I couldn't see the screen. I just knew it sounded different. Anna's slowly unzipped my pants. "This is not God's plan" a voice said.

What? And then it repeated. "This is not God's plan at all." Although it sounded way too much like a voice from above saving me from a horrible mistake with Boratch's daughter, I knew it was something else. Even Anna was shaken out of the moment. We both turned and watched the screen. Me with pants hanging down. Anna with her hand mindlessly on top of my underwear as if she forgot it was resting there. Robert San Sebastian was on the screen.

I removed Anna's hand and zipped up. San Sebastian continued. "What we are doing is a sin. It is wrong and we will all be punished for it. I have tried to make amends but they will not allow me. I am faced with a life of physical pain and imprisonment in this world or eternal damnation in the next. There is no good answer."

Anna looked at me. "Who's that? What is he talking about?" she asked. I walked over to the TV and turned it off. "What was that?" Anna asked. "Part of a very important case me and your father are both involved in. You shouldn't have seen that" I said. "What was he going on about? What did he do that was freaking him out so much? Murder someone or something?" I looked at Anna very seriously. This was bad. What she had just seen could get her in a lot of trouble. "You didn't see that. Ok? Listen to me. This case involves very, very, powerful people. You could get hurt and your father could even end up getting killed over this." That got her attention. "You're serious?" she asked. "Yes, very. Please, just forget you saw that. Don't talk about it with anyone. Not your friends. Not your father. Anyone" I said. She nodded.

"Your fly is still undone" she said. I looked down at my pants. I was fully unzipped. "That's a nice look for you. You should try it at Headquarters sometime" she said. "What are you, five?" I asked. I looked at her a minute not saying anything as I zipped up, I tried, in vain, to regain my composure. Her mood had totally changed. I even questioned for a second how drunk she really was. "If you're still hoping to get laid? Don't. The moment is over. Gone" she said. She tried to make a gesture with her hand to emphasize the gone. It didn't quite work. Reassurance that she was still really drunk and this wasn't a total ploy on her part.

The phone rang. Mercifully, the cab had arrived. "Your cab is here" I said. "You sure you don't want me to stay?" she asked. It seemed like an odd question after her previous statement. A trick. "Yes" I said firmly. She gathered her things and opened the door. Then she leaned in and kissed me again. Like, that kind of kiss. And before I could stop myself, I was kissing her back again. It didn't last very long. But it was nice. A little too nice. Then she whispered in my ear. "Goodnight, Chief Inspector." She walked out the door and gave me one of those over the shoulder "see you soon" looks before disappearing around the corner. For a spoiled, whining, too old for me woman, she had a certain appeal. Kind of like a rattlesnake in heat.

I sat on the sofa thinking about what had just happened. How was I ever going to explain all this to Boratch? Not that there was all that much to explain. It was just a kiss or two. And her hand in certain places it shouldn't have been. Or should be more often. What in heaven's name was I doing? She was Boratch's daughter. And clearly unstable. And really not that great looking. Except for that terrific ass and those amazing tits. But other than that. She was Boratch's daughter! And married. And kids. Kids! What was I thinking? It started to occur to me that I had just dodged a lethal bullet. Not entirely. More like I was just grazed by a potentially lethal bullet. A flesh wound, if you will. But imagine if that video hadn't changed and things had continued. The way she would have grabbed me. The way I would have ripped off her pants and taken her right there on the floor. The intensity of...I needed to stop thinking about Anna. This was bad.

I decided to focus on the video. That would pull me out of my salacious state of mind. I turned on the TV again. San Sebastian was there on the screen. He looked like even more of a wreck than I did. I almost wondered if some drunk, manipulative woman with a great ass just messed with him too. He was moaning about God's plan or something before. But I had been too distracted to make sense out of it. I rewound it. San Sebastian stared right into the camera. His words sounded like those of a man thinking he would be dead soon. Honest. Sincere. Desperate.

This is what he said. "This is not God's Plan. This is not God's plan, at all. When Rasheed came to me to discuss our findings, he imagined a world unified by a love of a higher power. A society in which every member would feel calm and at ease knowing they were part of a much greater whole. I voiced my reservations, even then. He was so persuasive. But the truth is that my ego got the better of me. Not just the paycheck and being put in charge of the project. But being told I could actually change the world. Being told that I was going to make the world we lived in better for each and every human on the planet. It was hubris. Pure hubris." I made a note on a menu sitting on the table to make sure I looked the word up. "Hubris." I thought I knew what it meant but maybe not. Then I scribbled down some other things. Rasheed. Secret project. Higher Power. Good of mankind. I wasn't sure what to make of any of it yet. But, at least it kept me from thinking about Anna for a bit.

San Sebastian continued. "Rasheed's argument was that we were going to make the world what it always should have been. A land of love and peace and devotion. When I voiced my concerns that we were dealing with things, manipulating things, that were better left alone, he refused to hear it. He convinced me that we were chosen. We were chosen by God to do his bidding. This was all God's plan. I knew even when he said it that it was a lie. A justification for tampering with the sacred. But I didn't protest. At least, not strongly enough. I did as he said and changed the focus of our research. What had started as a study in mapping the brain for research into Alzheimer's became Rasheed's cause. I hate to question his motives but sometimes I wonder if the fact that his parents were not Christian had something to do with it. But, as I said, he is by no means alone in his guilt. I did as he said. It was I that started to refocus the research. To try to attain the unattainable. I was even there with Deborah the day we thought was our big breakthrough."

San Sebastian got very quiet and introspective looking. It took him a minute to say anything more. When he did, there were tears in his eyes. "We thought we were witnessing a miracle. A divine act that would change mankind forever and please God. Instead, we have done the unthinkable. I deserve the eternal damnation that awaits. I deserve eternal pain and suffering." And then he leaned forward and shut off the camera.

A man's voice started yelling. "SUCK IT BITCH. SUCK IT GOOD. OH, YEAH. THAT'S IT. THAT'S IT." I grabbed the remote in a panic and turned down the set. "Three on a Dick" had resumed its normal programming. A man in a meat locker getting his own meat tended to by a woman on her knees. I hit pause. The woman on her knees was actually quite skilled. Talented even. Realizing that I was getting distracted, I turned off the set. The silence was much appreciated.

Why did San Sebastian put his final words on a porn stick, anyway? Was it self-debasement for him? Did he loath himself so much that he felt he deserved humiliation and degradation right up until the end? And if that was his suicide note, why didn't he leave it out by the table? I guess he figured somebody would eventually take the porn home and watch it. That some poor schmo would go from a night of private entertainment to hearing his overly wordy, and, in my opinion, somewhat pretentious, confession.

At least it explained the lab in his house. I guess. Kind of. The office was where San Sebastian and his team did research on some super-secret thing that made everybody love one another. Was it an ecstasy lab? I heard rumors that people were trying to make that drug fashionable again. No way. San Sebastian couldn't have really been going on and on like that about something as basic as "X." Are they really that fascinated by the drugs of the late Twentieth Century? So, what was he on about then?

Maybe it was just some sort of tranquilizer. Something that made people just feel calm and happy. But there were already so many of those drugs on the market, I had trouble imagining what made his so special. The best way to figure it out would be to get a hold of the actual research and have someone knowledgeable, like a scientist, explain it to me. Not very practical given I had no way of getting the research. Not to mention that bringing in some outside scientist would put Boratch and I at extreme risk.

The second best way was to find somebody else that knew about everything and to just get them to explain it to me. San Sebastian was dead. So was Deborah Marky. But there must have been other people involved. That was a big office. And then there was the corporation's Chief Innovation Officer, Rasheed. He would certainly know the answers.

My brain suddenly did one of those little tricks where it's telling you that you know something but you're not seeing it. Come on brain! It was office space. Just office space. No, not my brain. What I didn't know I knew. There were no labs. No scientific equipment. No brain scanners or medical gear. Just office areas. The labs must be in other locations. Are they still doing this research San Sebastian was rambling about?

My phone rang. I let it go to voicemail. When I listened to it a few minutes later I heard an uncomfortably familiar voice. "Hi, it's Anna, I just wanted to let you know I got home safely." And that was it. Why she thought I cared was beyond me. Especially now. I had bigger issues to deal with than Anna Boratch.

I decided to take another drive out to Life Gen. Which turned out to be a very bad idea. I got to the gate and was let through to Ridgecrumb's office tower. I got out of my car and was making my way across the parking lot when a black sedan pulled up behind me. Two guys in poorly tailored grey jackets got out. And they were identical. The jackets, not the men wearing them. "Chief Inspector Hastings?" the taller of the two asked. "Yes" I said. "I'm Ken Davis with Corporate Security. Could you come with us please?" I looked at him, shocked at the request. "No, actually. I'm here on very important Agency business." A second sedan pulled behind me. Two more grey-suited men got out. "Chief Inspector Hastings. You are not authorized to be on these grounds." "I disagree. I am a Chief Inspector with the People's Protection Agency, here investigating a case. Now, get out of my way before you get yourself into more trouble." They didn't move. "Did you hear what I said? I am Chief Inspect..." My phone rang. From the ringtone I knew who it was. "You might want to get that, Chief Inspector and avoid any further embarrassment to yourself." I picked up the phone.

"What do you think you're doing?!" a voice yelled. I started to answer but was cut off. "Answer me. What do you think you're doing Chief Inspector?" the voice demanded. It wasn't just any voice but one I knew well. It was my boss, or maybe now, former boss, Superintendent Kim. I started to answer his question. He wasn't done yelling. "You are off duty, as I recall. Furthermore, you told me that the San Sebastian case was closed anyway. So, I ask again, what do you think you are doing there?" The grey suits all chattered among themselves as they watched me sweat. I was really in a bind. Even worse than they knew. Not only had I disobeyed orders by being there when I was supposed to be taking some time off, I couldn't tell him the truth. I mean, I guess I could tell Superintendent Kim that the San Sebastian case was not really closed and connected to a powerful government minister on one side and an even more powerful cardinal on the other. And that Boratch and I had covered all that up. And that I was scrambling to make sense out of what the San Sebastian case was really all about before someone on either of the powerful sides came and killed us. And..." I was so screwed.

"It was personal, Sir." I said. "Personal? What are you talking about?" "I was out here previously just getting some information on who to notify about San Sebastian's death and..." The Superintendent cut me off. "I'm looking here at the case log, and I see that the case is not even marked for closure any longer. Do you want to explain that to me, Chief Inspector?" "Well, like I was saying. I was here today because there was a very friendly receptionist I met. A very friendly, pretty receptionist, and I thought I might ask her to dinner" I said. "Then why did you say you were there to see Miss Ridecrumb?" he asked. "Well, because, the receptionist, Geena, would have possibly gotten into trouble having a personal visitor on company time." "As she should" the Superintendent said. I kept up the lie. "No, I understand. It was a mistake. I'll just try to find another way to contact her." "I think that's a good idea" he said. "Yes, I agree. I'm sorry. My mistake. I'll be leaving Life Gen right away."

The grey jackets were snickering at my story. I guess it was pretty pathetic that a man like me would try to sneak his way back onto the corporate campus to hit on a receptionist. But believable. I thought it was a very good lie, actually. Given the not ideal circumstances, I thought it was quite impressive. Not to mention who it had thrown the Superintendent off "And the case?" he asked. Shit. "Excuse me, Sir?" I asked. "And the case? Why is the case still marked "open" when you told me it was closed and cued for processing?" I waited for another brilliant, believable lie to pop into my brain. Nothing. Nothing that I was thinking made one bit of sense or could explain that. So, I did the next best thing. I bought myself some time.

"Sir, that's actually a very complicated answer. I would prefer to explain it to you in person." "Fine. Then come to my office immediately to straighten this out. This reflects very poorly on you, Chief Inspector. At the moment I am gravely disappointed in your unprofessional behavior and am seriously questioning my earlier regard for you. Clearly, I had an unjustifiably high opinion of you. I thought you were better than this." Oh, did I hate when people used that phrase. Such a cheap shot. Such an annoying method of insulting somebody and trying to make them feel like crap about themselves. But I let it slide and told Kim I would see him shortly. He hung up without saying goodbye.

One of the grey suits started to approach me. The short one. "Do you know your way out?" he asked. "Yes, I think so" I said. "Ok, we'll follow behind you just to make sure." Great. How humiliating. Being escorted off the Life Gen office park by Security. I'm a Chief Inspector, damn it! As I was about to get into my car, the taller grey suit approached me. "Which Geena?" he asked. It took me a second to realize what he was talking about. "Sadly, I don't think I got her last name. Tall, dark hair, late twenties..." I said, throwing out one random thing after another. The grey suit nodded. "Malving, Geena Malving. Tower Ten, level three." "Yeah, that's the one" I said. "You should just call her. I think you're her type" he said. "Really?" I said, stunned that this gorgeous, fictitious girl not only existed but possibly had a thing for me. "Yeah, she has a real daddy thing and loves older guys like you." Older? I couldn't have been more than ten or fifteen years older than this kid in a grey jacket. Older. Wait, but he said she was into that. "Malving, you said? Geena Malving?" I asked. "That's correct, Inspector. Now, if you wouldn't mind leaving the property."

As I drove off the Life Gen campus I waved to my departing escorts. I made sure to give an extra nod of thanks to the grey suit that informed me of this older-guy-loving, tall, young thing named Geena Malving. Unfortunately, I couldn't really enjoy it too much given my impending meeting with Superintendent Kim. I still had no idea what I was going to tell him.

What I came up with was brilliant. Just brilliant. I walked into Agency HQ brimming with confidence. I had come up with something that was not only going to satisfy Kim but make me look like a real hero. This is what I said. "I was protecting you, Sir." And then I gave it a good pause for him to contemplate my nobility and loyalty to him. "I was protecting you because, as it turns out, the San Sebastian case may be more than it appeared at first" I said. "And you didn't see fit to inform your Commanding Officer of this finding?" he asked. "I did, Sir. And, normally, would have gone to you immediately, not only to report but for your insights and advice." Oops. Too far. I could tell from his expression that he sensed the brown nosing and got defensive.

I had to push on. "But then I remembered your impending promotion, Sir. The last thing I figured you needed right now was a case that was, potentially, very political." "Political in what way?" he asked. "Political in that it could reveal things powerful people are sensitive about" I said. Kim stared at his desk. It was killing him not to ask "what things?" but he was nervous. Nervous that I might actually be right and was trying to save him from stepping into a big pile of political poo. I rushed on before giving him too much time to decide. "By handling this case, off record, it gives you the very thing you will need most should it all explode the way it potentially could." I paused again for effect. I was getting good at this. "Plausible deniability" I said. He stood up and looked right into my eyes. "Plausible deniability?" he asked. "Yes, Sir. If you know nothing about it, you certainly can't be held responsible for any of the repercussions." He thought about what I had said. I could see him pondering every word. Finally, he replied.

"Are you an idiot, Chief Inspector?" he asked. I wasn't going to answer that but he clearly wanted me to. "No, Sir" I finally said. "You don't think I would be held accountable if one of my agents became involved in something? I am responsible for this entire department. Do you understand that?" "Yes, Sir." Then who do you think would be blamed if any agent or agents in this department got caught up in something they had no business being a part of?" he asked. I didn't answer. Luckily, this time, my silence was enough of a reply. And then he did something that totally baffled me. Actually two things.

The first was he kept ranting, very loudly. "Are we clear, Chief Inspector? I am to be informed of every facet of any case you are working on no matter what?" which sounded like he wanted to know everything about the San Sebastian case. But, this was the baffling part. He, ever so subtly, moved his head in a "no" motion as he said it. I think. Maybe. Which meant he didn't really want to know anything about anything. That is, if he really moved his head like that and I didn't just imagine it. He was still waiting for my answer. "Yes, Sir. clear." Except for the fact that I totally wasn't and really wasn't sure what he wanted from me.

Then he whispered something to me which, I think, helped me figure it out. "Can you drag it out and just let it die quietly?" he asked. "No Sir, there are people that..." He cut me off. "I understand. There are those that want things done quickly" "Right and those that..." I started to explain. "Understood" he said. And then he started yelling again. "I expect to have that report and know every detail by this afternoon. Got it?" I responded almost equally as loudly. "Yes, Sir. I understand, Sir." "Good, that will be all." And then he looked down at his desk. I put my hand on the door to leave. As I did, he called my name. "Daniel" he said, barely audible. "Thank you" and then he winked. Yes, winked.

I left his office in total disbelief. I knew it was a good lie but I had no idea that it would really work. I mean, I hoped it might but when it came down to it, I expected to get totally busted and have to tell Kim all of it. The whole San Sebastian thing would have boiled over and Boratch and I would both be in deep shit. But it worked. It actually worked. Superintendent Kim was so afraid of screwing up his impending promotion he didn't want to touch the case with a ten foot pole. I was left to go about my investigation completely independently but with his full support. It was great.

Of course, me being me, I decided to ride my wave of good fortune and make a phone call. I called one Geena Malving at Life Gen. The operator connected me and I began my play. I told her I had been in the other day and couldn't stop thinking about her. I told her that I would love to take her out to dinner sometime. Her reply was along the lines of "I'm sorry, I don't remember you, which means I'm probably not very interested. But thanks." Crap. Oh, well. At least I had my thing going with the Superintendent. I really was kind of a genius sometimes. Plausible deniability. Man, I'm good.

The stress was starting to get to me. I had so many things I felt I needed to take care of that I felt like I couldn't take care of any of them. Overwhelmed. Paralyzed. Lame. I should be looking into the background of Deborah Marky. I should be trying to decipher how San Sebastian's previous work with pharmaceuticals could have led to some super-secret drug. I should be making sure that Mike Laughton's kidnapping by the Clear Thinkers had nothing to do with me. Most of all, I should be getting laid. Sadly, that was the one that was top of mind when I woke up the next day. Impending death be damned. I was horny.

Obviously, I was in bad shape on that count if I was willing to do the nasty with Anna Boratch. Aside from all the moral questions; married, kids, friend's daughter, blah, blah, blah, the woman just wasn't really that hot. What had I been thinking? And then there was Isabella Laughton in all her spoiled, rich kid glory. Every time I saw her on the news as the concerned family member talking about her kidnapped dad I kept waiting for a long shot so I could check out her little body. And the lead terrorist was totally working for me. Big brown eyes and curves like that. At least I had Geena Malvich. I know she would have said yes to going out if we had ever actually met. I was sure of it.

Anyway, my main point is that with sex on the brain I was having trouble thinking straight. We are all just animals programmed to engage in basic biological functions. And I was being programmed to do something really fun and really dirty with a young, hot, somebody, somewhere, that I was having trouble finding. It was really, really distracting. Depressing even. It had been a long time since I had been with someone. Too long. Years, I think. Oh, Man, that is depressing.

I needed to deal with this issue before I could think about the case in any coherent way. My need for sex had become that pressing. I decided to talk to Father Mike. I met him at his mission and we went for a walk. When he asked why I was there, I told him I needed to get laid. "And, you mistook me for a pimp?" he half-joked. I told him it had been a long time and I was really feeling it. He said that he understood. "So, can you introduce me to someone?" I asked. "Yes, if you come to church more often. I would be happy to introduce you to some other members of the congregation." "Is that a bribe?" I asked. Father Mike just grinned. Bastard.

"Daniel, let me ask you something. Is it really just sex you are after? I have the feeling that you came to me because there is something more serious you are feeling." "Like what?" I asked. "I think you are lonely. I think you have been lonely for a very long time." I decided to steer the conversation in another direction. "I know you've explained this before but tell me again. Why does the Church insist people stay in bad marriages?" I asked. "Because they made a promise before God." "But people change. Things don't always work out..." I said. "It can be very difficult. Why do you know someone having trouble in their marriage?" And so began our conversation about Anna Boratch.

At first it started off as if I was concerned for a friend. And that Anna was that friend. Then it sounded more like I was concerned for her for Boratch's sake. Then it sounded like complete bullshit and Father Mike called me on it. "So, you want to sleep with this woman?" he asked. "No, I really don't. But I almost did. Which is really why I came here." I then launched into the sordid tale of Anna's visit. Which was a mistake. Not because Father Mike was going to be all judgmental about respecting the sanctity of marriage. He was pretty good at not being condescending and trite about such things. But for a much more practical reason. He asked me a question I couldn't answer very easily. Not like a big moral thing I didn't know the answer to. Something purely informational. He asked what had stopped Anna and I from going through with it.

The reality was the bizarre suicide speech from Robert San Sebastian had killed the mood. But I couldn't really say that. The last thing I wanted to do was involve him in this whole thing with San Sebastian. I just said "We got interrupted." "Someone walked in on you?" he asked. "No, it was more like a phone call but not a phone call. Something to do with a case that I'm not at liberty to discuss." He looked at me with a bemused expression on his face. "What?" I asked. "Not at liberty to discuss? That sounds mighty formal. You do remember who you're talking to here, right? Father Mike. The guy that knows about..." I didn't want him to get into what he knew about. But he was right. It was a bit formal.

Luckily, he let it slide. "Maybe that little pause in the action gave you time to think about what you were doing. Maybe it was God's way of giving you a chance to prevent yourself from making a horrible mistake" he said. "Maybe it was God's way of giving me blue balls" I corrected. Father Mike laughed. "So, do you wish you had slept with her? Do you regret that you were not able to that night?" he asked. "She's not even that pretty." "But?" "But, yeah, I regret it. It would have been nice." I couldn't believe I had just said that. What was wrong with me?

"Even though you know how wrong it is?" he asked. "But that's what I keep struggling with. Why is it so wrong?" I asked. I expected him to go on and on about marriage being sacred and so on. But this was Father Mike. He didn't even bother with all that and cut to the chase. "Because it will be a huge mess and it isn't worth it."

I let his words sit there. "If you sleep with this woman you will have taken a very big step into the quicksand. There is no guarantee you will not be sucked into it and unable to escape. "How do you know she isn't worth it?" I asked. He looked me right in the eye. "Alright, is she? Is sex with Anna Boratch worth all the complications to your life that it will cause? What are you going to do if her husband comes after you? What about her children? What if she wants to leave her husband to be with you? Are you ready to marry her and assume custody of her children?" "Wait, What? Who said..." I stammered. "And what about your loyalty to her father? You've said to me time and time again what a good friend he has been to you. And you would do this to him? In spite of knowing his feelings on his daughter and her marriage you would work against him?" he asked. Without thinking, I nodded. Father Mike was stunned. "Yes, yes, you would work against him just for sex with his daughter? Even with all those consequences, and quite a few more I haven't even mentioned, you would still sleep with her? Then maybe Anna means more to you than you are letting on" he challenged. I almost lost it. "No!" I yelled. Nothing else. Just "No!" He waited for me to clarify. I tried. "The nod wasn't "Yes, I'm going to do it anyway."" The nod was "Yeah, what you said. Exactly. I knew all this and just needed to hear it. Anna is a mistake. Bad news. A harlot" I said. "Let's not go overboard" he said.

His words had been true. All of them. And all so practical. Father Mike had just done a truly admirable job of pointing out how the risk/reward equation landed far too heavily in risk and not nearly enough in reward. It wasn't like she was a super-model or a movie star or something. Maybe that would be worth it. But given that she was an aging, not all that fit, self-centered, kind of bitchy, mother of two, she was clearly not worth the hassle. I breathed a sigh of relief. I could now do what was right and forgo temptations of the flesh with her. As I always knew I would. I had my principles.

I thanked Father Mike for his advice. He was such a good guy. I asked how things were going for him. They sounded slightly troubling. There was a movement afoot to decrease the funding to charitable organizations unless they started to require drug testing and proof of living a clean, Christian life. Father Mike was totally against such requirements and would never allow his mission to become so overbearing. But if certain powers that be in the Church and government got their way, the cost for his independence would be a slash in the very funding he required to keep his doors open. As good as he was with money, a total cut-off would be too much to make up with his own efforts. "So, what are you going to do then?" I asked. "Politic and lobby during the days and pray a lot at night. There isn't much else that I can do" he said. I offered him my sympathies and wished him luck. I also thanked him again for his sage advice. Such a good guy.

Mike Laughton was released. The State News Channel had video footage of Laughton being escorted from an ambulance to St. Joseph's Hospital. I turned up the volume. "...in good condition following five days of captivity. He said he was treated well and never threatened with physical harm or death. Exactly what led to his sudden release is a matter of speculation. It is extremely unlikely that the terrorists' demands would have been met. As you know, our government has a very, very, strict policy about not negotiating with terrorists..." I turned down the lies.

As I watched the video footage repeat, I saw another familiar face in the frame. Isabella Laughton was by her father's side. Mike Laughton had a beard and looked like he needed a shower but otherwise looked completely normal. No fingers cut off. Both ears still in place. My guess is that Energex had paid the ransom. Or, technically, the insurance company did. Every CEO and VP worth anything to anyone had a K & R policy. The K was kidnapping the R was ransom. Some added an E to make it KR & E insurance. The E was for extortion. Not quite as catchy sounding, in my opinion, but whatever. It all amounted to the same thing. If someone with a policy was kidnapped, the insurance company would step in and pay it.

The most interesting thing about it was how much a company decided to insure any given individual for. More than one CEO had been shocked to learn his up and coming VP had been insured for more than he. He was, literally, less valued to the Board of Directors than his colleague. I can also imagine how awkward it would be to learn the amount of coverage you had was lowered after a few quarters of bad earnings. If you're not getting shareholder value out of the company, then maybe it's really not so bad if you get killed by terrorists. These things just had a way of working out for the good of the corporation.

Anyway, Laughton was free. Isabella was with him. All was fine. In spite of Kapinskov's threats, Mike Laughton was alive and well. Unless Kapinskov was just waiting. Just waiting because he didn't get the chance before the Clear Thinkers stepped in. And now...No, Laughton was safe, now. He was far too high profile at this point for Kapinskov to touch. The video looped again. I have to say, Isabella really was quite the attractive young girl. I turned up the volume again. "the investigation has lead only to an empty warehouse in the small town of Freemont, about two hours east of the capital."

I flipped the channel. The local news had a photo of Brown Eyes, herself, on it. She was all wrapped up and hard to identify but I remembered my encounter with her at the Church of Foam. A "WANTED" caption was below the photo. "...believed to be very dangerous and known for their zealotry. The earlier crackdowns on the group, calling themselves the Free Thinkers...Sorry, the Clear Thinkers, at the time were derided by some as an over-reaction. However, given their recent involvement in this kidnapping, it appears that the government's zero tolerance policy was absolutely correct and completely justified..." I turned the television off. It was about as good a news as possible, given the circumstances. At least I could rest easy that I wasn't to blame for anything that happened to Mike Laughton. He could go on living a happy life and paving over nature preserves with Astroturf without fear.

I sat at my kitchen table and reviewed my notes. I had attempted to learn more about Robert San Sebastian and his career in the pharmaceutical industry. There wasn't much more to discover. His early career had been all about pushing Sensoral and keeping old ladies sexed up for their husbands. Then he moved on to the growing Alzheimer's market. He had a few minor successes but nothing major. There was one drug he oversaw the development of that was briefly considered a breakthrough in reversing dementia. However, later tests not only proved that it didn't work but that it occasionally caused minor dementia to bloom into several major psychiatric disorders. These side effects included bipolar disorder and schizophrenia. It was withdrawn from the market after only nine weeks.

I was also able to learn a little more about Deborah Marky. In the weeks preceding her untimely and crispy death, she had purchased a state-of-the-art alarm system for her house. She had also legally purchased and registered three handguns and a fully automatic assault rifle. There were no records with any law enforcement agency of her filing a complaint or receiving any threats from the Hand of God or any other fringe group. But, clearly, she felt threatened.

And then, as experienced investigators like myself are prone to do, I had a very clever thought. If the special drug project was still running, they would need somebody else to be in charge. Who would San Sebastian's successor have been? If I could find that man. Or woman. Then I would be able to trail them and learn what the whole Special Program was all about. Or I could just ask their CIO, Rasheed. That is, if I were ever allowed to get near him. And if he felt like answering the question. Which I couldn't and he wouldn't. Unless someone a lot more powerful than me made him. The Minister wasn't big enough. Crap. I had been down this road before.

It had been my hope that there would have been phone records from San Sebastian's underground office to somewhere. But if there was, I couldn't find them. Which meant either the office had never been occupied, a distinct possibility, or the records had been swiped clean. I remembered a contact I had at National Telecom. I hadn't spoken to him in years. He was kind of a creepy guy. The sort that was way too familiar with people he hardly knew and always wanting to hang out. It was so irritating, I stopped using him as a contact just because I couldn't handle it after a while. But I did what I had to do. I called him.

It didn't surprise me at all that John Griggs was still at the phone company. When he picked up, he was as chirpy as ever. "Hey Dan? Long time. How's things down at the Agency?" I tried to keep the small talk to a minimum. It was a battle in futility. John wanted to talk about sports, the weather, if I was dating, how we should go out again soon, etc. It was truly painful. Finally, I was able to get to why I had called. "Is there a way to track phone records from an address rather than a number?" I asked. "Sure" he said. "The number I'm looking for isn't the official one but one people wanted hidden." "I don't follow" he said. "I think there was a phone system, installed secretly, without any official records, at a particular address. I need to find out what that phone number would have been and then get a record of all calls from and to it." Silence. And then more silence. Finally, John spoke again. "You want me to find the records of something there are no records for?"

I tried to make myself more clear. The phone system was probably installed secretly. So, there would be no record of that. But I assume whoever had this secret phone system had to pay for it. So, there would be some records, somewhere, of a phone number billed to San Sebastian's address besides his own cell phone. I asked John if he understood. "Yeah, sure. But there are no records of it. You just said so." I was losing my patience. "Can you give me any information relating to phones and that address. Anything" I pleaded. "Sure, hang on. Give me the address again" I did. I heard him typing into a computer. "Here we go!" he said. I grabbed a pen. "We have an unlimited wireless plan for a Robert San Sebastian at that address. And it looks like he missed his last payment." Unreal. John clearly was missing the point of this whole exercise.

"Yes, I know about that one. And the reason he didn't pay his bill is because he's dead." "Really?" John said. "Are you sure of that?" he asked. "Yes." "Ok, let me make a note of that in his record. Hang on." I heard John banging away at the keyboard some more.

"What else?" I asked. "What do you mean?" he asked. I was getting increasingly frustrated. "Are there any other records related to that address?" "Let me check" he said. I heard him type some more. "No, I'm sorry. That's the only record we have of a phone tied to that location." "Are there any other phone bills sent there?" I asked. "Why would there be? He only has the one phone." I was going to kill him. "Please check, John" I pleaded. "Okee-dokey. Here we go." More keystrokes. "Bingo!" he yelled. "What? You found one?" "Well, no, there's only the one phone like I keep saying. But there was a repair call made from that location. Our technician requested that the networking router be reset for a number there." "So, there's a number? I mean, besides San Sebastian's cell phone?" I asked. "Yeah, it looks that way." he said. "Can you look up all the information on it?" I asked. "Sure thing."

I waited as John typed in more information. If there were logs from that number, it would tie everyone involved in the Special Project together. All the labs. All the sales calls. All the Church and government contacts. All of it. "Huh, that's strange" John said. "What is?" I asked. "There's not a single record of anything for that phone other than that one repair call." Crap. "Are you sure?" I asked. "Yeah, I'm sure. How strange." "Kind of like somebody erased them all" I suggested. "Exactly." I tried to get John to find a way to pull the, now erased, records. "No, sorry. They just don't exist anymore. Gone." Totally frustrated, I asked him one last thing. "Can you possibly tell me why they were erased?" I asked. More typing. "Yeah, that's easy enough. You guys told us to."

After a moment of confusion on my part, I figured out what he meant. It turned out John didn't mean "You guys as in the People's Protection Agency" but more generally, someone in law enforcement. The order to erase all records tied to that address had been sent from Anti-Terror. Specifically, the soon to no longer be Chief, Chief Windsor.

I got a panicked call from Boratch. Actually, four or five, panicked calls. His voice message was about how he needed me to pick up the cake before the party. But, since the party was already over, I assumed it was something else. I went for a walk to a small park in the Vietnamese section of the city. When I called him back, he picked up almost instantly. "Thank God, you called. I need to discuss the details of the party for you. He knows" he said. "Who knows?" "The guest of honor on my side of the family. He knows." "Who he?" I asked. I could tell from Boratch's reaction that I was missing something. "Just meet me somewhere in an hour" he said.

"Ok, how about some Pho for lunch?" I suggested. "Fine. I'll be there." And then he hung up. I still didn't know what he was talking about.

"Guest of honor on his side of the family?" Oh, shit. The Cardinal. He meant the Cardinal. No wonder there were so many phone calls. How did the Cardinal find out so quickly? Had my visits to Life Gen tipped him off? Crap. Crap. Crap. Crap. Crap. My heart started to race. The theory of someone like Rooney being after you is a very different feeling from the reality. He could crush Boratch and I in the blink of an eye. Maybe I was jumping to conclusions. Maybe that's not who Boratch meant.

I had an hour to freak out, calm down and then freak out again. If it was Rooney he was talking about, I was screwed. I didn't have any answers yet. My only powerful friend was Kapiskov who wasn't all that powerful, when it came down to it. And I had no good plan about how I would just run away and hide. I paced back and forth trying to think of various options. None of them were good. Maybe I was wrong. Maybe I was getting all worked up over nothing. I saw Boratch huffing and puffing as he made his way toward the Pho place. I started walking toward him. The expression on his face was not good. He was very worried and upset about something. This wasn't good.

Before I could even ask the question, Boratch blurted out my worst fear. "He knows." We were so screwed. I was so screwed. "He found out last night" Boratch said. I didn't really know what to say. "Crap" was about the best I could do. "What were you thinking?!" Boratch asked. That was a ballsy question. "What do you mean? I did it for you." I said. "You did it for me, Daniel? Explain how what you did benefits me" he said. "I went out to Life Gen to learn more about what San Sebastian was up to. The more we know, the more we can find a way out. Or could have. I guess we just ran out of time." Boratch looked completely confused. "What are you talking about?" he asked. "I went to Life Gen but was thrown off the property before I could do another round of interviews. What are you talking about?" I asked. "Steve" he said. "Steve? Who the fuck is Steve?"I asked. "Anna's husband. You don't even know the name of the man you cuckolded?"

I actually laughed. Not a loud, uncontrolled, long belly laugh. But an audible laugh. Steve. Steve I could deal with. I mean, it was annoying. But it sure beat being hunted down by the Cardinal, H.O.G. and whoever. "Who did you think I was talking about?" "Cardinal Rooney" I said. I explained what I had been thinking to Boratch. The nightmare scenarios playing in my head. I was smiling the whole time. I had a new lease on life. I had time yet. Time to solve the great San Sebastian case and wheel and deal my way out of the whole mess. Boratch wasn't smiling. In fact, he looked kind of angry.

"I'm glad you think cuckolding a man is such a laughable issue" he said. "Please quit using that word. It sounds ridiculous" I said. "No, what's ridiculous is that you are my friend, who I trusted, and you betrayed that trust by sleeping with my only daughter. My only, MARRIED, daughter." "I didn't sleep with her" I said. "What do you mean you didn't sleep with her? She told Steve she came over to your place drunk the other night and the two of you had sex." What a bitch, I thought to myself. "What a bitch" I said out loud. "And now you have the nerve to call my daughter a bitch to my face?!" Boratch grabbed me by the collar and breathed his vodka breath right into my face. I pushed him away. "Calm down!"

He turned and walked away. "Samuel, don't walk away. You're being misinformed. Anna and I did not sleep together." He turned and made his way back toward me. "No, then why did she say that she did?" He asked. "To make her husband angry and jealous." "Why would she do that? Why would she pick you?" he asked. "I was the first name that popped into her head. Maybe she thought naming someone at People's Protection would make him nervous. I don't know. Why don't you ask her?" Boratch looked so frustrated he could explode. "I did ask her. And you know what she said?" "No, what?" I asked "She said, she would be happy to talk to me about her problems if I would talk to her about mine." "I'm not sure what that means" I said. "She accused me of being an alcoholic. She said if I refused to let her intervene for my good, I had no right to pretend to do so for hers." That sounded like Anna. Not that I really knew, all that much, what Anna sounded like. I can't believe she did that and told her husband like that.

"So, the whole thing is a lie. You and Anna never slept together?" he asked. "No," which was true. "You never had sex?" "No," which, thanks to San Sebastian's weird confession, was also true. "She didn't even come to see you that night, like she claims?" Uh-oh. Boratch kept looking at me, waiting for my reply. The choices were bad. Blatantly lie, which would make the meeting sound far more sinister than it was, or tell the truth. Tell the truth and wait for the follow up questions that would probably lead to lies, anyway.

"No," I said. Boratch kept looking at me. He wasn't buying it. Why wasn't he buying it? "Alright she did. But it wasn't anything like you're saying." Boratch got in my face again. "No, then what was it like, Friend?!" The way he said friend the word could have easily been replaced by Asshole, Shithead, Scumbag or maybe all three at once. I don't think I had ever heard so much hatred and disgust packed into a single word before. "She came over to talk about your problem with alcohol" I said. "I do not have a problem with alcohol!" he protested. "Yes, you do. You're an alcoholic and Anna and I are both very concerned about you."

Boratch's entire posture changed. He went from looking ready to beat me to death with his bare hands to a man trying not to cry in public. He broke down in front of me. "I know I have a problem. It's the stress. You understand. I know you understand, Daniel." I nodded sympathetically. "I do. Nobody is blaming you for having the problem. At least, I'm not. I just want you to realize that it IS a problem and to deal with it" I said. He nodded and started tearing up. "I know. I know. I have actually tried. I've gone to meetings but I could never get myself to stay. They start discussing the damage drinking has caused them...I just can't take it and leave." "Would you like me to go with you?" I asked. "To a meeting?" he asked. "Yes." "You would do that?" he said. "Of course, I would do that. We can even find one this afternoon, if you like." He nodded. "I would. I would. I am so tired of the way Anna looks at me. I want her to be proud of her father, not ashamed." "She isn't ashamed. She just wants you to get help" I said. Put like that, Anna didn't sound like nearly the selfish brat she really was.

We spent almost another hour talking. Mostly it was Boratch talking about how liking the occasional drink had become a crutch he used. He was miserably unhappy with his life since his wife died. He was lonely and his poor relationship with Anna was a constant source of pain for him. He knew a lot of people. But when it came down to it, I was the only real friend he had in the world. He even apologized. "I'm sorry for being such a jerk. I know you would never sleep with Anna. You have far too much respect for her, and for me, to ever do something that hurtful" he said. I prayed my face wouldn't give anything away that was going on inside my head. Memories of Anna. Drunken kisses and groping in front of the TV. Thankfully, Boratch turned and just looked down at the ground. "You are a good friend, Daniel. I don't know what I would ever do without you."

I turned my attention to Chief Windsor. I needed to find out how much he knew about San Sebastian and the Special Project. I went back to HQ to talk with Superintendent Kim. "Chief Inspector Hastings, what can I do for you?" he asked. I wasn't even sure if I was officially back from my unofficial suspension yet. But it felt like I was. Ever since our little "plausible deniability" discussion, Superintendent Kim and I had become very close. At least in his mind. "I have a question about timing, Sir" I said. "Meaning, what, exactly?" he asked. "I've come across some information in my investigation..." Superintendent Kim visible stiffened. He really, really, didn't want to get involved in the San Sebastian mess. I continued more delicately. "It's still too early to get into exactly what that is" I said. Kim relaxed again. "But it...well, if it comes out, I would like to know at what point it would be best." He looked at me trying to figure out what I had just said. He wasn't getting it.

"May I ask, purely as a colleague of course, how your appointment to Anti-Terror is looking?" I asked. "It's all sealed up. We're just waiting for the right time to announce it." "That's great. Just great. So, Chief Windsor will be retiring soon, then?" I asked. "Transferred, actually. He's going to Tax Enforcement and Collections." TEC was a graveyard for careers, if ever there was. The salaries were extraordinarily high and the benefits included a huge pension. But it was dull and out of the public spotlight entirely. A sure sign that Windsor was being put out to pasture. "But it's not official yet?" I asked. "No, I believe the announcement will be made on the fifteenth of next month." "And you will be taking over Anti-Terror, shortly afterward?" I asked. He looked at me and started nodding. "Chief Inspector, I thought you would be a little more subtle than this." I wasn't sure what he was getting at. "If you want to know if I'm still going to recommend you for my current seat, just ask." His promise of promotion was the last thing on my mind. I had written it off and made it a fairly low priority given everything else going on. "So, will you?" I asked. He smiled. "I think you have learned your lesson. Assuming you continue to do the good work you have been, I think you can expect to be in this chair very shortly."

I forced a smile on my face. I really didn't want the promotion. It was a very boring job being Superintendent. But I put that out of my mind. "Do you have a date, yet, Sir, when you will be taking over the Anti-Terrorism Agency?" I asked. He stood up looking far more jovial than I had seen him in a while. "Anxious to ascend to the throne here, are we Hastings?" I faked my enthusiasm. "Yes, I supposed I am. Not that I have anything against being a Chief Inspector but..." He cut me off. "But it's not the same as being the boss, is it? Getting a seat at the table, as it were." Getting a seat behind a desk filled with forms and paperwork was more like it. But whatever he needed to believe.

He finally circled around to the answer I had come looking for. "I think it's shaping up like this. Windsor will be moving on by the middle of next month, I will take over immediately, and you, assuming you continue to do good work, will take over here about the same time." "The middle of next month?" I asked. "Think you can wait that long?" he asked. "It will be difficult but I guess I'll have to. Thank you, Sir. For everything." I felt completely transparent but people believe what they want to believe. He walked around and put his arm around my shoulder. "I am glad our professional relationship is developing the way it has. I think inter-agency cooperation will be key to success. Both for our departments and ourselves." "I couldn't agree more, Sir. I will be your little bitch forever, waiting to please you for making me your successor." Alright, that wasn't exactly what I said. But the message was the same. He really wanted to believe he was a kingmaker and I was his puppet. I let him. I had gotten what I had come for. I needed to have a talk with Chief Windsor. Maybe in return for helping him, he would help me.

"I can save your career" I said. Windsor looked at me with disbelief. I felt like a used car salesman trying to sell him a car known for spontaneously combusting. Getting him to even meet with me had been extraordinarily difficult. As the saying goes, the more you watch others the more you are watched. But, somehow, using my exemplary powers of persuasion, I had gotten him to meet with me for a drink.

"My career is just fine, Chief Inspector, in fact, I'm about to get a promotion" he said. He almost looked like he believed it. No. There's no way he could see the move to Tax Enforcement and Collections as anything other than what it was. A way to get him off the public radar and sit out his final days in government. "So, I've heard. The new head of TEC. Very impressive" I said. "How did you know that?" he asked. "I'm a Chief Inspector. Finding things out is my job." I cringed at my own words but let it slide. I had to press on. "So, you won't miss the action and glamour of Anti-Terror?" I asked. His expression suddenly got more angry. I had hit a nerve.

"So, what is it you want?" he asked. "I want to help you, Sir. If you want my help, that is?" He glared "And how are you going to do that?" I had to be very, very careful how I answered the next question. "There are things people don't know about the person being brought in to replace you. If those things became known at just the right time, the embarrassment might slow things down for a while." I waited for a reaction. And waited some more. Windsor could have done anything next, from arrest me on the spot, to hug and kiss me. I had no idea what he was thinking. "Go on" he said. Well, at least he was interested. "If the appointment of your successor should explode in their faces, they might be persuaded that keeping you on is the best thing for everyone." He paused again. He liked to pause. "And you know something which could derail that appointment at just the right time?" he asked. "I do." And I did.

Superintendent Kim had done a very poor job of hiding some things in his past. Admittedly, we were talking twenty-three years ago, now. But still. It was the sort of thing that was a political nightmare. In fact, I was very surprised it hadn't come out in the vetting process for Kim's appointment to Anti-Terror. But I could fix that. I could drop that big secret from his past on him at any time. The secret, by the way, was this. When he was younger, Kim used to cheat on his wife, a lot. That, alone, was bad, but not that big of a deal in the scheme of things. A good PR person could find just the right words of contrition to smooth that all over and make it all go away. But it was worse. Kim got one of his playmates pregnant. That's pretty ugly. Maybe even enough to damage his career, right there. But there was even more. A deep, dark secret that could totally destroy him which, through my own efforts and investigations, I had uncovered. Said playmate had gotten a secret, and obviously illegal, abortion which Kim had arranged and paid for. Superintendent Kim was a hypocritical baby murderer.

And then Windsor threw me a curveball. A very unwelcome, unpleasant, unexpected curve ball. "Sorry, not interested" he said. "You understand what I am offering you?" I asked. "Yup. And, like I said, I'm not interested. My days of ruining a man's reputation are over. I'm actually really looking forward to a quieter life over at Tax Enforcement. I think the change will do me a lot of good." I was speechless.

Which was good because Windsor wasn't done talking yet. "What interests me more is why you would offer me that information. Is this a personal or professional issue?" he asked. "What?" I replied, oh so brilliantly. I still couldn't believe he turned down my offer. "Are you doing this because it furthers your career somehow or because you have a personal dislike for Superintendent Kim and want to see him destroyed?" he asked. Windsor was like a different man. He was not the politically unaware buffoon from the press conference at the foam incident. He was not the desperate politician doing whatever it took to keep his grip on power. He was a cop. A mean, driven, interrogating the hell out of me, cop. I can't say I liked the change. "Neither" I said. "So, you offered me this damaging information on your boss out of the goodness of your heart?" I didn't answer. "What confuses me is how that would benefit you. My people are telling me you have been chosen to take his position at People's Protection. If he doesn't move on, isn't there a chance he could keep his post and put you out of luck?" "It's got nothing to do with that" I said. I felt like I was sweating. "So, it's personal then. You just really dislike the man and don't care what it costs you as long as it hurts him?" "What? No." I was not doing well in this conversation and knew it. What was I going to do when this got back to Kim? Oh, what a mess.

But I shouldn't have worried. My years of experience and working with people had given me the instincts necessary to turn the situation to my favor. Windsor kept asking questions as I prepared my counter-attack. Just when he thought he had me trapped. I hit him. "The truth is, Chief Windsor, I am here as part of an official People's Protection Agency investigation." That got him. "I wanted to know why you erased the phone records of one Robert San Sebastian's secret office and how deeply you were involved in the work that he was doing there." Windsor turned pale. Take that, Pal!

But Windsor was good. Very good. He tried to deflect the conversation. "And what does all this business about revealing confidential information about your boss have to do with any of that?" he asked. "It was just an interrogation technique. As a fellow law enforcement officer, you should understand these things. Never ask the suspect what you want to know too quickly or too directly." "So, now I'm a suspect?" He looked pissed. "No, no. I didn't mean it like that. But you do have information I need to further my investigation" I said. "The San Sebastian incident." "Yes." "Well, why didn't you just come out and say so instead of all this other garbage you've been talking about?" he asked. "Alright, I will. Can you tell me why you erased all the phone records of that secret office?" "No."

I waited for him to elaborate. He didn't. "No?" I asked. "But it would help in an official investigation..." He cut me off. "No. That information is classified. In fact, I strongly, strongly, suggest you forget you ever learned about that. The best thing you could do for your department, the government and, most of all, yourself, is to just forget about the whole thing and move on." He started to get up. "You might also want to think twice about offering damaging information about your superiors to people. Everybody already knows about Superintendent Kim's past. Everybody who matters, anyway. Pretending you're some skilled political trickster just makes you come across as an incompetent ass." And with that, he left.

The rest of the day was uneventful, which normally would have been perfect. However, given that it was only a matter of time before the Cardinal became involved in things, not so great. Frustration seemed to be the theme of the day. In all sorts of ways. Anna appeared at my door again. This time she wasn't drunk. Which was kind of regrettable. I liked her much better when she was drunk. This time around, she was her usual stick in the mud, selfish, self. "Aren't you going to ask me in?" she said. To which I replied, simply, "why?" And then she did something I'm not sure I ever saw her do before. At least when she was sober. She said "please."

She took her jacket off and sat on the sofa. She was wearing a very nicely fitting little top, skirt and boots. Harlot. For an old pair of legs, I had to admit they were holding up quite nicely. She saw my glancing at her and took it as sexual interest. "You like my skirt?" the harlot asked. "What are you doing here, Anna?" "I actually came by to thank you." This was a trick if ever there was. "My father told me about your discussion and how you were going to help him start going to meetings. I can't tell you how happy that makes me feel." Her words seemed sincere. But it was still a trick. "I didn't do it for you" I said.

She actually seemed a little hurt by my response. "It doesn't matter if you did it out of friendship to him or for me. The fact is that you did it. And I think that is very, very admirable." I sat there trying not to enjoy the praise. "Will you make sure that he actually does it and it's not just empty words?" she asked. "Of course." "It's easy to say you're going to do things but much harder to actually do them." "I couldn't agree more" I said. "Alright, that's all I really came over to say. I'll leave you to your porn" she said. "I was NOT watching porn. "Ok" she said in a way that made it clear she didn't believe me. "It was part of an investigation. Really, it was" I insisted. "Alright, I believe you. I saw the confession too, remember?" she said. How could I forget. "What does it matter anyway? Nobody cares" she added. True enough. Memories came flooding back to me of our previous encounter. Her hand. The kiss. And then I realized that was exactly what she had intended. Harpy. I needed to make sure my position was clear on all this.

"Anna, did your father tell you about the rest of the conversation he and I had?" I asked. "He did" she said, and then wouldn't say any more. "What did he tell you?" I asked. "That you lied to him" she said. "What?" "Don't worry, he doesn't know you told him lies. But he told me what you said." "And what was that?" I asked. "That there was nothing sexual between us and we just discussed ways to help him with his drinking problem." "That wasn't a lie!" I protested. Which, of course, was a lie. But...we had to straighten this out. "I didn't lie. We didn't have sex that night" I insisted. "No, we didn't" she said. "Well, at least we agree on that much." She came closer to me. I could almost hear the sound of her rattlesnake tail, rattling. "But we would have" she said softly. Snake tongue! I stepped back a couple of inches. "No, we wouldn't have. One or the other of us would have come to our senses, realized what we were doing and stopped things." Her eyes drifted, lower and lower down my body, until she was staring at my crotch. "If you say so" she said. And then she smiled. A very, very smug, "whatever you need to believe" sort of smile. Oh, I hated her sometimes.

"Regardless, it didn't happen and it never, ever, will happen. Do you understand? I promised your father and I intend to keep that promise." She stepped closer again. I really wished she would stop doing that. "Sure." Her short, little, flippant answers were really annoying me. "We won't ever have a physical relationship like that. Do you understand?" I said. And then she did something only a heartless shrew like her could do. She leaned over to me, very, very close and whispered right into my ear. Then she said "I find you repulsive and could never sleep with you anyway unless I was incredibly drunk." I stood there paralyzed by the insult.

"Bullshit! You would totally sleep with me!" I blurted. "Yeah, if I was drunk like I was the other night, I would have slept with the homeless man in the parking lot." What a bitch. What a totally cold, manipulative, lying bitch. "Now, you're the one that's lying" I said. "So, you admit you were lying before." "What?" I said. "You just admitted that you were lying before." "I did not. What was I, supposedly, in your twisted world, lying about?" I asked. "You tell me. Wanting to have sex with me, I guess." "What? I said no such thing." I couldn't believe she had twisted the conversation the way she had. How did I get on the defensive?

"Admit it, you wanted to have sex with me that night and you still want to have sex with me, right now" she said. "Oh, your ego knows no bounds, Anna. You're not even that hot." That must have gotten her. But if it did, she wasn't showing it.

"Is that what you told my father. You had no interest in me because I wasn't hot enough for you? What about all that garbage you told him about friendship and loyalty and just wanting to help him?" she asked. "All of that is true" I said. Although, honestly, I wasn't even sure I said all of that and Bortach didn't just hear it the way he wanted to.

Anna was still waiting for me to answer the question. The one about wanting to sleep with her or not. Which I wasn't going to do. She just stood there looking at me looking very angry and very confident. Which, Ok, I admit, was kind of hot. Between that attitude and the skirt and boots...We kept talking and just as we seemed to agree that we found each other totally repulsive. And that sleeping together would be a betrayal and source of incredible pain to her father. And...Yeah, we did it. We had sex. After all that, we had sex anyway.

The reasoning and logic went out the window even though she really wasn't that hot. But she was, kind of. I mean, she was. At least, right then. All angry and in my face. And that, aging, but still very, very nice set of legs. And the skirt...It just all came together. So, to speak.

I guess my years of (completely voluntary) celibacy had taken a toll on me. I couldn't get enough of her. We went at it first on the sofa with her keeping on almost all of her clothes. Then her shirt came off and that was another go round. Then, down to just the boots. And so on. For an old guy, I have to say, my energy and recovery times were mighty impressive. I felt like I was nineteen again. Except for the embarrassing timing issues. And not having a clue what I was doing. And...The point is, it wasn't one of those encounters where it was wham, bam thank you ma'am and then out the door. Or, in our case, deep regret over what we had just done. It was an all night celebration of the flesh. One, which I fully admit, that I thoroughly, thoroughly, enjoyed.

Of course, just as I was convincing myself that I had judged Anna Boratch too harshly all those years, she ruined everything. She started talking. She started talking about her tacky house and how she absolutely, positively needed to renovate the kitchen that has just been re-done four years ago. She talked about all the clothes her husband was too cheap to buy for her. And how he was a cheating asshole. And how much she would appreciate it if I would pay him a visit and just threaten him a bit with my People's Protection ID. All in all, as good as the sex had been, and it was, I realized I really and truly despised the person I woke up to that next morning. Which, as it happened, wasn't a bad thing.

Over coffee, I brought up how what we had done was a mistake. She once again tried to use her harpy ways to twist my words into something else. "You mean it was wrong?" she asked. "Yes, it was wrong. You're a married woman." "I am." "And I promised your father" I said. "You did." She was being way too glib about things. Just as I was about to get more harsh she cut me off. "Maybe that's part of why it was so hot for you" she said. "What do you mean, for me? Like it wasn't hot for you?" I asked. She just shrugged. "It was fine" she said. Fine? I was going to kill her. "I'm joking. It was nice." Nice? "Good" she added. That's better. I guess. "But I think part of the turn on was how wrong it was. You don't think so?" she asked. "Not really." "So, you just thought it was hot because you were so into me?" she asked. Oh, I was so going to kill her. But, she finally stopped with her word games and clever conversational ploys and we had a serious discussion. She realized how much it would crush her father if he ever learned what the two of us had done. We agreed that, no matter what, he must never, ever, find out. We also agreed that it could never, ever, happen again. Which is what made the next part rather confusing.

As she was gathering her things to leave she asked me if I would do it. I wasn't sure what the "it" was that she was referring to. When I asked for clarification, I couldn't believe my ears. "Talk to my husband. Just let him know if he goes too far threatening me and the kids that you'll come down on him like a ton of bricks" she said. I didn't answer. She looked at me, hair still a bit of a mess from last night's activities. "Please" she said. "I really don't want to abuse my power like that, Anna. I could get into a lot of trouble if my boss found out I was using my position like that." "Oh, come on. You know that you guys do it all the time. My father tells me story after story about how his law enforcement friends, you especially, always do things for him." True enough. "So, why won't you do this for me?" she asked. "I really don't feel comfortable about it" I said. And then I braced myself. I had a bad feeling about what was about to come next.

She was about to threaten me. She was about to threaten to tell her father about us unless I did what she asked. How had I let myself fall into this trap? That's probably why she even came over here last night. It wasn't to thank me and leave. It was to seduce me. To get me to betray her father so she could hold it over my head. I tried to think of what it was like to be in her position. Trapped in a bad marriage with a husband that really and truly did sound like a douche bag. A father that kept insisting she stay in that horrible situation rather than try to help her out of it. But that was no excuse for blackmail. That was just evil. And wrong. I couldn't believe she had done this to me.

But she was full of surprises. She kissed me again. A perfect goodbye kiss. And then she said. "I understand. Don't worry about it. I'll find another way to deal with Steve." And then another kiss. A little bit more passionate. A little bit more everything. So much so that I started to contemplate how late I could get to the office and have nobody notice. And then she pulled away and rested her hands on my shoulders and looked up at me. "And I don't find you repulsive even when I'm not drunk" she said. "Thanks?" I said. "But everything you said is true. We can't do this again. Ever. Even if we want to." That is what I said, isn't it? "Take care, Chief Inspector." And then a peck on the lips and a quick exit. As I watched her leave I was overcome by a feeling I had not expected. One that caught me completely off guard. Sadness. I really wanted her to stay.

My day did not get any easier. I went into HQ to find a note at my desk from Superintendent Kim. "See Me. NOW!" There was also a voicemail from him saying the exact same thing. He did not sound happy. He had found out about my visit to Chief Windsor. How was I ever going to explain my way out of this one?

I walked over to his office and knocked on the door. He saw me through the glass and glared. He waved me in. I shut the door behind me and took a seat in front of the firing squad. He was in his Zen Death Master mode. It wasn't good. It wasn't good at all. He looked right into my eyes and didn't say anything. And kept looking. I tried not to look away. I knew he wanted me to look away from his judgmental gaze. But I was...Fine, I looked away. But that didn't mean anything. "What I don't understand is "why?" he said. "Why what? Sir?" I asked. He let some more silence build up. He was good at that. Long, uncomfortable silences seemed to be part of his Zen technique. "I think you know what I'm talking about" he finally said. I did, I think. But I wasn't going to take the chance that I was wrong. It was a very rare thing that I made mistakes. But this was one I could not afford to risk. I was not about to admit that I had used embarrassing information that would destroy his career to further my investigation into San Sebastian.

But that gaze. That unearthly, burrowing into your soul, gaze. "I never meant to hurt you, Sir" I said. I immediately regretted how flamboyantly gay the words sounded coming from my mouth. The Superintendent didn't seem to care. "Are you saying you meant to help me by offering Chief Windsor that information about my past?" he asked. "Not exactly." "So, you admit you wanted to use it to hurt me?" he asked. "Well, no. Not really." He got up from his chair and looked out the window. He spoke to me as he looked out upon his empire. "There's no use in playing games and giving vague answers at this point. My contact at Anti-Terror has told me all about your meeting with the Chief" he said. I didn't reply. He turned and sat down again. "I ask you again, Chief Inspector, why?" I would have thought that, whatever your personal dislike and obvious disrespect for me..." I cut him off before he could finish the sentence. "I respect you a great deal, Sir." "No, I don't believe you do. You wouldn't have done what you did, if you did" he said. I paused a second to decipher his poor grammar. "But let's put your intense hatred and disrespect for me aside..." he said, "Sir...I" His hand silenced me. He wouldn't let me interrupt anymore. "What I don't understand is how it was in your own interest to sabotage my promotion. I had already promised you the position here. How does making sure I remain in charge of this office help you? I really and truly just don't understand." He looked to me for an answer. I didn't have one.

Kim went on. "Unless your hatred for me is so intense and so irrational, torpedoing your own career was worth it to you in your demented, hate-fueled little mind?" Demented and hate fueled? Oh, come on. "Sir, I'm telling you, I have no personal ill will toward you at all. You've been as good as boss as any and..." "As good a boss as any? Completely average. I had hoped our relationship was a bit more that that." he said. He was being a total cry baby about this. All sensitive and taking everything I said personally and in the worst possible way. I wouldn't have been surprised if he broke down in tears the way he was acting.

He let more silence build. "So, am I fired?" I asked. "Of course. There's no way I can condone such disloyalty. I think that's pretty obvious." I got up to leave trying not to think about the implications of a life without my job. "Sit down" he said. I really just wanted to get out of there. Which he knew. Which is why he was torturing me. "I would really like some explanation of your actions. It won't change my decision to dismiss you, either way, but I think you owe me at least that, after what you have done."So, I told him. At least, I tried to.

"It all has to do with the San Sebastian case, Sir. You have no idea how many, very, very powerful people are trying to influence the findings and..." The hand went up again. Kim's hand. "Enough. Your hatred for me knows no bounds. You're fired, regardless, and yet you still will not do the courtesy of telling me the truth." "But I was..." I protested. "I suppose it is a little embarrassing to admit how far you over-reached" he said. I wasn't sure what he meant. The San Sebastian case? I had over-reached on the San Sebastian case? I had to ask. What, on Earth, was he talking about? "What, on Earth, are you talking about?" I said. And then quickly added a "Sir" to the end of it. Kim's explanation was astounding.

"Your inflated view of yourself made you reach out to Chief Windsor to get me knocked off the Anti-Terror Chief list." "And I would do that why? Sir" I asked. "That's obvious. Because you wanted it for yourself. You thought you saw an opportunity to skip your place in the cue and to leapfrog me. To grab the spotlight of Anti-Terror for your own grandiose and foolish ambitions. It was a bold move, Hastings. But a reckless one. There was no way they would have considered you for that slot even if I was not given the position. You're not nearly capable enough." I suddenly forgot about everything else and just felt insulted. Very, very insulted. I had never thought about trying to get the Anti-Terror slot for myself. But, now that he mentioned it, why not? Why wouldn't be a good fit for the Chief position after all my years in law enforcement. I was one of the leading investigators in the Agency. Easily top five and the other four were all losers and lacked the social finesse and political awareness I had. I would make a damn good Chief of Anti-Terror. "Not capable enough." Screw you, Pal.

I didn't realize it at the time, but Superintendent Kim had done me a huge favor. I might have actually felt a little guilty for using the mistakes of his past for my own needs. Before. But not anymore. After his put down about how I was so out of my depth and how completely unrealistic it was for me to consider myself capable of handling the Anti-Terror slot...Screw him! Just screw him! He deserved everything he got.

"Are we done, now?" I asked. The lack of "Sir" being intentional and a clear insult to Kim. "To say the least, I am very disappointed" I was getting irritated how much he was dragging this out. I was fired. Fine. Let's get it over with. But Kim rambled on. "Disappointed, not only in you, but even more so, in myself. I had judged you to be a talented and loyal colleague. Not the overly-ambitious, unrealistic traitor you turned out to be." Like he was the first one to ever call me such things. Whatever. And then he used that phrase that I so very, very much despise. "I know you're better than this." Fuck you, Bub.

"Can I go, now? I'm fired, right? So, please. Let's say this my exit interview and call it a day." He was not pleased with my tone and said so. Good. Boo-hoo. "Yes, you're fired. You will also be receiving a copy of a very negative reprimand and explanation for your dismissal which will be registered with the Central Law Enforcement Records Department. In short, you will never work in law enforcement again. Ever. I will make sure of that." I ignored the words as best I could. I would sort it out later. Alone. With a source of alcohol handy, should it be required. I got up to go. Kim's death gaze was still upon me. "Leave your ID and weapon with me" he said. I took out my wallet and fished out my ID. I also turned in my official weapon. "Anything else?" I asked. "No, just make sure you stay clear of this or any other law enforcement agency office or you will be arrested for Obstruction on sight. Are we clear?" he asked. "Yes, we're clear." And I left. "Not capable." Screw him. Later, Baby Murderer.

It was only that afternoon that I started to really absorb what had happened. I had been a law enforcement officer of one sort or another for my entire adult life. From uniformed grunt at nineteen to Chief Inspector of the People's Protection Agency in my forties. And now? Now, I was nothing. And what was I going to do for money? I suppose I could go into private security the way many of my fellow officers did. Apparently, there was a lot of money in protecting one corrupt oligarch from another. My untoward dismissal might even help me in certain circles. There's nothing like a disgraced former law enforcement official on the payroll to impress the neighbors. Then again, it was for disloyalty and revealing secrets. I'm not sure your average oligarch would like someone with those habits standing around as they made their deals. I would figure it out. I always did. But right then, it was time to drink.

I called Boratch and invited him to the bar. He would have plenty of time to be sober and go to meetings later. And this way, he could look at it like his final, big blow out. His farewell to bars and vodka and drunken camaraderie before a life of meetings, coffee and donuts. Kind of like a man sentenced to prison but given a week to get his affairs in order before reporting in. Besides, it was a pretty unique circumstance. It's not everyday my entire career got flushed down the toilet. A lifetime in law enforcement turned to rubble. So, I called him.

At first Boratch was angry that I was appealing to his weak side. Then I made my pitch about how this would be his goodbye forever to booze. To my amazement, it still didn't work. Then I told him the short version of what had happened and how my career was over and done with forever. That got him. Playing the old "I really need someone to talk to" card. He agreed to meet me later that afternoon.

When he arrived, I was already a little drunk. I had gotten there a couple of hours earlier. I really didn't feel like waiting. Of course, I paced myself, like the seasoned, responsible drinker that I was. But I was still feeling a bit buzzed already when he finally showed up. Boratch was all sympathy and support. He said all the right things in all the right ways. He made a great case how it wasn't as bad as it looked. How private security was where the money was, anyway. How I would have ended up behind a desk doing a job I hated if I hadn't stepped in and taken control of the situation. I loved hearing every word. Between that and the alcohol, life wasn't seeming nearly as bad as it did earlier.

I still tried to correct him on the last point. I was actually trying to find out from Chief Windsor what this whole drug project thing was all about and knew I needed to offer him an incentive. Believe it or not, getting fired really wasn't the intent.

Boratch did an amazing job of making it all seem alright. He reminded me how dangerous this whole San Sebastian thing really was. The Minister, Cardinal Rooney, H.O.G. idiots and their weird pyromaniacal death rituals...It really wasn't pretty. So, therefore, ipso facto, if you will, I had no choice about what I did to Kim because it was a matter of life or death. Not only my own life and death but that of thousands, possibly hundreds of thousands of others. We had no idea what San Sebastian was involved with. We just knew that it was secret and it wasn't good. And that it was probably very, very bad. And a threat to innocent, God fearing, law abiding citizens everywhere who counted on the People's Protection Agency to protect them. So, that's what I did. I protected the people. What I had done was not wrong. Not wrong at all. Or stupid and miscalculated. What I had done was nothing short of a knowing self-sacrifice. I had sacrificed my own career for the good of the people and the good of the nation. I was a hero!

It all sounded so wonderful at the time that I ended up in a shockingly good mood. A few "damn straights" and "exactlys!" on my part and a lot of very, very wise and encouraging words from Boratch and I looked at the situation in a whole new light. Yes, my career was over. But it had to be done. I had no choice but to make that sacrifice. What was far more important than my professional integrity and reputation was the good of the people. It was for them I had done it all. And it would be for them that Boratch and I would figure out the San Sebastian case and stop whatever terrible thing that could happen from happening. It was just the sort of noble, heroic men we were!

And then I threw up. Not just once or twice. Like, all night long. First in the bar. Then on the way home out the window of the cab. Then at home, many, many times, well into the night and into the next morning. My only explanation for such a violent illness was food poisoning. Yes, I had drunk a lot. But I had also eaten some very greasy fish sticks that I vaguely remember did not taste quite right. In any case, it was a very unpleasant experience. It was only the afternoon of the following day, after an endless chain of black coffees, that I started to remember things a little differently. Somewhere after the discussion about me being a national hero and before the one on how golf is not a sport...No, it was after the golf discussion, too. Not that it mattered. The order wasn't important. It was what had gotten said. I think somewhere in there I said something to Boratch I shouldn't have. Something that I really, really shouldn't have. I think I told him I had slept with Anna. Oh, crap.

I tried to call Boratch and got his voicemail. I asked him to call me back as soon as he could. I needed to meet him and try to figure out how much had gotten said or not said. I also needed to figure out how much he remembered. I seemed to recall Boratch being as drunk as I was. I think. It was all so hazy after the golf debate. I could call Anna. Boratch probably would have talked to her. But I didn't really know the facts yet. Maybe I hadn't said as much as I thought that I had. Maybe I was worried about nothing.

There was a knock on my door. A very loud, official, sounding knock. For a moment, I wondered if Kim had come up with some false charges to arrest me. I know it's hard to believe, but such things happened when dealing with the People's Protection Agency. My heart started to beat faster. I really didn't want to be taken down to the basement for a more physical "talk" with Superintendent Kim. The knock repeated. Louder. More impatient. I stayed really quiet and didn't answer. Finally, the knocker went away. Before doing so, I heard something drop against the door. Making sure that I gave it a moment for the mysterious visitor to disappear, I finally went over to my door. Nobody was there. I opened it and a package fell against my feet. It wasn't a box but a large envelope.

The first thing I noticed was that the package had stickers all over it saying "NEXT DAY RUSH" even though the postmark was four days old. Some much for guaranteed, on time, delivery. The second thing was that it also said quite clearly, "signature required." They hadn't gotten my signature but had left the package anyway. Right there. At my door. In the open where anyone could take it. What incompetence. But all that went out the window once I brought the package into my apartment and opened it. There was a note inside. It said "You're still an incompetent ass but someone needs to know."

There was no signature on the note. Given the number of people that would disrespect me and call me an incompetent ass, that alone didn't tell me who it was from. For a moment, I thought the nasty name calling note was all that there was in the package. Then I saw the DVD. No label. Maybe someone had given me some more leverage against Kim. A way to get my job back or to still get his. Not that I really wanted his.

I put in the DVD and watched the screen. A title appeared. "LIFE GEN" with the little, official logo. And then another title card. "EPIPHANY." I had no idea what Epiphany was. I mean, I knew the regular meaning of the word. I think. I was educated, after all. The title changed again. And then I realized that I was watching some sort of corporate presentation. Some dreadful thing in Power Point or one of those other hateful software programs that middle managers spent their lives working on. It even had bullet points. Oh, how I hated bullet points.

The next screen said "EPIPHANY BENEFITS" at the top. Then said "1) Increases sense of well-being." Then "2) Increases compliance with authority" And finally, "3) Reduces need for immediate reward." So, "Epiphany" was the name of a drug? The next few screens were all about the chemical make-up of the product. I couldn't make heads or tails out of it. I fast forwarded. In fact, I got all the way to the conclusion screen which repeated the "Benefits" page. And then the final page, which just said "EPIPHANY BY LIFE GEN."

Right. That was clear as mud. It sounded as if Life Gen had figured out a better way to make people feel more content and less anxious. I suppose if they drugged people up enough, that made total sense. But it certainly didn't seem like the sort of thing that was groundbreaking.

There was a lot more information on the DVD. I really didn't have the patience to read scientific data or test results. So, I skipped to the video section. There was one called "The Great Discovery." I liked the title, so I cued it up. It was a presentation by San Sebastian, himself.

He stood there in a suit. A very expensive, well fitting, suit, I might add. He stood there in a suit looking right into the camera. He was not the weirded out, ready to kill himself, man that I had seen on the memory stick. This was San Sebastian at his slickest and most magnetic.

He spoke with absolute confidence and seemed almost giddy talking about what he talked about. Which was this... "We have found a way to re-connect mankind with the Creator. Epiphany is not a serotonin uptake inhibitor or antipsychotic medication. It is the result of a startling discovery which occurred during our research into the effects of Alzheimer's. That discovery is this; There is a region of the human brain which, through a combination of synaptic impulses and chemical responses, makes us, as humans, crave a higher power. This region of the brain, in essence, connects us to God." He stopped for a moment to let that last, rather lofty, claim sit.

"And the beauty of it is that it is as natural as any other involuntary human reaction. As natural as keeping the heart beating, lungs breathing, or pulling away from a hot stove. The need for God is an innate, basic, human need which is biologically driven and has been found in culture after culture, around the world, for thousands of years. This is not an accident or a coincidence. The need for God is fundamental to human existence and a biological imperative. And now we have the science to prove it." I wasn't sure that I heard what I had just heard. Or maybe I had misunderstood. I was expecting something about people pulling themselves out of depression or something. Nothing Like that. What I really didn't get was how San Sebastian had the balls to say such a blasphemous thing out loud and record it on video. Not only record it, but intentionally show other people. His claims were the sort of thing that could get him a life sentence in a re-education camp. And he only dug himself in deeper as the presentation continued.

"By understanding and controlling this biological process, a process which we have named "Ascension," we can do remarkable things. There will be no more individuals condemned to a life of questioning or disbelief. Faith can be restored. And that's just the beginning." I couldn't believe my ears. What this man was saying was against everything I had been taught. Ever. But he knew no bounds. He kept staring at the camera making statements and claims that I found remarkable.

"Epiphany not only restores this brain center into functioning properly for those that have lost their spiritual connection, it enhances any connection that already exists. Let me say that again. Epiphany restores the spiritual connection for those that have lost it and enhances and strengthens it for those that already have it. Epiphany makes us all, once again, God's Children."

I paused the DVD and tried to fully understand what San Sebastian was saying. There had been hallucinogens that I remembered hearing stories about. People claimed all sorts of new emotional and spiritual insights after taking them. Maybe Epiphany was just some new form of LSD or something. "God's Children." "Restoring faith." The whole thing made me very uncomfortable. I really just wanted to go through my day solving murders and crimes against the state and so on. All pretty basic, down to earth stuff. This thing San Sebatian was talking about was the kind of crap that just gave me a headache. And got people thrown into special prisons. Prisons that made normal prisons look like easy living, in comparison. I really didn't want to know about any of this. How things worked in my brain wasn't really an issue of concern for me. Just that they worked. Period. Leave the rest of it the Church and the philosophers. Life was too short to worry about such grand issues.

After watching the presentation, I knew enough about Epiphany and San Sebastian's involvement to understand why so many people were interested in his death. That DVD was a bomb just waiting to explode. What made it worse was the web of connections around it. Life Gen was owned by the Church. Their involvement in this blasphemous research would be considered a scandal of epic proportions. Just having watched that DVD could get me killed a thousand times over. The DVD which had been so carelessly dropped outside my door by the delivery person.

It was then that I finally remembered who recently had called me an incompetent ass. It wasn't Kim. I was a traitor and disloyal, but incompetent ass wasn't among his preferred names for me. It was Chief Windsor. Chief Windsor of the Anti-Terrorism Division who had just sent me a DVD that made me one of the most wanted men in the nation just because I had viewed it. Yes, it helped solve the mystery of the San Sebastian case. Sure. But I really wasn't thrilled with seeing what I had seen or having it in my possession. This whole thing was way, way above my pay grade. Drug companies and God. Why did Chief Windsor do this to me? What had I ever done to him?

I needed to talk to Chief Windsor again. And Boratch. Now, that I knew about Epiphany, it was clear to me why Cardinal Rooney wanted that case closed as quickly as possible. I could only guess that Kapinskov actually wanted the case exposed to undermine the power of the Church. I'm sure as a businessman and government official, he was getting increasingly tired of their power and influence. It would all be...Someone knocked at my door.

"Let me in, Daniel. It's Anna." I so didn't need this. "I know you're in there. Open the door" she said. I stood for a second trying to think. "Daniel!" She was so annoying. I opened the door angrily. "What?!" I asked. She pushed her way in. "Why did you tell my father about us?" she asked. "I didn't" I said. "You didn't? Then why did he call me last night and tell me I was a cheating, lying, unfaithful slut?" I stayed quiet. "Well?" "Did he really call you that?" I asked. "He was drunk, of course. Which is another thing. I thought you were going to help him get sober? You really invited him out to drink with you?" Between the haziness of my memory and the weird facts swirling around in my head about drugs, faith and re-education camps, it hardly seemed to matter. At least not right then. But it clearly mattered a lot to Anna. She had worked her way into a state of total fury and sadness, both happening at the same time. The yelling and tears continued simultaneously for at least ten minutes as I kept giving her truthful, but vague, answers. Finally, she tired herself out and we sat down.

"What do you want me to say? I got fired. I got drunk. Your father got drunk. Things got said that probably shouldn't have been," I said. "You think?" was her a little too snotty and succinct response. "Where is your father anyway?" "At work, I would guess. Why aren't you?" I just told you, I got fired. Really. I am no longer with the People's Protection Agency. I am no longer a law enforcement officer." "So, why did you tell my father about us?" I couldn't believe how little she cared about me getting fired. Doesn't she understand what a big deal that was? I was going to tell her about Epiphany and how explosive that information was but I didn't even bother. As usual, all she cared about was herself. "Well?" she asked. "Well what?" I replied. "What did you tell him?" she asked. "Do you want to know why or what?" I said, feeling a bit combative. "Both." I couldn't really think of an answer. "I don't know" I finally said. "You don't know why you did it or what you said?" "No." "I don't believe this" she said.

I told her that I was in a very bad state and it all just kind of happened. I think I even apologized. I know I said how wrong it was of her father to say the things he did. The Boratch she knew was not the same man I knew. "I hope you realize what you have done" she said. I didn't. "My father and I aren't talking anymore" she said. "He'll sober up and come around. Have you talked with him this morning?" I asked. "Yes, he called and said he was sorry he overreacted" she said. "So, you've patched things up?" She shook her head. "No, not after what he said. I can't deal with it anymore. Maybe when he gets sober." "But he's your father" I said. "He's a drunk first and my father second. Until that changes..." And then she got all teary eyed again. I really wish she would make up her mind between pissed off and crying. The back and forth made me nuts.

I promised her that I would talk to her father about what he had said, drinking, their relationship, Anna and I, etc. But what I really wanted to talk with him about was this Epiphany thing. The Cardinal was not going to let this one slip by. In fact, he probably already knew that the case was still open and that I had been investigating. I also needed to see Chief Windsor again. If he had known all this, why didn't he do something with it himself? Or bury it? Giving it to me just seemed like an unlikely option that he would choose to exercise. I suppose he could have done it just because he didn't like me. Sending me that DVD was like sending me a steaming pile of turd. Sure, it answered some big questions in the San Sebastian case. But it also opened up a whole new world of things that I had no real interest in dealing with. I had to talk with Boratch and find a way to just let this whole thing die quietly and to get us off the hook.

Anna kept staring at me. I had almost forgotten she was there. "The least that you could do is pretend for a second that you care about all this" she said. "I do care" I insisted. "Yeah, that's why you keep staring off into space and not listening to a word I say?" I wasn't in the mood to hear her tirade again. "Look, I'll take care of it. I'll go talk to your father and straighten it out." "And how are you going to do that?" she asked. "I don't know yet. But I will, Ok? Now, please go." "Will you call me after?" she asked. After what?, I thought. Talking to your father about Epiphany? Oh, right. "Yeah. I will call you. I promise." She looked at me and then nodded. I was so distracted that I barely noticed how good her tits looked in that particular shirt. I pulled myself together and waited for her to leave. I needed to see Boratch.

I got in my car and drove to HQ. I got the parking lot and realized that without my ID I could no longer get in. I even had to park in the city lot for eight dollars an hour, which was outrageous. But it was worth it to try to see Boratch. I carried along the DVD Chief Windsor had sent me. I had thought about leaving it in my apartment but I wanted Boratch to see it as quickly as possible.

My phone rang. It was Superintendent Kim. I made the mistake of picking up. "I need you to come into the office" he said. "Why? I thought I was fired." "Do you want to be fired?" he asked. "No, I don't," I answered before thinking it through. "Ok then. So, come to the office and pick up your weapon and ID. I have something I need you on." It was certainly not what I had expected to hear. The last time I had seen Kim in his office the man wanted to kill me. I had betrayed him and was a completely disloyal, overambitious son of a bitch. This didn't feel right. How many times could Kim fire and rehire me without losing credibility on the issue? "How long before you can get here?" he asked. I really needed to talk to Boratch first.

I was just about to lie and say an hour when Kim spoke again. "Is that you near the gate?" he asked. I looked up and saw Kim standing at a window looking right at me. Oops. "Yeah." "What are you doing here?" I didn't have an answer. "I'll explain when I come in" I said. "Alright, meet me in my office" he said and hung up. How was I going to explain why I was there? I suppose I could just tell him it was a personal issue and I needed to see Boratch. That was true enough. Whatever. Given the way things had unfolded, what to tell Kim was the least of my problems.

As I walked through the office, my fellow Agents or formerly fellow agents, looked at me strangely. I guessed they wondered why I was there. I know I wondered why I was there. This whole thing with Kim rehiring me just felt too good to be true. This was some sort of sadistic payback and I knew it. I knocked on the door and went into Superintendent Kim's office. "Thanks for coming so quickly." "Sure" I said. "Although it looks like you were already on your way here" he said and looked at me for an explanation. I saw my ID and gun on his desk and decided to just go with it. "Believe it or not, I was coming to apologize to you, Sir. Not to try to get my job back. I never expected anything so wonderful in a thousand years..." I was laying it on too thick. I pulled back the brown nosing a little. But I had to get one more little bit in. "I came to apologize just because it was the right thing to do. You are a good man and were a fine boss. You deserved better." He ate it up. I swore his head grew two sizes bigger right before my eyes.

"I'm glad you realized that, Hastings. I always tried to treat you well and...Well, let's just say, I was rather surprised and hurt about some of the choices you made." I nodded. "Yes, Sir" I said. He handed me back my ID and gun. "But let's not dwell on the past. I need you to look into something that's quite sensitive. Since you are familiar with this type of case and the suspect involved, you are uniquely qualified to handle it." I felt a giant hammer about to be swung into my face. "It looks as if Chief Windsor has committed suicide." Oh, how annoying. Why did people keep throwing me back into the heart and center of a case I wanted nothing to do with?

"We got the call about fifty minutes ago from a neighbor. He's at his apartment. The lab techs are already out there." Well, at least I could see Boratch. Which was good. I think. Maybe.

It was then that I noticed the way Kim was looking at me. He had this evil grin on his face that he was, unsuccessfully, trying to hide. "Was there something else you wanted to tell me before I go out there, Sir?" I asked. "No, nothing at all. I know you'll do your job as well as ever." I wanted to slap the look off his face. He knew he was sending me to something unpleasant. Something that was revenge for my betrayal. But it got me back into the Agency. So, I just went with it. "Welcome back, Agent Hastings." "Thank you, Sir." It was only as I walked away I realized I had been carrying the DVD about Epiphany with me the entire time. Nothing like walking around feeling like you have a bomb strapped under your coat and are just waiting to become a martyr.

As I paid my ridiculously, outrageously high, parking fee, it occurred to me why Kim was all smiles. If Windsor killed himself it would be very embarrassing for a lot of people. I would be pressured to cover it up. But Kim wasn't going to let me do that. He was going to make sure that I called it as it was and made enemies all over town. It was his way of dumping more pain on me and saving one of his other agents from a difficult situation. Stupid man. If he had any idea how badly I was already screwed over, how many massively powerful enemies I already had, or how I was already screwed beyond belief, he would realize his little trick was a failure. Stupid, stupid man. Take that Superintendent, Sir. I'm so fucked over already, you can't touch me!

Boratch wouldn't talk to me. Literally. When I arrived at Windsor's apartment, Boratch was in the bedroom with the body. Seeing Windsor dead shook me up a little. I mean, aside from the usual unease of seeing a corpse with part of his head gone. Why always guns? I mean, there were pills, hanging, jumping from things. But no. For some reason when people killed themselves now, it was always with a gun. I just didn't understand it. Anyway, Boratch. I saw him there and he didn't acknowledge me. I said "hello" and he didn't answer. I tried to break the ice. "It looks like I got my job back. So, I'm here." Nothing. "You're not going to talk to me all day? That's not very professional." He turned to me. Oh, he was pissed. I had never, ever seen him that angry. I almost waited for the fireballs to shoot from his eyes and destroy me. He went back to looking over Windsor's body.

"I'm sorry, Samuel. I really am" I said. He stopped inspecting the corpse, turned and looked at me again. And then he gave me the finger. At least it was a reaction. Maybe now we could talk. But no. He just went back to his work. I wondered how much of him being pissed off was about me getting him to drink again and how much was about Anna. Probably both. "I'm sorry about inviting you out to a bar. That wasn't very sensitive of me." He clenched his jaw. Oops. That made him more angry. I guess it was about Anna. "And I'm sorry about things with Anna. I never meant for our relationship to..." He charged me like a bull and got right into my face. His usual stale vodka breath was even worse than usual. "Don't EVER say her name again. EVER!" He stuck a meaty, old finger in my face. I stepped back. I expected him just to go back to the silent treatment but he didn't. Instead he said. "You claim to be my friend and then seduce my married daughter. You are filth!" he yelled. One of the uniforms looked in from the doorway. I glared at him and he disappeared again.

"I didn't seduce her. She came over..." Once again, he interrupted me. "So, now my daughter is a slut? You have the nerve to stand there in front of me and tell me my own daughter is a slut?" he accused. "I never said that." "She is a slut. A cheap, disloyal, ungrateful brat who thinks only of herself!" In spite of telling myself that he wasn't that far wrong, I was actually offended by his words. He shouldn't talk about Anna that way. Boratch walked off and returned to the corpse.

I was shocked at what came out of my mouth next. "Anna is not any of those things you called her. Maybe if you weren't drunk all the time, you would see what a great person she really is." I don't know what surprised me more, that I was defending Anna or that I was accusing Boratch. Either way, I was surprised. Boratch shook his head but continued to focus on the shattered skull fragments which had been blown to the floor. "Just don't talk to me. Not now. Not ever. We are through, Daniel. Do you hear me? Through." I was still dealing with the fact that I had defended Anna. I really didn't understand what was happening to me. But Boratch was my friend. Not to mention, I had information he needed to know.

"Samuel, even if you hate me now, which I guess you do, I have something I need to talk to you about. It's important." He didn't say anything. "Boratch, seriously. It's very, very important. It's about that other thing." He looked at me for a second, didn't say a word, and went back to his work. I looked at the pistol lying by Winsor's hand. I had no problem writing it up as what it clearly was. Consequences be damned, it was a suicide. Windsor was more depressed about the humiliation of being forced out of Anti-Terror than he was letting on and ended it. Or. Crap. Maybe he was so afraid of what would be done to him for knowing what he knew about Epiphany, this was the better way out. A controlled, quick death instead of a lingering, unbelievably painful one under torture. I started to feel sick to my stomach. Maybe Windsor really did hate me so much that he wanted me to face the same fate. What a total bastard. I felt like spitting on his increasingly odorous corpse.

"This man didn't kill himself any more than he sprouted wings and flew away" Boratch said. He still wasn't looking at me. But still. The fact that he was talking to me was a great thing. "What do you mean?" I asked. "The angle of the wound, the bruises on his arm. Someone forced the gun to his head and pulled the trigger for him." "Are you sure?" I asked. "Of course, I'm sure. Now you even question my professionalism? After all you've done. You have the nerve to question my years of experience and the validity of my findings?" he accused. "No, not at all. It was more of a rhetorical thing. Really." Either way, it wasn't what I had expected. At first blush, everything about it looked like a suicide. The mechanics of it. The sudden change in Windsor's life being thrown off of Anti-Terror. All of it. Well, except for when I met him and how he really did sound Ok with a quiet, well-paying retirement at Tax Enforcement. Between that and my professional trust in Boratch, anger and alcohol aside, the suicide conclusion had bitten the dust. Windsor had been killed. Probably for the DVD I had in my own jacket pocket at that very moment.

"Samuel, we need to talk after this. There are a lot of very, very important things I need to tell you." "Like I said. We are done talking. Forever. At least about anything not required to do our jobs." "It's about our other case" I said, hoping the uniforms hadn't overheard me. "Not interested" Boratch said. "Not interested? Don't be ridiculous. As complicated as things were before, they have gotten worse. Very, very much worse."

He looked at me. "I doubt that very much. If things were as bad as you say you would have saved your own skin already and gone into hiding." Which was meant as an insult. And it was. But he was kind of right. If I hadn't concluded the particular people and powers that we were dealing with wouldn't have tracked me down anyway, it might have been a more serious consideration. But that wasn't the point. The point was that I was there, in the room with Boratch, and I wanted to patch things up with him and find a way for us both to avoid untimely and/or painful deaths. No matter what it took, I was going to show him that DVD. After that, my hands would be clean and he could do what he wanted. But I owed him, at least, that much.

I tried again. "Can you meet with me tonight? Please. I really have to talk to you." "Not interested" he said, again. "Samuel, please. I can't tell you enough how important it is." He walked closer to me again. "Maybe you should have thought of that before defiling my married daughter." I couldn't take it anymore. Defiling? Does he have any sense at all of who his daughter really is? I told him that I was headed back to HQ and would be awaiting his report. Honestly, I should have spent a lot more time investigating the crime scene. It was a murder, after all. Not just a murder but one directly connected to me and the DVD I possessed. At least, I thought it did. But right then, with Boratch and his anger and acquisitions, I really just didn't care. I needed to just leave and get out. So I did.

Of course, I realized, right after I left, that it would be a little difficult to write up my report. I had been so focused on dealing with Boratch that I hadn't exactly done a bang up job investigating the crime scene. With enough "maybes," "possibilities," "it appears," and other qualifiers, maybe I could still write something up. I trusted Boratch enough that, when he said the man was murdered, that the man was murdered. As for who did it, though, I really should have put a little more effort into that. I mean, for my own sake. Boratch had just pissed me off so much.

I stopped my car. I still wasn't ready to go back there and face Samuel. Maybe, I would just wait for him to leave then go back. Superintendent Kim wouldn't care one way or the other. He was just looking for a willing neck to put an Albatross on. Of course, the suicide Albatross had morphed into something else. Possibly, a murder by H.O.G. incident. Or maybe another political assassination of some sort. Either way, it was still one very large, ugly bird.

I turned on the radio and listened to some, not very good, songs that had been played over and over again for as long as I could remember. At this point, I enjoyed listening to them. The songs hadn't gotten any better. It was still hackneyed, clichéd nonsense. Banal, I think is the word certain folks would use to describe it. Or trite. But their familiarity brought me a level of comfort. The truth was, this whole thing had been very upsetting.

As I thought about what a bad day it had been, I remembered that I had promised to call Anna. I really didn't feel like talking to her. However, I knew that if I didn't, she would just phone me and hassle me until I replied. If I didn't answer my phone she would just show up at my door yelling and screaming. Such were the ways of Anna Boratch. One thing was clear. Anything with Anna was done. Friends. Sex partners. Whatever. It was way too complicated and there was way, way, too much drama. Not to mention that she was married, her father, my former best friend, hated me and, when it came down to it, I just really didn't even like her very much. I decided that I should just call her and get it done with.

"How did it go?" She asked. "He won't talk to me" I replied. Silence. I clarified "I mean he will. But only about the case." "So, he is talking to you?" she asked. "Yes, but only about the case" I said. "So, he didn't say anything about me? I find that hard to believe." I remembered the long train of words Boratch had used to describe his own daughter. Slut. Cheap. Disloyal. Ungrateful Brat. "No, he did. He's pretty angry at both of us." "He's an ass." "He's your father." "My father is an ass." I really didn't have anything else to say to her. I mean, other than please stay the hell away from me and get out of my life forever. Which I kind of said. But not really.

What I said was, "Alright, well, I promised to call you and bring you up to speed. Now that I have, I should get back to work." Silence.

"Anna, are you still there?" I asked. Silence. No. Crying. I could hear Anna crying softly through the phone. "Anna, it will be Ok. He loves you more than you can imagine" I said. Louder crying. Not exactly the reaction I had been trying to elicit. "Anna, it will be Ok" I said again. Still more crying. I couldn't take it anymore. "Do you want to meet again, later, to talk about this some more? You could come over again." I couldn't believe my own ears. What a stupid, stupid thing to do. "No. Thanks. I should go" she said. "Alright. Well, if you change your mind..." And then she hung up.

I sat there in my car. I couldn't believe how annoying this whole thing was. I had all sorts of people who wanted to do some serious damage to me and I was sitting there listening to Anna Boratch cry. What the hell was wrong with me? I finally drove back to the crime scene. Boratch's car was still there. I walked in again. He was not happy to see me. "What are you doing back here?" he asked, as rudely possible. "My job. Why don't you just do yours and not worry about what I'm doing?" He snorted. Actually, more of a chortle. I thought we were about to get into it all over again. Instead he turned and walked off into a different room.

I desperately needed to urinate. Another factor, albeit a minor one, in not waiting around in my car any longer. I wandered around Windsor's large, but bland, house until I found a bathroom. As I was taking care of things, I noticed that the window was slightly ajar. Possibly a point of entry for the people that did this to Windsor. I would think that there were two people, at the very least, involved in the murder. It would take that many to overpower Windsor, hold the gun to his head, and pull the trigger. I washed up and found a tech.

"Make sure you dust the bathroom window for prints" I said. The tech nodded. I noticed two uniforms talking quietly to each other across the room. "Tell him" one said. "Tell me what?" I asked. The other uniform stepped forward. "There's a chance that you might find my print on there, Sir" he said. "And why is that?" I asked. "I used the bathroom earlier and opened the window after I was through." I kept staring at him. "It smelled really bad and I was embarrassed. Sorry" he said. Outrageous. And I told him so. "You used the bathroom at a crime scene and possibly contaminated the evidence? What were you thinking?!" I said. "But didn't you just..." I cut off his insubordinate questioning, immediately. He had a point. But that wasn't the point. I was a Chief Inspector, and that still meant something. How dare he question me? I heard Boratch saying that he was leaving to the uniforms. I thought about following after him and making one more attempt at conversation. I decided not to bother.

After about an hour or two of poking around Windsor's house, I hadn't discovered much of anything useful. From the look of it, there was no sign of forced entry. He let his killers in, voluntarily. If I had to guess, and I often did, I would think that they were law enforcement officers. Law enforcement officers who were also members of the Hand of God. But I had no way of knowing for sure. There were probably cameras on Chief Windsor's house. Maybe even a spy satellite. But getting access to those recordings required a top level security level. One far beyond mine. Which was annoying. Because that meant there were people that probably already knew exactly who did this and how they did this, but didn't want to share any of that information with me.

The day didn't get any better. I stalled on turning in my report. I needed Boratch's official findings about the bruises and so on before I could safely call the crime a murder. And then there was the whole "God is just a bunch of chemicals" thing weighing on my brain. I wasn't sure why I even cared. It wasn't exactly something that affected my day to day life. All the same, I felt the need to see Father Mike. Or get drunk.

In the end, I choose the latter. Which turned out to be a mistake. Not because it gave me a brief moment of relaxation and peace. That was all good. But because when I got home there was someone waiting for me outside. Someone I really, really didn't want to see. He wasn't a particularly large man. But there was something sinister about him. And he was in very, very good shape. He had the kind of body of someone that spends hours in the gym and does triathlons on weekends, just for fun. Luckily for me, I had my gun back. I put my hand on the grip and was about to pull it out when this, unusually fit, athletic man leaped at me. In the vast majority of cases, my experience, training, and cat-like reflexes served me well in physical confrontations. Not that I had been in any in over twenty years. But, regardless. I liked to believe I could hold my own. Which is why it was such a shock to find myself laid out on the sidewalk staring up at the sky. This overly aggressive, massively-muscled man had sucker punched me right in the jaw.

I tried to get up. "Stay down" he commanded. The tone was right but the man actually had a fairly high, feminine voice. It was very hard to feel threatened by him, in spite of the fact he had just floored me with a single, lucky punch. I started to sit up. "I said, stay down" he said again. That wasn't going to happen. I went for his knees. A kick. A well aimed kick right for his knees. Which actually hit his shin. Either way, it worked. The man bent over in pain to grab his shin and I was able to get off the ground. As he was hopping around like some demented bunny rabbit, I pulled my gun and aimed it at him. "Put your hands up" I said. He was too busy grimacing and dealing with my devastating blow to his shin to react. "I said, hands up."

He glared at me.

"Put the gun away" he said. As if that's all it would take. "Who are you?" I asked. "I'm Steve, Anna's husband" he said. Crap. I really didn't have time for all this drama. It was all very, very annoying. Steve finally let go of his shin. "Why are you here?" I asked. "Because you're banging my wife and I think we should talk about it." "You just struck a federal law enforcement official. I could get you put away for years for that." He didn't seem rattled at all. Quite calm, in fact. "Yeah, but you won't do that" he said. "Why not?" I asked. "Like I said, you're banging my wife. I'm sure you're man enough to understand how I'm well within my rights to punch you out for that." That really wasn't the point. The man had hit me. Hard. In the face. It hurt and I might even have a bruise. I should put him down in the basement for a while. That would teach him. I certainly wouldn't be the first person to put a romantic rival in prison. Romantic rival? What was I thinking? There was no rival. Or romance. What's wrong with me? I put my gun away.

Steve stuck out his hand. It was a weirdly gentlemanly gesture. I reciprocated. He was right. There was no reason we couldn't be adults about all this. "Why don't you come in and we can talk about things?" I suggested. Keep in mind, I was also a little bit buzzed from my time at the bar while all this was going on. Normally, I wasn't nearly so gallant or mature. Especially considering the man had committed an act of violence against my face. We sat down in the living room and I poured us some drinks. I found Steve to be quite different from the initial impression I had of him. He was not the brutish barbarian that had attacked me. Nor was he anywhere near the bullying, belligerent thug that Anna had described to me. He was actually a really good guy. At least I thought so for a while.

"I understand why you are having an affair with my wife. She's a strikingly beautiful, intelligent, caring woman." None of those words matched my actual perception of Anna. Not one. But I let it slide. Whatever the man needed to believe. "It's not that I approve of what the two of you are doing. But I understand" he said. And then he asked me a very odd question. "What I would like to know is if it is serious." I wasn't sure what he meant. "What do you mean, "serious"?" I asked. "Do you plan on asking her to leave me for you? Have you already?" he asked. I was very confused. What was he talking about? Anna and I had sex once and this guy was already picturing me stealing her away and whisking her off somewhere. Talk about deluded. "No, we have not talked about anything like that. Either one of us. It really hasn't come up" I said. "Yet. But it could, right? I mean, you do love her, correct?" I didn't answer. The man was on a roll. So, I just let him get on with it.

"See, this is the situation, Daniel. I have been known to have the occasional fling on the side, myself." So, I heard. "I completely understand such things. What worries me about this particular situation isn't that the two of you are having sex together. That's bad enough. But that it might lead to even more serious consequences. Do you understand what I'm saying?" I looked at him blankly. No. No, I did not understand what he was saying. What was he saying? "If you ever, ever...ever try to talk Anna into divorcing me and taking my children away from me, I will make the rest of your life a total hell." He waited for me to look suitably threatened. I was too drunk and confused to really care. But he kept at it and leaned toward me. "Do we understand each other?" he asked. Part of me wanted to reassure him that Anna and I had no such intentions. I mean, how ridiculous. Anna and I, together forever. Kids. I just wasn't seeing it. At least I wasn't seeing it before her husband had painted such a clear picture of that possibility for me. But all of that was secondary to the fact that this imbecile was in my living room, drinking my whisky, threatening me. I wouldn't stand for that. No way. No how.

"You better think twice before making threats, Pal. Don't you know who I am? Who I work for? What I do for a living? I could have you down in an interrogation cell with electrodes attached to your balls in three minutes. Wanna try me?" I tried to put on the most aggressive, threatening look on my face possible. Steve got up. "You're not going to do that" he said. "Yeah, why's that?" I asked. "Two reasons. Because you're an adult and know that's just not the way these things are done." A crap answer, if ever there was. "And because I know people that know people that are already very unhappy with the way you have handled certain investigations." So, that was why he was being such a tough guy. He knew people who knew people that knew that I was screwed. "Who?" I asked. He put his finger to the end of his nose and pushed it flat. And then he snorted. Twice. In rapid succession. H.O.G.. He had connections with H.O.G.. Unfortunately for him, given that I was a little drunk, I actually found the way he looked and sounded pretty funny and not intimidating at all. Steve the piggy man. I started laughing. Out loud. A lot.

"You laugh all you want. You watch yourself with my wife or my friends who like bon fires are going to find you" he said. "Whatever. You, H.O.G., and all the rest can just get in line." "You're drunk" he said, pointing out the increasingly obvious. "And you are a Piggy Man" I retorted. He shook his head, not so much in anger but in frustration. He had come to scare the wits out of me but I just kept thinking about how silly he looked with his pig nose, snorting. Silly, Piggy Man.

After a morning of dealing with a nasty headache and a very impatient Superintendent Kim wondering where the report was on Chief Windsor, I finally found some time to visit Father Mike. Between the tiredness, hangover and recent events, I just really needed to talk with him. He was just one of those people that ten minutes with seemed to make everything a lot clearer. I could use some clarity. Clarity would be good. So, I went to see him at his mission after lunch.

As usual, when I said "I need to talk with you" Father Mike dropped everything and made some time for me. We went for our usual walk and he waited for me to begin. Which was a problem because I really didn't know where to begin. I had this feeling like I really needed to talk with him but now that I was with him, wasn't sure what to say. He waited patiently.

"I have something I want to talk to you about but it could get you killed" I said. "Ok" he said. "Ok?" I asked. "If you need to tell me something, just tell me. I'll deal with whatever consequences it brings." What an odd man. But I just went with it. "What if I told you that the Church sponsored scientific research which proved God was just a bunch of chemicals in your brain? And that a whole lot of people had died already because they wanted that covered up? And that you could die just because you heard me say this? And that I could die? Painfully. And that...Just, what would you say?" I asked in a long, breathless ramble. He didn't seem ruffled in the least by the bombshell I had just dropped on him. Perfectly calm, in fact.

"Do you understand what I just told you? God is just a bunch of chemicals in the brain" I said. I would have thought telling a man that spent his whole life devoted to serving a higher power would have been upset by this news. But no. Apparently not. "Ok" he said. I guess he could tell from my reaction that I had expected something else.

"Whether God exists in my brain, up in heaven, or any specific place doesn't worry me. The fact is, God exists. What you have said, or what this research you're talking about shows, doesn't change any of that. What concerns me is your fear of people coming after you because of what you know. Who is it that you're afraid of?" he asked. "I wouldn't use the word afraid, exactly. Just concerned" I corrected. "Fine, who are these people you are so concerned about?" he asked. "Everybody." "Everybody?" he asked. "It's the sort of information that would be embarrassing for a lot of people. It goes against the teachings of the Church, for one thing." "A lot of things go against the teachings of the Church. We do the best we can but we don't get it right every time." I couldn't believe he just said that. Admitting something so openly like that. Then again, I could. He was that sort of guy.

"Are you really worried about harm coming to you? You don't seem particularly nervous about it" he asked. I thought about it for a second and then I realized he was right. Given how many people probably wanted me to just go away, forever, I wasn't really too anxious about it. Which was weird. It was almost like I wanted to think I was a big problem for all these hugely powerful people but knew otherwise. Which I guess I did. And I hated it. I wanted to be on their radar. I wanted to be a threat. I wanted to matter. "Maybe that's what bothers me." I said. I explained to him how insignificant I felt and how I really, really hated it. I was somebody, damn it. But nobody seemed to care. At least, not anymore. Father Mike made a valiant effort to talk about all the influence I had and how important my role was with People's Protection. But we both seemed to know it was just empty words.

"You need to realize that you are part of something much, much, bigger" he said. Uh-oh, he was getting into priest mode. "You are part of God's plan" he said. I really wasn't in the mood to hear it. I already had my moment of self-discovery. I was nobody and I hated it. I really didn't need to hear the "God works in mysterious ways" lecture again. I thanked Father Mike and started to walk off. "Isn't there something else you would like to talk about while you are here?" he asked. I looked at him, baffled. "The woman. The married woman you were tempted by..." Oh, Anna. I didn't answer. "You slept with her anyway, didn't you?" Again, I chose silence for my response. He started to shake his head. "Daniel, you agreed with me that it wasn't a good idea. Yet, you did it anyway, didn't you?" "Yes" I admitted. "And how is that working out for you?" he asked. "It's a mess. Just like you said it would be." He breathed a sigh of frustration. "So, tell me. What's going on with it?" he asked. So, I did. I told him about my conversations with Anna. I told him about Boratch and how our friendship might be over. I even told him about Steve and his conditions and threats.

"H.O.G.?" Father Mike asked. "Hand of God. The people that burn people at the stake in the name of God." "There are many who have done evil in the name of the Almighty." Yeah. Anyway. "So, what is your relationship with Anna now?" he asked. "We don't have one." "So, you stopped seeing her?" he asked. "Yeah, I did." "I think that was a very wise thing to do. It must have been difficult though" he said. "What was difficult?" I asked. "Telling her you couldn't see her anymore, even though you cared so much about her." I wasn't sure how to answer. "Yeah. I mean, not really. It was a mutual decision" I said.

I wasn't sure why I wasn't being completely honest with Father Mike. I knew I was making it sound like Anna and I had discussed things and, very maturely and calmly, decided that it had to end. No such thing had happened. At least not yet. But I guess it would. Which would suck. But would be good. And was necessary. But would suck. A lot. I stopped listening to Father Mike as he went on about healing and moving on. I had just realized something horrific. In spite of the fact that Anna Boratch wasn't that attractive, was self-absorbed and really kind of a bitch, I might actually be in love with her.

I thanked Father Mike and pulled out my phone. I needed to speak with Anna. Maybe if I just faced her in person. The real her. The always complaining, wanting something from somebody, her, I would realize that I wasn't in love with her at all. Maybe I was just a romantic at heart. The sort of tough, but sensitive, guy that loves to be in love. That craves the idea of timeless romance. Maybe Anna just happened to be there. The wrong girl at the right time. It was the only explanation that made any sense to me.

Just as I started to dial her number to get this all cleared up, another call came in for me. It was Samuel. "I was hoping to get your voicemail" he said. "Sorry, to disappoint you." "You've already disappointed me so much, what's one more little thing?" he said. I didn't respond. I was not about to be lured into his childish games. "So, what did your report say?" I asked. "What? You want me to read it to you over the phone, now? You can't read it for yourself" he said. "Boratch, quit being a pain in my ass. This is work. What did your report say?" I asked. He responded angrily. "It says exactly what I told you it would say. Chief Windsor was physically held and forced to shoot himself." "You're sure of that?" I asked. "You're questioning my professional confidence again? Of course, I'm sure of that!" He was really starting to irritate me.

"Are we done now? I have bodies to attend to" he said.

"One more thing" I said. "If it's not about work, don't even bring it up. I have said all there is to say on the issue of you defiling my married daughter against my express wishes." The way he said it, it made it sound even more fun and dirty than it actually was. By a lot. I was tempted to say as much but, somehow, restrained myself. "Well?" he asked, rudely. "Would it take one person or two to commit the crime?" I asked. "Either." "Either?" I asked. "That's what I said, either.

It could have been one very strong individual or two. I wasn't able to tell such things from the bruises on the victim's body." "Ok, thanks." "Ok? It's far from Ok. How you can even live with yourself is beyond me. Maybe the next suicide I am called to should be yours!" he yelled. I was speechless. I knew Boratch was angry with me but his statement was still a bit over the top. Even for him. He hung up without saying "goodbye."

I went to the car and phoned Anna. This had to end. Even with my incredibly confused feelings for her, it just had to end. Samuel had been a good friend for a very, very long time. Losing him over this wasn't worth it. Not to mention, all the complications with Steve and her being married and having kids and so forth. There was no answer. I didn't leave a message.

At HQ, I was almost immediately summoned back into Kim's office. "Where were you? I tried to call you on your cell phone" he said. "Really, I don't remember hearing..." And then I looked at my cell phone. He had called and left three messages. "Sorry, I think there must be something wrong with my phone service. I swear it didn't ring." Kim just stared at me.

"So, where were you?" he asked again. "At the crime scene" I said. "I called the uniform at the location when I couldn't reach you. He said you left several hours ago." "He was mistaken" I said. Kim wasn't buying it. "I actually left and then went back." He still wasn't buying it. "Seriously." "And why did you do that?" The bigger question was why he was grilling me like he was. As a Chief Inspector I expected, and was normally given, quite a bit of freedom over my own schedule. I was not some lowly rookie who was expected to clock in and out of my assigned shift. "Because I thought of something that I wanted to check out."

Kim just kept staring, waiting for me to explain. I was not happy with his new hands on approach to my work. If this was the way it was going to be working with him, from now on, maybe I shouldn't have taken my job back. Then again, he would be leaving soon to take charge of Anti-Terror. "The Medical Examiner believes that Chief Windsor was forced to kill himself. It wasn't a suicide" I said. "It wasn't a suicide?" he asked. "No, Sir. It appears someone, or more likely, two people, forced him to shoot himself" I said. "And this conclusion is based on what evidence, if any, Chief Inspector?" I ignored his tone and gave him a straight answer. Which, as it turned out, was a very stupid thing to do. "The Medical Examiner found bruising on the victim's arm to indicate someone had grabbed the victim and forced the gun up to his head." "He's wrong" Kim said, flatly. I didn't respond. "Do you understand me, Chief Inspector? The Medical Examiner is mistaken. "If you say so, Sir" I replied. "It's not what I say that's important, it's what you, the lead investigator, says that matters" he said. Right. Then the Superintendent closed the trap. "So, I'm asking you, is it likely that the Medical Examiner, a man well known to have problems with alcohol, may have been incorrect in his findings?"

What a bastard. There was no way that I was going to do that to Samuel. Not after all the things we had been through together. Friendship and loyalty had to count for something. Kim kept staring. He was waiting for me to give him my answer. "No, Sir. I have always found Medical Examiner Boratch to be highly competent and professional in his work." Kim sent me the most lethal looking death glare possible. I was toast. "Are you sure of that, Chief Inspector. You are absolutely certain that the Medical Examiner's findings are not mistaken?" He kept the death rays coming. "Yes, Sir. Although not an expert in his area, I would stand by Medical Examiner Boratch and his findings unless someone proved, definitively, that they were incorrect." Kim didn't see anything. He just exhaled in a way that made it clear that he was frustrated and angry. "Alright" he said. And with that, I was dismissed.

I arranged to meet with Boratch immediately. He refused at first but I insisted. It was important. Very important. He needed to know that I had just been pressured to turn on him and had risked my job, and possibly personal safety, in defending him. I had stood by him as a loyal friend in spite of his disrespectful behavior toward me. It had been a difficult test of my personal character but I had passed with flying colors. I was a good and loyal man. In fact, as far as I was concerned, it kind of made us even again. Whatever his misgivings about Anna and I, he would see now that my friendship was something to be cherished and not so easily discarded. Surely, it would make things better between us.

"You idiot!" he yelled. "Why did you tell him that?! Why did you tell him about my findings!!!" Boratch was bellowing at full fury. I reminded him that, even though we were in the parking lot, we were still near HQ and that he needed to lower the volume. "I'm done for anyway, thanks to you. I will scream as loud as I want!" he said. I tried to deescalate the situation by talking very softly to him. If I could speak very quietly to him, maybe he would do the same back. It was a trick I had learned from years on the job dealing with uncooperative suspects.

"Do you realize what you have done? Do you?" he asked. "Yes, at great personal sacrifice I stood up for you to my boss even though I had just gotten my job back." "Sacrifice?! The only sacrifice here is me. You have offered me up as the person they need to discredit and get rid of. Why did you tell them that?" he asked. "Because that's what you determined." "Since when do the facts on a case have anything to do with what we write in the report?!" He had a point. "I need to know. Was this really just stupidity on your part or was it intentional?" he asked. "Intentional? Was what intentional? Kim is the one that pointed to you right away. I wasn't." "AFTER you told him about my findings!" he yelled.

Honestly, I was getting very, very tired of being yelled at by Boratch. It just wasn't right. He kept trying to make me look like I had done something wrong. Like he wanted me to apologize for standing up for him. I had done right by him and here he was berating me for it. "You still don't understand what you have done, do you, Daniel?" he asked. "No, I really don't. I was pressured to turn on you and, instead, I stood up for you. How was that wrong? I mean, for you? It's obviously not very helpful to me. But you don't seem to care about that. How does my standing up for you, hurt you?" I asked. Boratch shook his head. Then he got very quiet. He put his hand on my shoulder.

"You have signed my death warrant, Daniel. And maybe yours as well" he said. I really wished he would stop being so over-dramatic. Then I saw the problem. Finally. Because of my insistence that the San Sebastian case was not quietly swept aside, the Cardinal was already less than pleased with us. By writing up a report that indicated that Chief Windsor had been killed by others, a hit, it drew attention to all of that. In particular, it drew attention to the Cardinal's buddies at H.O.G.. As a result, Boratch and I moved up much higher on the list. That list being people that needed to be removed. We had gone from irritating and incompetent to a serious problem that should be dealt with.

"Why didn't you tell me?" I asked. "Tell you what?" "I don't know. To keep it between us. To wait until we could discuss it. I don't know" I said. "Because, I just assumed that was common sense." I looked back at the moment I was summoned into Kim's office. I hadn't been thinking straight. I was tired. And hung over. And thinking about everything and anything not to do with the Windsor case. Threatening husbands, a future, or lack thereof, with Anna, God chemicals...I was so damn tired and confused that I had committed the ultimate act of stupidity. My boss had asked me a question and I had answered honestly.

"There's something else you need to see" I said. I handed Boratch the DVD about Epiphany. "What is it?" he asked. "San Sebastian talking about the secret drug research the Church was doing through Life Gen." "Research into what?" he asked. "You'll see. All I'll tell you is that we were already very, very much, on the Cardinal's hit list. What happened today probably didn't matter one way or the other." Boratch shook his head. "Of course it matters." And he was right. It did. Every action I had taken and every bit of new knowledge we had gathered made us more worthy targets. Sometimes, I wondered if I wanted to piss someone powerful off just so they would kill me and I wouldn't have to deal with all this crap anymore.

He looked at the DVD in its case. "When did you get this?" he asked. "A couple of days ago" I answered. "And you're just letting me know, now? Unbelievable!" he said. "You're the one that wouldn't talk to me!" I replied. I was sure that Boratch was going to start yelling at me, again. But he didn't. Which was far, far worse. The aggressive, bullying man he had been, just moments before, now looked completely different. Small and old. More than anything, he just looked tired. "I'll fix this, Samuel" I said. He answered so softly I could barely hear him. "No, you won't. You can't. Either can I. It's done."

The day did not get any better. I was fired by email. Not face to face. Not even with a phone call. One day back on the job and then my career ended with an email. Said email read as follows:

"Chief Inspector Daniel L. Hastings,

It has been brought to my attention that you knowingly, and recklessly, compromised the integrity of an active crime scene. Specifically, on the morning of Thursday, 2/15 you were sent to investigate a possible suicide at 3459 Morningside Drive, Bellhaven, and failed to properly follow procedure."

So, it was about Windsor's death. That was fast. The email continued.

"Specifically, you used the bathroom on site rather than respecting the obvious importance of keeping the scene intact and uncontaminated."

That fucking uniform must have ratted me out. He probably got hit with the same thing from someone else and pulled the "but he did it" defense, assuring that we both got nailed.

"Please present yourself to Agency headquarters to return your weapon and your People's Protection Agency credentials.

Best of luck on your future endeavors,

Lynn Baumgarden, Human Investment"

I couldn't believe they put in the "best of luck" line. Unreal. You're fired. Thanks and good luck. Oh, how I hated the H. I. people. So, that was it. I was officially out on my ass. Again. That was possibly the briefest return to work in history. Fired, rehired and fired again in the drop of a hat.

And then there was this thing with Boratch. It had been there before. The Cardinal and H.O.G. had every reason to go after us, me especially, just for knowing about Epiphany and the drug research. But Boratch was right. We, I, kept finding ways to piss them off and make ourselves bigger and bigger targets. Boratch would have been content to just keep his nose clean and to keep the Cardinal happy from the beginning. But, what was done was done. I had to focus on the here and now.

I needed to talk to Anna, more than ever. I called again and left a very insistent voicemail telling her we had to talk as soon as possible. I still wasn't sure she would call me back. The last time we had spoken, she was almost as angry at me as her father was.

She didn't call. She just came over about nine o' clock that evening. She did seem to like the drama of just showing up unannounced. She looked very suspicious. I told her that I had something very important to tell her. I told her it was about her father. Which it was. Not nearly as much as it was about me. But still. It involved Boratch. I offered Anna a drink but she refused. She even kept her coat on.

"Well?" she asked. I didn't say anything. "What is it?" she prodded. I thanked her for coming. She looked at me, impatiently. "Some things have happened that have put both your father and I at considerable personal risk..." "What does that mean?" she asked. ""Considerable personal risk?" I wasn't quite sure where to start.

"I got fired again" I said. She laughed. "Really?" she said through her laughter. "Yes, really. I'm glad you find that so amusing. My entire career is down the toilet and you think it's funny." She tried to get more serious. "Sorry. You're right. I'm just surprised they called you back in if they were just going to...Anyway, my father. What does that have to do with my father?" I explained that her father and I had both been involved in a very politically sensitive case. One related to that video of San Sebastian she had accidentally seen part of. It was a situation that became very complicated and put her father and I in the very awkward position of having angered several, very powerful, well connected people, all of which seemed to have lost their patience with us. She seemed to be listening. "And the thing is, we are both in danger. Very real, very serious danger." She looked like she believed me.

I stopped talking and waited for a reaction. She didn't say anything. "He'll figure a way out. He always has" she finally said. "I hope you're right but it's not that simple. This is a very serious situation. One involving some extraordinarily powerful people and some information that could damage them." "And this has to do with that weird speech that came on your porn video with the cucumber?" she asked. "It wasn't MY porn video! But yes."

I suddenly realized the conversation wasn't going the direction I had hoped for. The idea wasn't to bring her up to date on the San Sebastian/Windsor/Epiphany/Deborah Marky Case. It was to talk about us. I had something I really, really needed to tell her. "I just thought you might want to know because it would be a terrible tragedy if things between people were not clear. And that those people had any doubt about how others felt about them." I looked at her and waited for the shoe to drop. Did I really need to spell it out? A thoughtful look came over her face. "I see" she said. Thank heavens. "And you're right. My father is an ass but, like you said, he is still my father." What? No. That's really not what I was leading up to. I mean, it's good. I hope they do patch things up but that really wasn't what I had asked her to come over for. "I just wish he wasn't such a judgmental bastard when it came to my marriage and my personal life" she said.

"About that" I interrupted. "Just where are you with all that?" I asked. "What do you mean?" she asked. "I mean, emotionally, practically, where are you when it comes to things like your husband and..." I couldn't even say it. "And what?" she prompted. "And us. Where are you with us? What do you want to happen?" I asked. "I thought I had been pretty clear about that. You messed things up between me and my father. I can't forgive you for that." "How did I mess things up? You were the one acting against his wishes?" I corrected. "And YOU were the one that told him all about it!" she said. "So, we're both in the wrong then. It's a wash."

It sounded like a pretty reasonable way to end that whole issue and move on to talking about more important things. But I was wrong. Anna wasn't going to let it go. "Like hell, it's a wash. You told my father things you shouldn't have, after I, specifically, asked you not to. How can I ever trust you again?" she asked. "Of course you can trust me. And you're right. I screwed up. Ok. I said it, I screwed up. That's no reason to keep holding onto things the way you are."

Anna walked away and poured herself a drink. I had expected more yelling. I guess the drink was a good thing. At least she intended to stay and talk more. That was a success of sorts.

"Daniel, what are you saying? I really don't understand what you're after. Do you want me to forgive you?" I hadn't thought about it but that would be good. "That would be a start" I said. "Then say it" "Say what?" I asked. "Say that you made a mess of things with my father, are sorry, and you want me to forgive you" she said. That was kind of bitchy, demanding something so detailed like that. But whatever. I went ahead and did. I apologized for telling her father about us. Which, I thought I already had. I guess she just wanted to hear it again. She remained quiet and just stared at me. "Fine, I forgive you" she finally said. Well, that was a waste of time and energy. But I let it go.

"Anna, I want to keep seeing you" I said. I hadn't meant to say it right then, but it seemed as good a time as any. "Didn't you just tell me that I needed to patch things up with my father?" she asked. "Yes, I hate the fact you two are fighting" I said. "And how would continuing to see you help achieve that objective?" she asked. She had a point. But still. And why was she talking like that. "Achieve the objective?" She was on a roll. "Well?" she asked. "I think, given time, your father would learn to accept our relationship" I said. "What relationship?" she asked. "What do you mean?" "What relationship are you talking about? Having sex?" she asked. It seemed like a fine plan to me. But I knew I had to say more. "What sort of relationship do YOU want?" I asked. "Don't put this back on me. What are you talking about? As far as I was concerned, you and I were done the moment you started getting my father drunk and telling him things you promised you would never tell him." So much for my apology smoothing things over.

"Tell me, Daniel. What sort of relationship are you imagining between us? More sex? Something more serious? Are you thinking I'll get divorced and go right from one marriage to another with you? Is that what you see? Anna and Daniel forever?" She was being really unkind about all of this. I had bared my soul to her and was being ground into dust for it. But, in for a penny, in for a pound. "Yes" I said.

"Yes? Yes, what?" she asked. "Yes, I want to keep seeing you and having sex with you and going out with you and being there for you during your divorce and being with you after and helping you raise your kids and all of it. I love you Anna. I love you and I want to spend the rest of my life with you." Yikes. I couldn't believe I had just said all that. Where did that come from?

There was absolutely no reaction from Anna. No words. No change of expression. She just kept looking at me the way she had before I spilled out my river of heartfelt and sincere words. I loved Anna Boratch. I don't know when it happened or how it happened. But it happened. I loved Anna Boratch. Even thinking those words made me feel strong and right. I was putting it all on the line to go after what really mattered in life. Love. It was all about love.

"What are you talking about?" Anna asked. I repeated everything I had said. Sadly, it came off less romantic and more like a quiet mumble the second time around. But I said it all again. I told Anna I was in it for the long haul and wanted it all with her. "Well, that's not going to happen" she said. "Because of your father? Your marriage? The kids? What? We'll work all of that out. I'm not sure how. But we will. I know we will" I insisted. She kept looking at me in that distant sort of way. I really was not enjoying it. Surely, she would see what I was saying and come around. Surely.

"All of that, any of that, are good reasons but that's not why" she said. "So, what is the reason then?" I asked. "Because I don't love you." Ouch. "I thought we had an understanding, Daniel. I thought it was clear that you and I were just occasional bedmates and nothing more. I didn't even think you really liked me. And now you tell me that you love me and want to spend the rest of your life with me?" "I know, I'm as surprised as you are" I said. And I was. I really didn't understand how Anna had gone from bitchy, self-absorbed, badly aging, not really that good in bed, daughter of my best friend, to the woman of my dreams. But she did. So, I just went with it. Why was she finding that so strange?

"Listen to me again. I don't love you. I don't mind having sex with you. At least, I didn't before you started babbling to my father about it. But that's about as far as it goes" she said. I wasn't having it. "I was the same way but there's more. You know there's more. You're just frightened to admit it" I said. "No there isn't. There is nothing more. There never was and, more importantly, there never will be. What do I have to say to get that through to you?" I was pissed. Fine. Whatever. But she wouldn't give it a rest. The hurtful words kept coming.

"I really don't understand you, Daniel. Are you really that desperate and lonely?" she asked. Obviously, I thought. Obviously, if I'm professing my undying love for some old hag like you there was something seriously wrong with me. Why are you being such a bitch? "Just go, Ok?" I asked. "I will. And please leave my father out of whatever mess you've stepped into. He's an asshole and an alcoholic but he's a good man. Don't drag him down with you." I wasn't even going to bother to respond to that one. But, even then, she still wasn't done. She did the little kiss on the cheek thing to say goodbye. Why do women like to do that when they leave you? Not that Anna was leaving me, exactly. But still. A kiss on the cheek. Why? Just, why?

The next three days should have gone as follows. Sleep. Drink. Sleep. Drink. Get laid by supermodel. Sleep. Anna pleads for forgiveness. Conditional acceptance of Anna's apology (the condition having something to with her providing me with oral sex on demand). Love. Love. Peace. Love. And somewhere in there, there would be a heartfelt and sincere reunion with Boratch, a new job offer at somewhere far better than People's Protection, and the H.O.G. people, Cardinal and Minister would all go away. And, maybe more sex with a supermodel. Believe it or not, that is not exactly how things, actually, came to pass.

Instead, it was more like this. Anger. Depression. Exhaustion. Rejection. More rejection. And more rejection after that. Drinking. Nausea. Exhaustion. More Nausea. And so on and so forth. Those three days after Anna straightened me out on where things stood were not fun. I had plenty of time to think about it. About her. About what would never be. And about work and how I didn't have any. And about friends, and how I had alienated them. And, shockingly enough, on top of all that, there were no supermodels involved. Three days just wallowing in emotional pain. A misery-cation, if you will.

However, some seriously messed up stuff happened that snapped me right out of it. Like, instantly. I walked home from the bar drunk but it wasn't a good drunk. More the kind you get from two beers because you hadn't slept much or eaten in a while. And the bad buzz was made worse upon my return. My apartment was trashed. Admittedly, I hadn't done the best job of keeping it neat and tidy. There were dishes in the sink. Magazines on the sofa. Nasty things growing in the toilet. But that's not what I'm talking about. I'm talking trashed. As in, someone got in there and intentionally destroyed the place. Furniture was broken. My TV was shattered. My stereo was stomped on. It was ugly.

My first thought was it was the act of a woman. An insanely jealous woman, crazy with rage. A hot, intensely passionate woman who would throw dishes at me one minute and have the most intense, psychotic, heated sex imaginable with me a minute later. Alright, actually, I didn't think that. If only I was so lucky. But, for a second, I did think it might have been Anna. But Anna was not the type to be so emotional. Or passionate. Or crazy in bed. At least not with me. So, screw her. So, this wasn't her doing. Which meant this was one of two things. A message that I had done something I shouldn't have, or someone looking for that DVD about Epiphany. Or both. Which I guess is three things. Whatever. The point is, someone made my already miserable life even more miserable. I liked my stuff. My TV and stereo, in particular. And these assholes had ruined it all.

Using my vast experience as a law enforcement officer, I quickly developed a list of plausible suspects. Steve, because I had done exactly what he had warned me not to do by making my play for Anna. H.O.G., either looking for that DVD or just letting me know they were unhappy with me on the San Sebastian/Windsor/Broken Television case. Or the Minister, who probably figured out by now I lied to him when I fingered Mike Laughton for turning on him when it was me. Or maybe Laughton himself because he found out about all that. Or maybe even Boratch who came over really drunk to talk with me and got so angry, he did this. Or Superintendent Kim for trying to use his past against him to gain favor with Windsor. Or...crap, I had made a lot of enemies. There were so many people that had reasons to want to make my life a bit more sad and pathetic than it already was. Too many.

I sat there in the debris of my former possessions, trying not to think about how poetic it was that I was, literally, sitting in the ruins of my life. Heaven forbid I was ever that pretentious. My mind, still slightly buzzed and greatly tired, mind you, tried to go through the suspects once by one. It was all very methodical and logical. And, as it turned out, a total waste of time. But I'm getting ahead of myself.

I started with the least likely suspects, to get them crossed off my mental list. Anna, first. Her motive would be anger. She was, indeed, angry with me about telling her father about us. It's possible Steve had mentioned we had talked as well. That might not have gone over so well, either. Especially, since I'm not sure I ever got around to mentioning that conversation to her. She had plenty of reason to be pissed off. She really was kind of hot when she was angry like that. I mean, for an older, married with two kids, not all that good looking, woman. But I digress. The fact was, my apartment was trashed days after our discussion. If she had done it right away, it would have made sense. In that passionate, crazy, plate throwing, psycho-sex having, sort of way. Which didn't really apply to her. No, it just didn't add up. When it came right down to it, Anna wasn't emotionally involved enough with anything regarding me to put so much energy into it. I just wasn't worth the effort to her. Haggard wench.

And then, her father. My former best friend and trusted confidant. Maybe he came over and...No, no way. I'd known the man for years and trashing somebody's apartment just wasn't his style. Punching people. Spitting on them. Calling them very imaginative and cruel names. All of that fit his M.O.. But not destroying an apartment.

Superintendent Kim? Would Kim have done this, or had it done, to send me off with style? He did seem oddly cool with the fact I had painted him as a Baby Murderer to Windsor. Too cool. He even gave me my job back. For a day. So, it was to set me up and spare his remaining officers problems. But still. I can't imagine he would do this. A calm, cool death glare was far more his style. Losing it like this was just way too out of character. Next.

H.O.G.. Yeah, Hand of God made sense. I mean, THEY didn't make sense at all, always talking about God's love and peace and coexistence, and then burning people alive. But, in terms of destroying the apartment. It could either have been a warning or a search for that DVD. The DVD I had already given to Boratch. I wondered if he still had it. Had they done the same to his place?

I called him to see if his apartment was still unmolested. I got his voicemail. I told him about the situation, to be on guard, and to call me as soon as he could. I wasn't holding my breath that he would do any of that. Especially the calling me part. Anyway, H.O.G. seemed plausible but I wasn't sure what to make of it. A search? A warning? Both. I moved on to the other suspects. For now.

Mike Laughton. Rich, oil executive and father of the young, firm and lovely, Isabella. Oh, how I wanted to spank that girl. In all sorts of ways. I'm not even sure what that means. However, it accurately expresses the difficulty I was having focusing on the task at hand. Instead of being able to methodically rule out Mike Laughton as a suspect I found myself enjoying certain thoughts about Isabella. Keep in mind, as I have made quite clear, I was slightly drunk at the time. Either way, the process of getting Isabella out of my mind and being able to rule out her father took a while. But I did it. I decided that her father was very unlikely to have ever been informed by Minister Kapinskov about what I had said about him. Unless, of course, Kapinskov told him himself. Which he might have. Which meant, Mike Laughton might have hired someone to do this to my place as payback. I put him down, mentally, as a "maybe."

And then there was Kapinskov himself. He had been pretty quiet of late. But, when it came down to it, he should really be quite pleased with me. He was clearly lining up opposition to Cardinal Rooney and the Church for some sort of political power grab. I had helped him a lot with this. I had let the San Sebastian case lead to all these other things that the Church was involved in. Most of which, I realized, I actually hadn't told Kapinskov about. At least, not directly. But surely he could piece together my visits to Life Gen with the whole SanSebastian/Windsor/Broken TV thing. I made a mental note to consider talking with the Minister directly, again, soon. I had good stuff for him. Especially that DVD about Epiphany, assuming Boratch still had it.

Where was I? So many enemies. Too little time. Right, Steve. Anna's husband with the weirdly twisted view of chivalry and marriage. I could totally see him getting all worked up learning of my impassioned plea to Anna to leave him and be with me. The plea she stomped all over and spit on because she is a heartless bitch. But I could see Steve not liking that at all. He was pretty clear that he wouldn't stand for that. But he was also pretty clear he wasn't man enough to go one on one with someone like me. He had said he would contact his buddies in H.O.G. which might have been what made them do this to my apartment. Which meant H.O.G. had just trashed it and probably still didn't know about San Sebastian's confession on the porn stick or the DVD. Unless Anna told him. No, she wouldn't do that. Would she do that? No, she wouldn't do that. So, yeah, maybe H.O.G. via Steve. Seemed like a mighty strong suspect to me.

Who else? Anna, Steve, Kapinskov, Laughton, Kim, Boratch, H.O.G., and H.O.G. again...Who was I forgetting? I guess it could have been just a random thing. Kids high on something that just thought it would be fun to break stuff. Such things happened. Which was the sort of violence and destruction I hated most. Everybody else I on my list had a reason to do this. Not a great reason, in some cases, but a reason. People just randomly making life worse for other people...the people that keyed cars, beat people up for fun, did crimes for a chuckle, sort of people...they deserved a special place in the basement of HQ. One where people laughed as they broke their bones one by one. "Having fun now, Apartment Vandal?"

I realized I was getting myself all worked up. Until then, I had been remarkably cool and calm considering that all my worldly possession had been destroyed. And the act might be a warning to do harm to my person. Or parts of my person that I really didn't enjoy the thought of getting harmed. I returned to being the consummate professional, analyzing the data and forming a hypothesis. In fact, my conclusion was thus. Whoever did this to me really sucked. That was about as far as

I got, that night, trying to sort through it all. I ended up just clearing a space in all the junk that had once been my furniture and falling asleep. However, things got clearer the next morning.

I awoke on top of my ripped sofa cushions, still in my clothes. I sat there just looking at my trashed apartment and trying to ignore my headache. I then remembered that I had tried to call Boratch. I looked at my phone to see if he had called me back. No. The man could certainly hold a grudge. It was then that I realized my mouth tasted of hedgehog or some other flavor just not right for a mouth to taste. I got up and made my way through the various piles of my former stuff on the floor and went to the kitchen to get some water. Cold water sounded ideal to me. I was already imagining how good the ice cold water would feel as I opened the refrigerator door. And it was then that the great mystery was solved. I knew, without a shadow of a doubt, who had trashed my apartment.

The severed head of a pig stared at me. Eyes, ears and the whole deal. A complete pig's head. Pinned to its neck was a note. "You're next." The threat seemed a little confusing and vague to me. But at least now I knew who was behind it. I knew who had ruined a TV I really liked and a stereo that was old but still really good. It was H.O.G.. I hated those guys. So, much so that I told them so, out loud. "Screw you, Piggy Man!" I yelled. And with that, I sent Sir Pork-A-Lot flying across the kitchen and onto the floor.

Much to my embarrassment, I took the next few minutes to enjoy the self-pity I had denied myself the day before. Life on this planet just seemed to be getting a little worse for me every day. Those minutes might have turned to hours were it not for a phone call I got. I had thought that it might be Boratch. So I interrupted my pity party and answered. It was not Boratch's number but Superintendent Kim's. I really didn't feel like dealing with him. I let voicemail pick it up. The message went on for a long time before the little phone display showed it. I wasn't even going to listen. Kim's firing, rehiring, and refiring of me had been part of this whole crappy thing. I wasn't in the mood to hear it. What was he going to do, rehire me, yet again?

But curiosity got the better of me. I listened to the message. "Chief Inspector, this is Superintendent Kim" (No, shit). "I need you to call me back immediately. It is very, very important. Please, call me back as soon as you hear this. Or just come down to Headquarters. Just contact me as soon as possible. It's important." The message wasn't what I had expected. Not one, but two, mentions of it being important piqued my interest. But then I remembered who I was dealing with. It was probably about me neglecting to turn in my official PPA ID last time around. It wasn't something I had done on purpose. Kim never asked and I certainly wasn't going to bring it up. That's what they get for firing such a distinguished veteran of the agency by email. Email!!! They weren't going to let that go, though. Having a People's Protection ID gained you access to a lot of places and a lot of information. Or maybe it would be forgotten about. I guess I could tell them I just lost it. It wasn't like they could fire me again for incompetence or being irresponsible. The phone rang again while it was still in my hand. It was Kim. Again. I still didn't answer. No message this time. But what was so important?

I tried to ignore it and started cleaning up my apartment. But Kim called again. And again after that. He even left another message. "I need to speak with you immediately. Please call me or come down to Headquarters when you hear this message." I kept piling the bits and pieces of my furniture and possessions into trash bags. I started in the bedroom. The living room and kitchen would have to wait. I just wanted to be left alone. Why couldn't people just leave me alone?

And then another call and message not ten minutes later. Enough. I was going to go down there and tell Kim what I thought of him face to face. I needed the outlet and he had offered himself up. Feel my wrath you tiny, little man! Fire me, will you?! Time to put him in his place. Instead of calming down while driving to HQ, I got more amped up. The ridiculous traffic along Calvary Road might have had something to do with it. Either way, by the time I got to HQ I was just itching to go off on somebody. Kim, Boratch, somebody, anybody. Anybody that had helped turned my life into the mess it was in. I refused to just stand by quietly and take it anymore.

I stormed into Kim's office. He wasn't there. "He's in the morgue" his assistant said. Fine. In the morgue. Probably with Boratch. Perfect. I could kill two birds with one stone and tell them both exactly what I thought of them and their recent behavior. The anger felt good. Anger was strength. I was no longer a powerless victim. I was all mighty and ready to take on anyone or anything. And then I walked into the morgue.

There was the corpse of a very, very, burned victim on the stainless steel examining table. A crispy critter, if ever there was. And there was a second burned corpse, mostly covered, at the table next to that. Superintendent Kim saw me. "Chief Inspector, finally..." I looked at the blackened corpse and looked back at Kim. "So, what's so important?" I asked. "Just to remind you, you fired me. Again. I don't work for you anymore" I added. "This isn't about that" Kim said. "So, what is it about?" I asked. He gestured toward the body. I didn't get it. "Yeah, so. You have another case. Give it to one of the incompetent kiss asses that still works for you" I said. "I'm sorry" Kim said. But he said it like he was really sorry. Not like, "excuse me" kind of sorry. He gestured again toward the charred body.

"Am I supposed to care about this lump of coal for some reason? Well, I don't. I'm no longer a Chief Inspector and have moved on." I said. Then Kim seemed to realize I wasn't understanding. "You don't recognize him?" he asked. "No. Should I?" I said. "Look closer" he said. And I did. I got close enough to smell the disgusting smell only a cooked human body can create. It turned my stomach. But I still couldn't recognize it. I shrugged. "It's Boratch. It's your friend Samuel Boratch. We found him last night."

I felt dizzy. Like, I was ready to fall to the floor, kind of dizzy. I was barely able to keep upright. "And that's his daughter Anna behind you." Oh, Man. I checked out. I just checked out. Boratch. Anna. No. I just thought about standing upright. And breathing. Breathing was somehow difficult for me. Anna. I needed to sit down. I stumbled over to a little stool and did just that. Kim just kept staring at me. It felt good to sit. But then I realized what stool I was on. It was Samuel's. The one he used when he worked. Samuel. Anna. Dead. Those things on the slabs were them. They weren't even human any more. Just chunks of flakey, black flesh and bone.

"We found them in a warehouse last night. Both had been tied to stakes and burned alive" Kim said. Burned at the stake. H.O.G.. Hand of God had taken two people I loved and let flames slowly engulf them. I could almost imagine their pain. Their terror as to what was happening to them. "How long?" I asked. "Like I said, we found them last night. The call came in shortly after eleven." "No, how long between when they started to burn and when they died?" I asked. "I have no idea.

That would be a better question to ask the Medical Examiner."
But Boratch was the Medical Examiner. Then I realized they
had brought someone in to cover for him or replace him
already. My thoughts were still not quite making sense.

"I asked you to come down because I know you and the
Medical Examiner were close" he lied. "No, you didn't" I
corrected. Kim waited for me to finish. "You brought me down
here because you know it's H.O.G. and thought maybe I could
help you with your case." "Can you?" he asked. I didn't
answer. He kept prodding. "There are obvious similarities
between this and the death of Deborah Marky. Were you able
to make any headway on that case?" he asked. I wasn't sure
what he was talking about. Deborah Marky? What? And then I
remembered how very, very little Kim knew. The poor man
was clueless.

Hand of God was all over the case Boratch and I were
working on. So was Cardinal Rooney. But Kim knew none of
it. He didn't know about Epiphany. He didn't know about the
DVD. He didn't know about all the people watching
everything Boratch and I did. He certainly didn't know about
the pig's head left for me in my refrigerator. Oh crap. It hit me.
"You're next." "You're next" suddenly made way too much
sense for my own comfort. I was so tired of these guys. H.O.G.
had done this. They had killed Boratch. They had killed Anna.
Beautiful, giving, tender, Anna. Not just killed, but made to
suffer pain unimaginable to any but those that have endured it.

The anguish of one's very skin covered in flames and organs being turned to blackened pulp. They had left me alive just long enough to make sure that I saw those I loved die first. Soon, it would be my turn. Well, if that's the way it was, so be it. Come on boys! Bring it on, Piggy Men! You think you can mess with me? You have no idea who you're dealing with. No idea at all.

Kim tried to ask me questions about what I and Boratch had been up to. I told him nothing. This wasn't about sympathy or understanding. He just wanted to question me. He knew he was in way over his head and wanted some answers. It's not every day a colleague at work is burned alive with his child. But there was still no offer to rehire me. None. And I wasn't going to bring it up. If I wasn't good enough for them then they were on their own. I would take care of this myself. H.O.G. was not going to get away with this. And if it came from the Cardinal, either was he.

As I left, I heard Kim yell something about turning in my ID and gun. I ignored him. For a moment, I worried that he would have some of the uniforms stop me. He didn't. Which was a good thing. Where I was going, I might need the gun to persuade someone to cooperate.

"Was it you?" I asked. Steve sat behind his desk still wondering how I had gotten into his office. "How did...?" he started to say. "Was it you?" I asked again. "Was what me?

What are you talking about? How did you get in here?" He wasn't reacting like a guilty man. But he was clever, that Steve. It would be just like him to act all innocent and ignorant of the horrific crime he had committed. "Did you tell your friends at H.O.G. to kill Anna and her father?" Steve's face went through a series of contortions. Confusion. More confusion. Denial. Acceptance. Grief. Anger. More confusion. "What?" he asked.

I told him where I had just come from and what I had seen. "Did you put your friends at Hand of God up to this? Did you have Anna and her father murdered?" "No. How can you ask me that? No." I reminded him of the threats that he had made to me. I pointed out how he feared Anna was going to leave him and take the children. I even told him that I had pleaded with Anna to do just that, and to let me be part of Anna's life forever. "You did what?!" he yelled. He started to get up from his chair. I pulled my gun out. "Sit down!" I commanded. He reluctantly did so. Steve still seemed very confused about what was happening. "Is she really dead?" he asked. I assured him that she was. The body had been positively ID'd. So had her father's. Steve actually seemed upset. The nerve.

"I really did care for her, you know" he said. "So, are you saying you never mentioned having her killed by H.O.G. because of her disloyalty?" I asked. "No!" he said. I wasn't about to let up. "Admit it. Just say it. You had Anna and her father killed because you couldn't stand the fact that she didn't love you anymore and was going to leave you." He shook his head "no." "She was going to leave you and take your children from you and you couldn't stand it." Steve kept denying it. "How?" he asked. "How what?" "How did they die?" Steve asked. "You know how. How H.O.G. always murders people. They were burned alive at the stake." I said. Steve got very quiet. "Admit that you did it" I repeated. "I didn't. I swear, I didn't" He insisted. "Even though she cheated on me and embarrassed me, she didn't deserve that. She was my problem to deal with, not theirs. They had no right. They had no right at all!" Steve was getting himself quite worked up about things.

"I will help you find the men that did this" he said. "And how are you going to do that?" I asked. "I know H.O.G.. I will help you find the men that did this. But only if you promise me one thing." "You're not in any position to make demands" I responded. "Do you want the people that murdered Anna, or not?" he asked. "Fine. What?" "If you find them, you don't arrest them, you kill them." Fine. "Slowly" he added. "Fine." "I want them to suffer" he said. "I get it. I get it. Fine. Done. Now, who are they?" I asked. The answers I got from him were bittersweet.

Steve and I left his office. It wasn't, exactly, easy to leave discreetly. Between my bold entrance, the yelling and the pulled gun, even the most jaded employee noticed something was up. Except for maybe this one guy in the corner with headphones on, doing some sort of web design thing. But, beyond that, all eyes were upon us as we left. He tried to reassure them that things were fine but, clearly, they all knew otherwise. You could hear the gossiping start before we were even out the door. I think I even heard one guy tell another that Steve was a drug dealer who had gotten addicted to his own product. A complete lie, as far as I knew. But people really did love to talk shit about other people. It's what kept the People's Protection Agency in business.

Getting the information from Steve that he had promised wasn't as easy as I had hoped. At least, not at first. It wasn't that he didn't want to cooperate. He did. A lot. He wanted the people that had killed Anna as badly as I did. But it took a while. To get it we had to drive all the way out to Steve's overly-large and tacky house in the suburbs. With traffic, it took almost an hour.

When we finally arrived, Steve told me the kids were both away somewhere. I wasn't really listening. I was too consumed by looking over the house. Over the years, I had heard about his house, their house, many times from Anna. It was nothing like she described it. "A chateau feel" to her was a resemblance to a kid's pizza place to me. But it still got to me in a way that I hadn't counted on. I saw her things. How she lived. The chair she sat on. The collection of pretentious books on her shelves. And the photographs. They were everywhere. Anna and her kids when they were infants. When they were toddlers. A wedding photo. None of it matched the images I had created in my own mind. Not that it mattered, now.

Steve must have noticed me looking a little too long at the photographs. "I didn't bring you here to be a tourist. This is my house. Anna was my wife. You're only here because we both want her killers to pay for what they did." True enough. Steve told me how his ties with Hand of God went back for decades. Several of them had gone to the same private university that he had. Whereas, he had chosen a career in the packaged goods industry developing new products for children to crave, many of his classmates went on to the military. He graduated at the height of the Islamic Insurgence and enlisting was the popular, and patriotic, thing to do at the time.

As he kept rambling, I looked at the stairs and imagined the bedroom at the end of the hallway. The place Anna had sex with the man I was talking to. And then I realized that they had probably had sex on the very sofa I was sitting on. Pretty gross. Really gross, actually. In all sorts of ways. Then again, Anna was far too uptight to ever risk her upholstery like that. So, no worries, I guess. But still, I kept thinking of Anna having sex all over the disgusting, suburban monstrosity that I was in. It wasn't a thought that saddened me. Or, even more shockingly, even aroused me. Instead, it brought me a weird sense of comfort. I have no idea why. The woman had just died and thinking of her having sex all over the house with another man brought me comfort. What on earth was wrong with me?

"You look deep in thought? Have you already developed some sort of plan?" Steve asked. "No. I was actually thinking of your wife fucking" I said. Steve flinched. He wasn't expecting that one. "You really are an ass, aren't you?" he said. I wasn't about to tell him the thoughts were about him, not me, having sex with his wife. Let him think the worst. Either way, I was finally pulled out of my private porno show. Steve had found what he had come there for. He had some photos to show me.

There was an image of five men on the screen. They were young. And in uniform. The uniform of our National Defense Force. "This photo was taken in Iran about twenty years ago. The man on the left is Rodrick, then Bollings, then Gretizowksi, then Fay." "OK" I said. "Bollings died a year later in a car bombing" Steve added. "These are the men you think murdered Anna?" "It feels like them but I'm not sure. I know Rodrick and Fay are members of H.O.G.." "What about Gretowski?" I asked. "Gretizowski" he corrected. "Whatever." "He went into massage therapy." "Really?" I asked. Steve didn't understand why I sounded surprised. "He went from military guy to massage therapist?" I asked again. "Yes, really. Why does that sound so strange to you?" "I don't know. It just does" I said. Honestly, what sounded strange to me was that I was talking about such trivial crap when my best friend and...whatever Anna was, had been murdered. Denial? Lack of sleep? Early signs of mental illness? I forced myself to focus.

"And the two that you said are in H.O.G., what can you tell me about them?" I asked. Much better. I felt like a professional, again, almost. "Rodrick is the one I know the best. He's with the local chapter by my office. I see him sometimes before or after his meetings." "Hand of God meetings?" I asked. "Yes, it's all very informal. They just meet at the Golden Sheep and get drunk together, most of the time." "But not always? Sometimes, they decide to go out and do God's work by torching someone?" I asked. "Yeah" Steve replied. "Yeah? That's all you have to say? This man is your friend, and kills people after he drinks too much, and all you have to say is "yeah"?" Steve glared at me. "I wouldn't be so judgmental, Inspector. Everyone knows that you agents at PPA do exactly the same kind of thing." "But we're official. Not some group of ex-military nitwits in a bar" I protested. "And that makes it better?" he said, a little too self-righteously. I ignored his implication and moved on.

"What about the other one, Fay?" I asked. "He's the one I really think is behind it" Steve said. "Why's that?" I asked. Steve continued. Fay was a professional military guy. Even more than the rest of them. He did four tours during the Islamic Insurgence. He was also a very religious man. After he returned from his final tour, he joined the Church's security force. The force was already well into the transformation from private, uneducated, security guards who made ten bucks an hour, to military-trained, hardened, and eventually very well armed, private little army. It was ideal for Fay. He was a believer with all the right training and skills for the Church's needs.

He moved up the ranks, quickly, and soon found himself a member of Cardinal Rooney's massive, bodyguard detail. Three years later, he became its commanding officer. "And all this time he was also with H.O.G.?" I asked. "He got into it about a year out of the military, through Rodrick. But they had some sort of falling out. I think it was over their attitudes." "What do you mean?" I asked. "Rodrick complained to me, one night while we were drinking, that Fay had become a religious nut job. Which is saying something because Rodrick is out there himself. Fay had come down on him and the other H.O.G. members for being far more interested in beer and a good brawl than serving The Lord." Fay sounded like a kind of a prick. "They still talk, now and again, but it sounded from Rodrick like all the heavy stuff that goes on with H.O.G. is handled by Fay and other members of the Cardinal's security detail." I let that sink in for a minute.

I had always pictured H.O.G. members much more like Rodrick. Idiots who were about as intelligent and threatening as a shrub. At least until they got really drunk and started misquoting the bible to each other and decided to kill themselves a heretic or two. What Steve was describing wasn't that at all. It was a group of highly trained fanatics that could, and would, kill you if God told them to. Or the Cardinal.

Which to them was almost the same thing. "Do you think the Cardinal personally ordered the murder?" I asked Steve. His reply wasn't what I expected. "Why would he do that?" he asked. My mind ran through a list of answers. Because of Epiphany, and Windsor, and Marky and San Sebastian and...And then I remembered Steve didn't know a thing about any of that. The only way he could have would have been if Anna told him. And she wouldn't. She hated him and would never let him know about any of that information.

"Why do you even care who killed Anna?" I asked. Steve looked right at me. "Because she was my wife" he said. I should have just left it alone, but something in me refused to do that. Something about his attitude. "So?" I challenged. "So?" Steve replied. "So, she hated you and planned to leave you and take the kids with her as soon as she could. Her death solves that whole issue for you." "You still think I did it?" he asked. "No. I don't. I just don't understand why you would turn against your buddies at H.O.G. like this. It seems to me that they just did you a huge favor." "Like I said, because she was my wife. Contrary to what you might think of me, Daniel, I still cared for Anna a great deal" he said. "We had a lot of history together and she was the mother of my children." "But you didn't love her. Not anymore." Steve didn't answer. "So, I ask again. Why are you going against H.O.G. and helping me, right now?" I asked. He just repeated the same answer. "Because she was my wife." And then I finally got it. Why

Steve was so upset about Anna. Why he was doing something that could, and would, come back on him in the form of financial ruin and/or physical harm. He was angry somebody had done this to something he owned. Or in this case, SOMEONE he owned. It was a challenge to his manhood. She was his to deal with, not theirs. What a dick. What a total, macho, stuck in the Middle-Ages, dick. I pulled out my gun and I shot him. Three shots. All to the chest. He died right there at his desk.

It would be easy enough to explain. Steve was a suspect and had tried to escape after his lies had caught him out. He had some very compelling motives to kill Anna. It also gave me something else that I sorely needed. A way to keep Kim and the others out of my way. I would tell Kim it was Steve that had killed Anna and Boratch. In the meantime, I would be going after the real prize, Roderick, Fay, and, if need be, the Cardinal, himself. It was perfect. But, honestly, I didn't think of all that until Steve was already dead and slumped over his desk. The reason I shot Steve wasn't any of that. The reason I shot him was that he was a total dick and it just really pissed me off.

What many people would have assumed was the most obvious problem, was actually the easiest of all. Steve hadn't been armed or trying to escape when I killed him. But it was a situation easily adjusted to my needs. I just searched around a bit until I found Steve's gun. I knew he had one because Anna had mentioned how much she hated having it in the house and around her kids. I placed said gun in Steve's hand and it all looked as it should. The bastard had tried to shoot me and I got him first.

I called Superintendent Kim and told him what had happened. Not what really happened, of course. What happened in my fictional scenario. Kim demanded that I stay at the scene and wait for the investigators to arrive. I said that I would be much happier giving my statement directly to him to avoid any weirdness with my former colleagues. Although annoyed, Superintendent Kim agreed that it made sense for him to come out to the crime scene himself, given the nature of the crime and identity of the shooter. That shooter being me, his former heir apparent. The one thing I had to make sure of though, was that I kept my People's Protection ID. The gun I could replace easily enough. I had a half a dozen throwaways in my car trunk. But I still needed that ID to get people to let me in places and to force them to talk with me. As intimidating as I was, which, all bragging aside, was pretty impressively intimidating, I was even more of a threat with the weight of the People's Protection Agency behind me.

So, I waited. In the hour or so it took Kim and the investigators to get out to the crime scene, I did three things. I reviewed the crime scene and my story to make sure it all felt solid. I thought about finding Rodrick at the Golden Sheep and getting the story from the piggy's mouth, as it were. And three, I snooped around Anna's possessions some more. I started in the bedroom, of course. Not just because it was the most likely place to find her lingerie, sex toys and what not. It was also the most likely place she would have hidden anything intimate like a diary. Maybe that diary would have some indication of her true feelings for me. The ones she was so frightened of. The ones she worked so hard at...Oh, who was I kidding? Anyway, she wasn't really the type to keep a diary. At least, not with Steve around. He was so possessive, he would have had no problem searching for it. And then he would have it against her in any way that he could. Yet another reminder of what a bastard he was and how I had done the world a favor by removing him from this world.

I found myself staring at a photograph in the hallway for a while. It was Anna and her children at some sort of party. Other than the slightly aging face, Anna still looked pretty good in the picture. Beautiful, in fact. Much to my annoyance, I found myself wondering what it would be like if she had become my wife and her children mine to shepherd through life. As shocking as it may seem, the idea of having a family suited me. I would have been a great father and caring husband. Instead of Daniel L. Hastings, People's Protection Agent, I would have thought of myself as Daniel L. Hastings, Husband and Father. But it wasn't meant to be. I knew that I was destined for things far greater. I had been for some time.

Being a husband and father was just not in the cards. Such was the way of things.

Superintendent Kim arrived with an annoyingly large group of others. There were the two agents he would dump the case on the moment it became convenient. Their names were Dalbry and Henderson. I knew them both well and thought they were incompetent asses. Dalbry had the highest closing rate of any agent in the department and had the attitude to match. His success wasn't due to his skills, I assure you. The man was just constantly lucky and had all the right connections to make things fall his way. Henderson was worse. He was a veteran Detective who had managed to stay with the agency longer than anyone else. Twenty-one years, in fact. The required politicking and ass kissing skills for such a record were extreme. It irritated me to even think of it.

In any case, I fed my lies to the anxious ears hearing them and explained how, and why, Steve had died. He had worked with H.O.G. to murder his wife and our beloved co-worker, Boratch. And then Kim started asking questions. The most annoying of which was "So, who are the suspect's co-conspirators at the Hand of God?" It was a good question. And, of course, the answer was Rodrick and Fay. But I didn't want to tell them that. At least not yet. I couldn't have them mucking up my whole plane to make Rodrick lead me to Fay and to do what must be done. So, I made up another answer on the spot.

"Growtowski" I said. "Who's Growtowski?" Kim asked. "An old schoolmate of Steve's who he knew from university." I saw Kim and the other agents write down the name. It occurred to me that I might even be saying it wrong. Was it Grotowski? The one that died. Grezowski? Something like that. I figured, by the time they realized what his name really was, and found out he died twenty years ago, I would be well on my way. Even if Kim came back to me and said it didn't make sense that a dead man could have burned Anna and Boratch alive, I had an answer. I could just say Steve lied to me. Sorry.

It was just as I was feeling very pleased with myself and my well-rehearsed pack of misinformation that I realized something. I was an idiot. It wasn't Grotozski that had died, it was the other one, Bollings. Oops. The guy I had named was the massage therapist. Depending on where he lived, they would find him much more quickly then I would have liked. After picking him up and interrogating him in all sorts of horrible ways, they would realize he couldn't have done it. I supposed that I could still say Steve lied to me. In fact, I could still go ahead and mention Bollings to buy myself even more time. Perfect. Some things just have a way of working out, I guess.

I went directly to the Golden Sheep on the off chance that Rodrick and his pals were there. They weren't. Intent on not making the stop a total waste of time, I ordered a pint. Maybe if I hung around a little, I could learn something. Of course, I could also flash my ID and ask directly. But that could scare them away. No, I would have to slowly sip my beer and spend some time in the bar. And if I didn't come across anyone or anything useful tonight, there was always tomorrow and the day after that.

About three pints in, I started to wonder about the name of the place. I thought the mythological reference was "The Golden Fleece." And that it had something to do with a God screwing animals and someone killing one and the constellations. Or money. It had something to do with money. Or some God screwing a sheep for money. All I knew, well I knew a few things, was that the bar was mercifully free of sheep decorations and that the beer was good. And syphilis is only found in two creatures. Humans and sheep. You do the math. In any case, Golden Fleece or Sheep, or whatever, seemed like a very silly name to me.

I finally gave up waiting around the sheep bar and headed home around ten at night. I was dreading going home. Unless the magic cleaning fairies had come while I was gone, the place was still going to be a wreck. I really didn't want to spend the money for a hotel. But the idea of staying in my trashed apartment was just too depressing. The plan was to stop by and get some clothes and things, and then get a cheap motel. Since it was just me sleeping, alone, there was no need for anything luxurious. Just a bed and a floor not covered in my former possessions.

It was a little more difficult to drive home than I would have liked. My tiredness was affecting my perceptions and reactions. But, I did it. Minor, almost hitting a pedestrian incident aside, it went just fine. I parked and walked into my apartment. Or what used to be my apartment before those assholes destroyed it. Those assholes that wanted to kidnap me and burn me alive for knowing about their super-secret, God drug thing. I really hated those guys.

Even a little drunk, I noticed that there was a loud buzzing sound coming from my kitchen. Not a refrigerator but something else. I walked in and saw my old friend, Piggy, right where I had tossed him, rather ungraciously, onto the floor. Some flies had joined him and were buzzing all around his porky, little head. Many, many flies.

I didn't want to deal with it and just walked away. I grabbed a few things out of the apartment and left as quickly as possible. If I could, I would never go back there. I wasn't sure how I was going to pull that off but, right then, that became a new goal. Never go back to the apartment. For reasons I couldn't quite explain, it seemed very important at the time.

The motel I ended up staying in cheered me up a great deal. It was just a chain motel off the main road. But it was large, had cable television, and there was a free breakfast served in the lobby. The anonymity of the place suited me fine. Just another traveler. A pilgrim of sorts. Well, not really. Not at all, actually. But, again, it sounded good at the time.

I woke up the next morning more determined than ever to find Rodrick. Kim had already started calling me and leaving me messages. It turns out it doesn't really take that long to track a massage therapist down. They knew Grotingowksi, or whatever his name was, was probably not a member of the Hand of God. Just to make sure, they were putting him through unimaginable pain down in interrogation. But they would have been surprised if he had anything relevant to say. Kim was already hounding me about why I had named him.

I could still buy a little more space by naming the, now dead, Bollings. But not much. I had to be much more aggressive in finding Rodrick before my time ran out. Waiting around in the bar might have been preferred but these circumstances called for much more drastic actions. So, I threatened the bartender. Which I kind of felt bad about because he seemed like a good enough guy. The night before, he had even chatted with me a bit. But I couldn't let that interfere with my task. I flashed my ID in front of him and forced him into the back room. I told him that as we spoke, another man that I was interested in was having his testicles sliced off in an interrogation chamber and that if he wanted to avoid the same fate...He crumbled immediately. I mean, why wouldn't he? As tough as the Hand of God clowns might be, they weren't the ones right in front of him talking about giving him an involuntary sex change operation.

According to the bartender, Roderick used to come to the bar for the meetings but that was only about once a month. However, lately, he had been in every Thursday night for the prime rib special, usually alone. Being that it was actually on a Thursday when all of this was happening, I couldn't have been happier. From what the bartender told me, Rodrick would be in just before seven to catch happy hour and the prime rib deal. Since it was only about four, that gave me some serious time to sit around. But, so be it. There are worse places to wait for a man you intend to kill then a good bar.

The Golden Sheep started to really get on my nerves. I couldn't trust the bartender to keep his mouth shut. He might try to warn Rodrick. But I had to pee. So, it came down to wetting my pants or leaving him alone for a few minutes. I could have tied him up or something too, I suppose, but that would have left the place without a bartender. So, I just threatened him and told him to make sure he acted normally and didn't warn anyone that I was there. I even went as far as telling him that if Rodrick didn't show up for some reason, I was going to take it out on him. He pointed out how unfair this was and how it was possible Rodrick wouldn't show up because he was sick or had to go somewhere else or whatever. But I stood firm. I was either going to kill Rodrick that night, or him. The bartender seemed to believe me enough that I could use the restroom without worry. So, I did.

The upside of all this waiting around was that the bartender didn't screw anything up for me. The downside was that, by the time Rodrick arrived for his slab of dead cow, I was a little more drunk than I had planned. It wasn't that I couldn't hold my beer. It was that I hadn't slept all that well and hadn't eaten much and had spent almost four hours in the bar before Rodrick arrived. All of which might explain what I did next.

I followed my own plan and waited until Rodrick went to the men's room, just as I had. Then I put my gun behind his head and walked him out a backdoor into an alley. So far, so good. It was then I kind of messed things up. I accused him of murdering Anna and Boratch. And he admitted it. He not only admitted it, he bragged about it. He said that Anna had been a lot of fun before she had been torched. She had offered to do anything to save her and her father's life and they took her at her word. Rodrick started to really boast as he described the things he and the others had done to Anna. Which, honestly, really wasn't very smart considering I had my gun pointed at him. But he felt that he was untouchable. He was one of the Hand of God, after all. He truly seemed to believe that because he was one of the Cardinal's favored sons, he could do what he pleased and brag about it. Even to me. Even to me, as I held my gun up to his skull.

So, yeah, I shot him. Not like Steve where I shot him quickly a few times and dropped him. One shot at a time the way I had learned from some of my co-workers. An elbow here. An elbow there. A kneecap here. And so on. The screams were loud. Very, very, loud. People came running out of the bar and some nearby stores and saw me there. Saw me shattering various bones and body parts with bullets from my gun. But I kept at it, even with an audience. "Where do I find Fay?" I demanded. Rodrick was too busy screaming to answer. "Where do I find Fay?" I repeated. Rodrick just kept being highly uncooperative and rolling around in agony. "Who's Fay?" someone asked next to me. I turned and saw a homeless guy watching the whole thing. He didn't seem very concerned with any of it. Kind of like seeing one man slowly maim another was an everyday occurrence for him. "Mind your own business!" I yelled. The homeless guy shuffled off. I glared at a few others watching. Most scurried off when I set eyes upon them. No need to get involved with these things. But more than I would have liked still remained to watch all the excitement.

Finally, Rodrick mumbled something. "You suck" he said. "You suck?" That's the best he could do? What a lame, lame thing to say. I mean, sure the man was in considerable pain. But "you suck"? How weak was that? I asked him where Fay was again. He didn't answer. So, I shot him in the crotch. Which wasn't good. I mean, it wasn't good for him, obviously.

I'm sure it hurt a lot. A whole, whole lot. But it also wasn't good for me. Not at all. In hindsight, I guess I kind of overdid it. Roderick died on me. Like, right then. I really hadn't expected that. I had planned to walk away leaving him all broken and shattered and in agony. But no. He died. Right there with me standing over him. Right there in front of eight or nine witnesses who had seen the whole thing.

I had to take control of the situation. I flashed my official ID. "People's Protection Agency. This is official business. Please move along. I'm with People's Protection. Quit gawking and move on unless you want what he got!" Most of the laggards did as instructed and took off. But, even after that, one or two people stayed behind to keep gawking. I was amazed. There was a time when the moment there was any sort of violent incident, people just scattered. Finding witnesses was next to impossible because people just didn't want to get involved. But now, it seemed, people had gotten over that fear. Anything for a bit of entertainment and stories to tell down at the beauty parlor.

I should have them all taken in and interrogated at HQ. That would teach them to be so nosy. Not that I still had the authority to do any such thing. But THEY didn't know that. Why were they all so bold? It was wrong and an affront. I was with the People's Protection Agency and had just tortured and killed a man right in front of them. Doesn't that mean anything to anyone? What's wrong with these people?

I gave up trying to sort it out. It was possible one of the zombies watching had called the police. I didn't want to deal with it. If I had to, I could probably lie my way out of it to Kim, just as I had about Steve. But it would still cause me problems. Kim was already suspicious of me. He knew I had gone rogue. A deadly Federal Agent that would stop at nothing to avenge the murder of his friend and...and...and whatever Anna was.

Given that Rodrick had died before giving me any information beyond the fact that he thought that I sucked, it really was not a rewarding night. I mean, it was in the sense that Rodrick was an asshole who had tortured and murdered Anna and my best friend and paid the price. That was all good. But in terms of where to go next. My only hope was that the Cardinal was such a high-profile man that I could find him and Fay together somewhere. It was plausible enough, given that Fay was the Cardinal's lead security officer. The problem was that finding Fay in those circumstances meant finding Fay in full private army mode. He would be well armed and combat ready. Not to mention, the rest of his unit would be around.

I had to find some means of getting Fay alone and dealing with him one on one. I sensed a stake out in my future. Which wasn't good. For one thing, I found sitting around waiting to see some suspect really boring. I just didn't have the patience for it. But, on a more practical level, a stake out meant more time. I didn't have more time. Not anymore. In the past few days, I'd killed two people in cold blood. It wasn't the best way of keeping a low profile.

In spite of being determined to do something quickly, I went back to the motel. I awoke the next morning feeling pretty rough. There was blood on my sleeve. A lot, actually. It was Rodrick's. I had fallen asleep in my clothes, again. The clothes I had been wearing when I sent that H.O.G. asshole to an early grave. An early, painful, grave. I felt proud. Worried, too, of course. Every time I heard someone in the hallway, I was sure that it was Kim coming to question me or Fay and his H.O.G. pals coming for their revenge. In actuality, the odds of either were fairly remote. I knew enough about how people were tracked down to avoid making the most common mistakes. No credit cards. Deactivation of all GPS systems. That sort of thing. The sort of things that were just common sense to an experienced law enforcement person like myself. Which is why it was such a surprise when I heard a knock on my door.

I pulled out my gun. I considered firing a few rounds through the door, catching my adversary before they could react. Then I realized it was probably the maid. No need to pump her full of lead, empty soap dish aside. I had forgotten to put the "Do Not Disturb" sign out last night. They knocked again. "Who is it?" I asked. "Room Service" said a female voice. Room Service? I hadn't ordered room service. In fact, I was pretty sure that that particular motel didn't have any room service. A fine breakfast buffet, yes. But room service? I don't think so. My finger tensed on the trigger. "Come on Inspector, I know you want to see me." My confusion cleared as I put a face to the voice. Someone from my past. Someone I already knew. Someone that had already caused me way too much trouble for me to ever want to see ever again. And why was she here? I looked through the peep hole and confirmed my conclusion. Isabelle Laughton was standing outside my door. Why was Isabella Laughton standing outside my door?

I put the gun to my side but still held on to it. I opened the door and was greeted by a huge smile. "Morning. You look like shit, Inspector." I pulled her into the room and shut the door behind her. I pointed my gun at her. "How did you find me?" I asked. "I followed you" "When? From where?" "Yesterday. You weren't hard to find after shooting that man and then yelling at everyone about how you were a People's Protection Agent." Her words hit home. I had really screwed the pooch on that one, I had to admit. But at least that little pyro murderer had suffered a bit and paid the price for what he had done. "Is that blood?" she asked. "Yeah" I said. She didn't ask me anything more.

"Why were you following me?" I asked. "Because" she said. "Because? That's your answer, "because"? I asked. She smiled but said nothing. "Is anyone with you?" I asked. "Yeah, in the car. They're waiting for us." "Who is?" I asked. "Friends of mine." I was getting really, really, annoyed that Isabella was being so mysterious. "Look, tell me why you're here and what you're up to. I don't have time for games right now" I said. "I'll say" she chirped, in reply. "I am really running out of patience here. What is this about?" I asked again.

She sat on the edge of my bed. In spite of the tension of the moment, I found myself admiring her long legs with their soft, almost glowing skin. She looked ready to vomit. "Don't be gross. I am, definitely, NOT here for that" she said, a little too definitively for my liking. "So, what then?" I asked. "Your questions will all be answered. You don't know it yet, but this is all a really, really, good thing for you?" she said. "Yeah, how's that?" I asked. "I can't tell you, yet. But trust me. It is. You have no idea how great this is. And how it's all about to turn out so amazing for you." "And I'm supposed to just take your word on it?" I asked. "Yep. It's not like you've got a lot of better options, right now." Sure I did. I could throw her out. I could kill her. I could do all sorts of things. For a girl so frightened about being taken to the back of my car not all that long ago, she was oddly confident of herself. I didn't get it.

"Well, what do you want to do? I can't stay here all day." she said. "I want you to quit playing games and tell me what this is all about." "Nope" she said with a smug look on her face. "Nope?" I asked. "That's right, you either come with me or you don't. Just make up your mind about it, would you?" I still didn't move. She finally caved and gave me a bit more information. "Alright, fine. There's someone you need to meet. Someone that can help you with what you're doing. That's all I'm going to tell you." It wasn't much. But it was enough. Although I knew that I might be walking into a trap, a trap that could end in agonizing pain and death, I took the leap. It was possible Isabella was working with H.O.G. and had put up to all this by her father. Very possible. He was kind of a right winger, being a politically active, energy executive and all. But it didn't feel like that. This was different. And Isabella wasn't the worst company in the world. So, I threw all logic out the window and just went with it.

I followed Isabella out to the parking lot. There was a car waiting for us. A nine-year-old Honda sedan. And it was red. Between that and the early-twenty something guy in the driver's seat wearing a ridiculous hat, it was not very impressive. Somehow, I had expected a black sedan, like we used at People's Protection. Or a massive SUV. Something with presence. Instead, as I climbed into the back seat of the Honda, I felt like I was going on a road trip. A very bad road trip for spring break involving cheap, watery, beer and people yelling "Woooo!!!!" really loudly all the time to give the impression that they were having fun.

"Hey Dan, I'm Frank" the insolent, young, spring breaker driving said to me. "Please call me Chief Inspector" I said. "But you got fired" Isabella pointed out. "Still" I said. "Alright, whatever, Man. It's all good. Got your seat belt on,

Chief Inspector?" Frank asked. I assured him that I did. Let the partying begin.

I tried a few times to get Frank and Isabella to tell me more as we drove. They wouldn't. They just talked about the weather and how nice it was to have some sunshine after all the rain. We drove for about two hours heading west out of the city. It was actually an interesting drive. We went past the industrial district. Then past the Seminary of St. Jude. Then past the park. And then, country. Wide open, green as could be, country. Of course, there were tacky houses scattered here and there behind faux stone walls. But still, the effect was all very pleasant. Just me and the kids out for a drive in the country. No fears at all. No H.O.G.. No worries that I was being driven to painful torture followed by a merciful execution. It all just felt right. As if it had always been meant to be.

We turned down a long dirt road and, eventually, arrived at a large farm house. A really great, old, house. One built back when people cared that places would stand more than twenty years. A couple of dogs off their leash walked up to the car to greet us. And there were horses. Lots of amazing horses just slowly roaming around their pen. I liked this place. I saw a few more people out in the fields. They were all young, like Isabella and Frank. They were also all disturbingly good looking. For a moment I wondered if I had discovered some secret cloning facility for the beautiful people. "Come on.

You'll have plenty of time to explore the farm, later" Isabella said. She led me into the house.

The house was a good size but not extravagantly large. It was the perfect size, really. I heard people down the hallway in what must have been a kitchen. At least, I assumed it was, the way they were going on about how wonderfully the tomatoes had turned out. Isabella stopped in front of a stairway leading to the second floor. She looked at me. "Go upstairs, end of the hallway to your right, into the bedroom. Then take off all your clothes and wait." I didn't move. Isabella just kept looking at me. For a moment, I briefly considered that I had already died. Maybe in the confrontation with Rodrick? At my apartment? Was I dead right now lying in my trashed apartment and didn't know it? How else could I explain it all. This all too perfect, idyllic house. This beautiful, young girl ordering me to her bedroom to strip and wait for her. It was all so..."Frank will be up to take your clothes and gun and to make sure you are not armed in any way." Oh, that makes sense. Wait. Frank? "I'd rather have you search me, if you don't mind" I suggested. "Don't be gross" she said. "Then it's off. I'm not putting myself in that position. I said. "Fine. Then we'll just take you back to your crappy motel or messed up apartment. Between the police and all the other enemies you've made, there's a good chance they will already be there looking for you." A valid enough point. But she wasn't done.

"Or you could go upstairs, do what I say, and find out who killed your best friend and the woman you loved." "I already know who killed them" I corrected. And who said anything about loving Anna? "Yeah but do you have any idea how to make them pay for what they did? You're never going to be able to get to Fay on your own" she said. "How do you know about Fay?" I asked. Isabella grinned. "So, it's up to you. If you want Frank to take you home, that's fine. Or you can quit stalling and show a little cooperation. Believe it or not, we really did bring you out here so we could help you" she said. "Who's we?" I asked. "Frank, it looks like you'll be driving Daniel home" she said. "Alright, alright. I'll go upstairs" I said. I hated being forced into things. But, whatever. It seemed as sensible a thing to do as any other option. What's the worst they could do to me, completely unarmed, naked, and in the middle of nowhere?

I went up to the bedroom and did as asked. It wasn't nearly as enjoyable as I had first imagined. It was a bit cold, for one thing. But the real downer was Frank walking in. Being strip searched by that little twerp was truly degrading. Did they really expect to find a loaded pistol up my ass? I tried not to think about it as it was happening and just stared out the window. The view could have been something out of one of those old, overpriced paintings. Lots of green and little clouds in the sky. But I wasn't exactly in a position to enjoy the view. And if Frank showed any enjoyment from what he was doing to me I would kill him. Luckily for both of us, he seemed to hate the process as much as I did.

"Satisfied?" I said, immediately regretting my choice of words. 'Yeah, you're good. Thanks" He threw me a towel. Put this on, if you want. I need to keep your clothes for now." "Why?" "Because you're about to meet somebody who has some answers for you" he said. "And they have a problem with people wearing clothes?" I asked. Frank just smiled. "It will be fine, Dan, I mean, Chief Inspector. Just trust us. We really are trying to help you" he said. "So you all keep saying." He took my clothes and left me there with my towel. It was very uncomfortable and very cold. I was not enjoying myself, in the least.

I didn't have my cell phone with me anymore or a watch. In fact, it was safe to assume these people were going through all my things looking for information. There were a few calls on my phone which might have been of interest to them. But they already knew about Rodrick and Fay. So, maybe not. Time dragged. And that little towel did not do a lot to keep the draft through the window from coming in.

Finally, I heard someone walking up the stairs. I really hoped it wasn't Frank again. Or someone about to kill, maim, or otherwise do horrible things to me. I was really regretting how I had let myself end up in this position. I had thought it was worth the risk to get the information I needed. But now I wasn't so sure. I was pretty certain, in hindsight, that allowing myself to be driven off to some secret location, disarmed and stripped was not really the best of plans. But it was too late now.

The steps got closer. Light steps. Female steps. Isabella? Perverse fantasies aside, I really didn't feel like dealing with the brat under these circumstances. The door opened. I saw a hand. A female hand. A woman walked in. A shockingly gorgeous woman wearing a white dress and heels. She was old. Close to my age. But her body was amazing. Not lithe and limber and gazelle-like but more porno actress amazing, except with real body parts. Maybe. I couldn't really tell through the dress. Then I saw her face and those eyes and realized who it was. It was her. It was the woman I had seen at the foam church incident. The leader of the Clear Thinkers.

"Hello, Daniel" she said. She walked in and closed the door behind her. I thought about standing up but, given the towel-only situation, thought better of it. "How do you know my name?" I asked. What a dumb question. But she answered anyway. "I know a lot about you. Not as much as I would like, though" she said. So, she was here to interrogate me. I get it. Not gonna happen. "Then you know I'm cold and really not enjoying sitting here in just a towel." She smiled understandingly. "I'm sorry. I know it seems extreme but there have been several attempts on my life recently. The last involved a woman who hid a razorblade on her person and came to me in my bed." I tried not to get distracted by the lesbian porn memories going on in my brain and went back to the security issue. The razor. "On her person? You mean, in her ass? Some woman shoved a razorblade up her ass and tried to kill you with it?" I asked. "Not her ass. Here.." She gestured to her crotch. Now, that seemed like a very bad idea all the way around. Anything for the cause, I guess. "Who was she?" I asked. "Just another misguided soul who had been brainwashed."

I finally understood why it was Isabella who had come to fetch me. She was one of them. A member of the cult. Was her father also? "What are you thinking?" my hostess asked. "Is Isabella Laughton one of you, then?" "Yes" she replied. "Is her father?" I asked. My hostess looked disappointed and confused by the question. "Don't be ridiculous. Michael Laughton is about as neoconservative, right wing, profits-at-all-costs as any man in the country. Isabella just helped us borrow him for a while to raise some money." "Don't you mean kidnap? For what?" I asked. "All in good time. I'll tell you that and a whole lot more, very soon." "Why not now?" I asked. She didn't answer.

"You know, it's really not fair that you have me here, like this, and you're just standing there refusing to answer my questions. I took a lot of risk by doing this..." "You had nowhere else to go" she said. "Of course, I did" I insisted. "They would have found you." "Who?" I asked. "I'm not sure. But someone. By now, one of them would have found you and killed you." It was a pretty cocky thing to say. It was probably true. But still. She really had no right to sound so sure of herself, like that. "Fine, can I at least get my clothes back then?" I asked. "Don't you want to know my name?" she asked. "Sure, what's your name?" "I'm Karen. I am the founder of the Clear Thinkers." "Well, Karen. I'm cold and feel really uncomfortable sitting here, like this, in just a towel. Can I please get my clothes back?" "I'm sorry. I can't do that" she said. "Look, I have no razors, guns, knives or weapons shoved anywhere they shouldn't be. I also don't have any sewn into my clothes. I'm just cold." "I'm sorry I can't take that risk" she responded. I was not happy with her attitude. Not at all. Which must have showed."Would you feel more comfortable if I took off my clothes, too?" she asked. I wasn't sure if I had heard right. Well?" she prompted. The strangest thing of all was that I knew I should say "no." Seeing Karen naked was going to be one mighty big distraction. A memorable one to be sure. But I wasn't there for that. I was there to find out how to get to Fay and the Cardinal and to make them pay for what they had done.

Too late. Karen must have taken my silence for a "yes." She had already started to slip off her dress. I could have stopped her. I should have stopped her. But who am I to demand that a stunning, built-like-a-brick-shithouse woman remain fully clothed if she felt like getting naked for me? So, she kept going. Layer after layer of her clothing removed. All at just the right pace, so that I could fully enjoy the show. Soon, she was standing in front of me wearing only her high heels. Oh, my, she was gorgeous.

"Better?" she asked. "Yeah, much." I replied. "I'm glad you approve. Very glad" she said. And then she walked just a little bit closer. "Now tell me about your investigation" she said. I felt sucker punched. Was this naked woman in front of me with the most gorgeous, perfect, body I had ever seen, really expecting me to have a serious conversation with her right now? No way. Couldn't do it. Not humanly possible. "Just kidding" she said. And with that, Karen walked over to me and kissed me. Kissed me in the best of ways. And then sometime, shortly afterward, my towel got misplaced. Oh, it was magnificent. Her body. The things we did to each other. The setting. We spent the next several hours getting to know each other, very, very well. If only I could just stay in that moment forever. But it wasn't meant to be.

The next morning, I woke up with Karen in my arms. She was so beautiful. And she even smelled good. My own aroma, on the other hand, I couldn't vouch for. A shower and some time alone in the bathroom would probably be a good idea. There was a soft knock on the door. Karen stirred awake just as Isabella peered in. "They're almost ready for you?" Isabella said. "Ok. Thanks" Karen said. And then Isabella shut the door again and left. Karen sat up and started to put her clothes back on. "Do you really have to do that?" I asked. "Couldn't you just stay here, with me, a little longer. I might get cold." "I got you a blanket last night" Karen said as she started to cover up that Aphrodite-like body of hers. "It's not the same" I said. "Do you want me to ask Isabella to come in here to take my place?" she asked. I couldn't tell if she was serious or not. So, I covered my bases. "Maybe, later. Right now, you. Here. With me" I said. "Sorry, there are things that need to be looked after. Things that matter to you as much as me." "What does that mean?" I asked. "Soon. Very soon, actually. But right now you should take a shower and eat something. It could be a long day." "Why?" I asked. She leaned over and kissed me. Seeing her in her dress made me only want to rip it off of her. "I'll have Frank bring your clothes and some clean towels up" I tried to think of a quip to make about the towel I already had but came up empty. "I'll see you in a bit" she said. And then she left, closing the door behind her.

I braced myself. At any second thugs could storm through the door and start doing horrible, painful, things to me. I knew I was being set up. As good looking and charismatic as I was, it didn't quite explain why Karen was so eager to get naked for me. And sleep with me. And be the most fantastic sex partner I had ever, ever, had. By a lot. I started to enjoy my thoughts and memories. Even indulge in them. But "no" I had to snap out of it and deal with the reality of the situation. I had been lured out here and seduced, or attemptedly seduced. I had, yet, to understand why. Why were Karen and the Clear Thinkers being so nice to me?

Frank brought up my clothes. The t-shirt, socks and underwear had all been washed. He showed me to the shower and told me breakfast would be ready for me when I came down to the kitchen. There was even a razor and shaving cream provided if I wanted to shave. Which I didn't. But it was a nice gesture. All in all, the service was better than any hotel I had ever stayed in. Everything I needed was provided. And breakfast, of course, was outstanding. Everything was from the farm. The eggs. The pork sausage. The potatoes. It was prepared very simply and in large portions. Exactly what I needed after a night of strenuous, mind-blowing, sex with Karen.

Which is why I was really annoyed when Isabella came to the kitchen and told everyone that it was time. "Time for what?" I asked. Nobody answered. They all just started walking out the door. I was really annoyed I didn't get to finish my eggs. But, I was the guest, after all, and should show a little gratitude. Isabella held the door for me as I followed the others out the screen door. They were walking toward a stone building out in the field. From the looks of it, there were at least twenty or thirty people all headed that way. I did not see Karen among them.

"Where's Karen?" I asked. "You really like her, don't you?" Isabella asked. "I just met her" I said. Isabella just grinned.

We walked across the field and waited behind the crowd of people trying to shove their way through the doorway. For a decent-sized building, the doorway was pretty inadequate. Then again, I suppose it's not every day that thirty people try to cram inside of it for whatever we were all doing here. Inside, I just saw a dirt floor and lots of people standing around. Isabella gently cleared them away and led me through. People were staring at me. I didn't like it. It wasn't a good kind of staring. And then I saw the top of the stake. A stake. They were going to burn me alive at the stake!

I turned and tried to get out. My way was blocked by the crowd. "Where are you going?! This is for you" Isabella said. Yeah, a stake and kindling made special, just for me, courtesy of H.O.G. and the Clear Thinkers. How did those two groups ever get together? I felt a couple of hands grab me. Large, beefy hands. An extraordinarily large, young, man, a real farm boy type, had stopped me. I was just about to deliver him an expert kick when I heard another voice. "Daniel!" it said. It was Karen's voice. For whatever reason, I halted what would have been a devastatingly effective attack on the young lad in my way and turned to face her. "Daniel. Where are you going? This is all for you. We brought him here for you" she said. It was hard for my eyes to leave Karen's ever so captivating face.

But they did. They slowly saw what was behind her. A stake and kindling, just as I had deduced. But the spot atop the wood was already taken. It was not me they were going to burn alive. It was Fay.

I recognized him from the photo Steve had shown me. He was gagged and bound to the stake. "How did you get him?" I asked. "It wasn't difficult" Karen said. Right. It wasn't difficult to kidnap a superbly trained, psychotic killer who commanded a well armed, private security force. But, I suppose that didn't really matter. What DID matter was that Fay, the man who had done something unforgivable to my friend and Anna was there in front of me. The anguish of that loss came welling back up within me. As wonderful as the last day had been, nothing could really erase that feeling. But watching Fay burn would help. A lot.

So, I stood there as one of the farm workers/cult members handed Karen a flaming torch. An actual, real, historic-type, torch. Which, honestly, took me out of the moment a little. Between the dress she was wearing and the way she held it, I found myself thinking of the Statue of Liberty for some reason. But then I turned to look at Fay again, and snapped right out of it. I hated that man more than I had hated anyone in my life. I knew that Roderick was just the dumb side-kick and that Fay was the real instigator. I couldn't wait to see him in agony.

I kept waiting for Karen to light him up. But she didn't. She stood there looking at me. They all stood there looking at me. I finally understood. I took the torch from Karen. Nobody said I word as I got closer to Fay atop his combustible pedestal. He saw me and struggled in vain to break free. Terror filled his eyes. I got within feet of him. He deserved this and a whole lot more. Then I stepped back and lowered the flame. And...nothing. The kindling wouldn't light. I tried again. Still nothing. Fay was freaking out. The false starts were a cruelty he hadn't expected. Karen came over to me. Her eyes met mine. Then she grabbed my arm with the torch in it and lowered it very slowly. She directed the flame to a very specific spot in the pile of wood. And held it just so. Her and I, together, managed to light the wood and send Fay to his excruciating death.

It was shortly afterward that I was handed the, seemingly empty, vile. The one everybody was in awe of. The one that, according to the members of The Clear Thinkers, would kill God and change the world forever. After the initial shock of the claim, it started to sink in. And, oddly, start to make a lot of sense.

The logic went like this...San Sebastian found, during his Alzheimer's study, that the craving for a higher power was biologically based. No matter who you were and where you were born, you had a certain amount of these particular brain chemicals. Which meant there was a very, very, good chance you would believe in some sort of higher spiritual power. It was as basic a human need as eating. However, the Church, being the Church, couldn't just leave things alone. Instead, they developed the drug, Epiphany, to make those chemicals stronger and, in theory, make people more fervent believers. Hence, more likely to follow their cause. It all sounded pretty logical. Like total heresy. But logical. So, the chemicals had been discovered and well researched by Life Gen with secret backing from the Church.

Unfortunately for them, San Sebastian's assistant, Deborah Marky, was a double agent. She had been a Clear Thinker for years. She delivered all the Epiphany research to Karen. I can only imagine the hot and lusty reward Deborah got for that, given Karen's lovely welcome to me. But...Crap. I forgot what I was talking about. Right, so Deborah Marky had the sex of her life but was discovered by H.O.G. and cooked Medium-Well on the stake for it. But she had done something absolutely huge for the Clear Thinkers. By studying the research from Life Gen, research that the Church, itself, paid for, they came to a conclusion. If God was only a chemical in the brain, and that chemical could be manipulated, why not go the other way? Why not find a way to remove that chemical or make it inactive? No chemical. No God. God is dead and the world is free from tyranny and religion for all time. Or maybe Karen said, the tyranny OF religion. I can't really remember. But it was something like that.

The difficult part for the Clear Thinkers hadn't been finding a way to make the brain chemical inert. Life Gen had done such good research, that part came quite easily. It was how they were going to get their new Reverse-Epiphany drug inside of people. They couldn't exactly go around and force people by gunpoint to take a pill. They needed to weaponize it somehow. Which is where Isabella had, apparently, come in.

It wasn't clear how long Isabella had been a member of the Clear Thinkers. However, it was really clear from Karen's mention of her role, and the applause from the others, that she had done good. She had arranged the kidnapping of her own father, Mike Laughton. Having his trust and all the inside information she needed, made that a fairly simply task. At least from the way they were talking about it. Nobody ever mentioned what would have happened if Laughton's K & R Insurance hadn't ponied up the ransom. I guess it didn't matter, since they did. They paid the Clear Thinkers a boatload of cash for Laughton's safe release. That money was then used for the research into how they made the Reverse-Epiphany drug something people could catch easily. They developed a process which made it airborne and highly contagious. In the end, everyone's brain chemicals would be altered. There would be no natural yearning for a higher power. There would be no God.

After the stake burning and presentation of the vile, the crowd started to walk back toward the main house. Karen, however, was leading me in the opposite direction, out further into the field. As much as I hoped it was for a quickie in the grass, I was pretty sure it wasn't. "You have a real gift for public speaking" I said. "Thanks." "You're a great leader" I added. She didn't say anything. Which was odd. Karen loved to talk. Especially about her cause. "Are you Ok?" I asked. She nodded. "Just nervous. You know how it is when you spend your entire life working toward something and then you finally get it. It's a head trip. And trust me when I tell you this is not something we do lightly. I have spent many a sleepless night asking myself what right I have to do this. Or if it makes me as evil as the very people we are trying to weaken." "Which people are those?" I asked. I got that little look of disappointment from Karen that I already dreaded. "I think you know the answer to that. Marx had it right. It just took us a while to figure out what to do about it." I nodded but, honestly, wasn't sure what that meant. I mean, of course, in a general sense...

My thoughts were interrupted as Karen pointed to a large structure in the direction we were headed. "That's where we do all of our research. It used to be pig pens. Kind of ironic, don't you think?" she said. "Ironic? Oh, H.O.G. Got it" I said. "I could show it to you but there's not much to see but a bunch of stainless steel machines. "No, that's Ok. So, where are we going then?" I asked. She pointed just past the larger structure. "There" she said. There was a very small house just up ahead. So small that it could have fit inside San Sebastian's kitchen. Or Anna's, for that matter. "What's that?" I asked. "Proof" she said. "Proof of what?" "That everything I've told you, and all of them for that matter, isn't just lies. That I'm not just some delusional crazy woman starting a commune." I wanted to ask more but decided the best thing to do was to just keep quiet. A rare moment for me.

A few minutes later we reached the tiny little house in the field. Karen knocked on the door. I was shocked when a very familiar face appeared and welcomed us. It was Father Mike. "Hey Dan, come on in." Mike was wearing street clothes. Not uncommon for him. He showed us into the house. I was still too stunned to say anything. He guided us into the living room. It was so small I had to sit right up against Karen on the sofa. "What are you doing here?" I asked. "I came yesterday when they said they were finally going to bring you out to the farm. It was my idea, you know. I recommended you." I had no idea what he was talking about. "What?" I asked. "They asked me who I thought was capable of doing it and I said you, right away." The way he was talking it felt like he wanted me to thank him. Given that I was still a little unsure about everything, I wasn't anywhere near ready to do that.

"You must be excited?" he said. "About what?" I asked. "Sunday." "Sunday?" I asked. "Yeah, the..." Karen cut him off. "We haven't gotten that far, yet. Daniel had some more questions first." "Alright, shoot?" he said. Father Mike seemed as chipper as ever. "How about why are you here?" I asked. "To help." Right. "Do you know what these people are planning? And about this drug-germ thing they want to release and what it, supposedly, does?" I asked. Mike smiled. "Sure." I kept sitting there. "And you're Ok with that?" I asked. "Yeah, I am" he responded. "But you're a Priest" I pointed out. "You mean, I was." And then he started to explain.

First of all, he corrected himself. He actually was still a Priest. But only technically. He didn't see things the way he used to. Yet, he never actually left the Priesthood. What had happened was a little complicated. Karen had approached him and challenged him. She said that she could make him see that he had spent his entire life believing in, and spreading lies about, something that didn't exist. And that people like him were being used by others for personal gain and to maintain a stranglehold on power. Father Mike, being Father Mike, accepted her challenge.

He openly admitted to her, as he had many times to me, previously, that religion was often abused and used in horrible ways. It's been that way since the beginning of time. But that didn't make religion wrong. It made the people that committed those abuses wrong. It was like blaming a handgun for a murder instead of the person that pulled the trigger. His words, not mine. Anyway, so, he debated with Karen for a while and he became more and more intrigued. Being that Father Mike was a straight up, always horny male, was probably a factor too. Karen was, obviously, someone men liked to spend time with. In any case, they talked and talked and finally Karen presented her claim that God was just a bunch of chemicals in the brain. Something created long ago but useless for modern man, much like an appendix. And, much like an appendix, something which could get inflamed and actually cause harm.

Father Mike seemed to love rehashing the whole back story. He was actually excited about the subject. "So, I kept telling her, if chemicals in the brain did such things, then God put them there. And that maybe it wasn't to make us crave God so much as to be able to hear him." That sounded like Father Mike, alright. A good point too, come to think of it. I guess. "But then she laid down the gauntlet. She said that if I was so sure God existed, and always would exist, that I would be immune to her drug. I said "yes I would be." But I had no desire to be messing around with the chemicals in my brain. So, I declined." Once again, I felt lost and wondering what the point of his story was. "And then Karen changed my mind" he said. He grinned. "She gave me the Anti-Epiphany infection when we had sex." How biblical of her. The Godless seductress tempts the faithful Priest and destroys him with one act of carnal passion. How absolutely annoying. What an idiot.

And why was Father Mike fine with that? She lied to him. Or at the very least, didn't tell him that she would infect him during sex. Wait. Did she do the same thing to me. Was I infected? "Do I have this thing now!?" I blurted. Karen turned to me calmly. "Yes" she said. "Is it dangerous?" I asked. "No more dangerous than the ideology and myths of religion" she said. "What does that mean? Don't give me that! I want a real answer!" I was angry. Really angry. I mean, the sex was great and all, no doubt about it. But I'm not sure it was worth scrambling my brain chemicals for. I felt violated. She had no right! Father Mike tried to calm me down.

"Dan, it's fine. There are no complications or side effects. I can personally attest to that. I feel better than I have in ages" he said. "So, shouldn't I be feeling something? Anything?" I asked. "There's no pain or loss of brain function, if that's what you're worried about" he reassured me. I looked over to Karen. She was looking very content. Too content. She had tricked me. I wouldn't forgive her easily for that. "As for the other thing" Father Mike added. "What other thing?" I asked. "The effects of the contagion on faith." "Oh, that" I said. "There's a seventy-two hour incubation period. You won't feel anything physical. You'll just look back at some of the things you used to do, and used to say, and feel very, very stupid."

For some reason, Father Mike's words really depressed me. I wasn't so worried about myself, I was used to feeling stupid. But I hadn't devoted my life to the Word of God. He had spent his entire adult life as the spokesman for something he no longer seemed to believe in. There was something incredibly sad about that. It kind of sucked. "You really regret all the things you used to do with the Church?" I asked. "No, not by any stretch. The idea of hope, charity, looking out for your fellow man...I still believe in all of that. That's why I don't mind staying with the Priesthood as long as necessary and continuing my work with the Mission." "As long as necessary?" I asked. "Until the bio-agent is released and starts to take hold in the populace" he said.

"So, you aren't angry with Karen? You don't want their plan to fail?" I asked. "No. I credit Karen for opening my eyes and seeing the world for what it is. It's an amazing, beautiful, astonishing place. We don't need myths to help us appreciate that." My head was spinning. Father Mike, my Father Mike, was saying things that went against everything that he had been telling me my entire life. He couldn't have made the adjustment that easily. "But that means you believe your whole life was lies!" I said. Father Mike looked at me very calmly. "Not all of it. Like I said, a lot of it I still believe in and think is worth fighting for. The world needs caring. The world needs compassion. But, yes, part of it was lies. I bought into the lies and now I know better. Soon you will know better too. Soon everyone will. The entire world will finally have clarity." Clarity. Like clear. As in Clear Thinkers. It was then that it occurred to me that there was another very plausible answer to

Father Mike's conversion. One far less complicated than brain chemical deadening, bio-agent, germs. Father Mike was pussy whipped.

Eventually, Karen said we had to get back. The rest of the group was waiting in the main house. I was feeling very unsettled. Seeing Father Mike disavow all that he had stood for was really a shock to the system. "Are you Ok?" Karen asked. "Not really" I responded. "Do you want to talk about it?" "Do you want to tell me why you did this to me?" I asked. "Did what, to you?" "Put me in this position. Gave me this brain altering germ thing. All of it" I said. "It's a lot to comprehend at once" she replied. "You think?"

We went back to the house. They were waiting for us. A meeting was about to begin in the living room. Everyone was standing around looking very happy as they waited for Karen to start. It was all fun and games for them. I suppose I could understand why they were so excited. They had spent years getting to this point. Years of silly conceptual art pieces masquerading as terrorism. Years of knowing that Windsor and his Anti-Terror Division were trying to hunt them down and kill them. And now they were almost there. The final plan was ready.

Karen was handed a map. It was of the city. There was something circled on it. "The Cardinal will be leading a sermon at St. Anthony's Cathedral." She pointed to the part of the map that was marked. They are returning to the site of their foam stunt. How original. How convenient...Then the penny dropped. Karen was as clever as she was hot. The foam incident I had witnessed was the rehearsal. A way of learning the ins and outs of the Cathedral. "We will release the bio-agent from here." She pointed to something on the map, several inches from the Cathedral. "The Bank of Nations Tower. Specifically, its roof." People nodded. "According to our calculations, the wind will blow the released agent directly toward the Cathedral and its occupants, including the Cardinal. He and his minions will be plunged into a crisis of faith. Their followers will question all the lies they have been told and all the evil they have done in the name of their God. The corrupt, dictatorial, Church leadership will be some of the very first, after us, to see the world as it is. They will be some of the very first to achieve clarity!" The crowd applauded. Which was really disturbing. The way Karen used the word "clarity" and the response it got reminded me way too much of a government rally. A very bad government rally involving lots of flags and brown shirts. Then again, she was mighty hot when she got excited like that.

Someone in the audience yelled a question. "Do we have any predictions how long it will take for the contagion to reach a hundred percent penetration?" What a dick. Why couldn't he just ask how long until everybody got brain altered? Penetration. What a pretentious ass. "Our computer models show a ninety-three percent conversion rate in no more than three months following the initial airborne release." "Worldwide?" someone else asked. It was Frank. The twerp who had strip searched me. "No, nationally. Worldwide we are a little less certain of but we think about a year" Karen said. "With the same success rate?" Frank asked. "No, probably, slightly lower. More like eighty-percent. But keep in mind, we always have the option of further dispersions." If this speech was supposed to get my all hyped up to be part of this thing, it wasn't working. People were sounding a lot like the officials I had to deal with at People's Protection when they came up with their latest schemes to make the world a safer place. They also seemed to gloss over a few tiny things.

"Excuse me" I said. "Yes, Dan?" Karen asked. "I can tell you, first hand, that the Bank of Nations Tower is a highly secure facility. How, exactly, do you intend to get up on the roof without being detected?" People looked at me. I mean, people already were looking at me because I asked the question. But people were looking at me differently. Like I was the class idiot. It wasn't a dumb question. Why were they all looking at me like that? "Sorry, Dan, we had already covered that, previously. The short answer is we won't" Karen said. "You lost me" I said. "We won't. But you will. With your position at the People's Protection Agency, I can't imagine you will have any trouble accessing the roof." I wasn't surprised. II had a feeling she was going to say something like that. How nice of them to assume that I was already on board. I was pissed. "It won't be that easy" I said. "Yes, it will. We have already made a reservation for you and your date at Cloud." "Cloud?" I asked. "The penthouse restaurant. You have a reservation for brunch on Sunday, the day of the sermon." "And the roof? How do I get from Cloud to the roof?" I asked. "I doubt with your official ID and professional demeanor that you will have any difficulty in that" she said. That was one of us. That is, if I was even going along with this whole thing. "And who is...?" I started to ask. "Me. I'm your date. If that's what you were going to ask." "It was. Thanks." I shut up then. I had too much to figure out.

There were two things I had to decide. The first was if I even wanted to be a part of this whole cause. I owed them something for Fay and avenging Anna and Boratch's death. And Karen being so nice to me in the bedroom. But she did infect me with something on purpose. It wasn't herpes or gonorrhea but still. She had no right to do that. And then there was the whole practical part of the equation. Would their plan even work? I could easily get busted in the Bank Tower. I wasn't, officially, even an agent anymore. Not to mention, Karen was my date. Karen, cult leader and now a wanted terrorist for the kidnapping of Mike Laughton. It all just sounded like a very bad idea to me.

I told Karen I needed to go somewhere to think things over. Somewhere other than the farm house with all those people looking at me. She asked me to come with her for another walk. It was good to just get away from the crowd. "There's another little house like the one Mike was in that you could stay in" she said. "That sounds good. A little privacy would do me a lot of good right now." She looked at me with concern. "You don't believe in our cause, do you?" she asked. Uh-oh. I wasn't sure if I was ready to get into that with her, yet. "I don't know" I said. A shockingly honest answer from the likes of me. "That's Ok. Give it a little time to absorb. People forget that they have been living with all these plans and ideas for months already and you haven't. It's all just common knowledge to them" she said. "I had a feeling everyone but me already knew the whole plan" I replied. "Yeah, they did. But I wanted to go over it with them again" she said. "To get them motivated" "To inspire them, yes." "You're good at that" I said. "Good at what?" "Inspiring people. You really are a natural leader" I said. "So, how do I inspire you?" she asked. I was expecting some sexual innuendo or at least a seductive look. I got neither. Just a very serious, calm, face. "Just give me some time" I said.

I asked about something else that had been bothering me. "Why didn't you just wait?" I said. She didn't seem to know what I was asking. "Why didn't you just wait until your drug had made me one of you?" I asked. "Being affected by the bio-agent wouldn't have automatically made you one of us" she corrected. "Fine. But you know what I mean. Why didn't you just wait longer until after we had sex before telling me the plan?" I asked. She smiled. "When did you figure that out?" she asked. "In the meeting. It doesn't make any sense to me. Couldn't you have found a way to have your way with me a little sooner?" She laughed. "Have my way with you? It seems to me, it was the other way around" she said. "Right. You bend males to your will. Not like I'm saying it's a bad thing. But you know you do. We are putty in your hands." "Yeah" she said. "Well, at least you admit it" I said. "Yeah" she said again.

"But to answer your question, we talked about it. A lot. There were a lot of people in the group that said it was too much of a risk to ask you to participate before your body fully processed the chemicals." "Which makes total sense to me. That's the way I would have done it" I said. "It absolutely, positively makes the most sense on a practical level. You would be much easier to persuade, probably, if we had slept together for the first time last week instead of last night. But it's more complicated than that." I tried not to focus on the wording of "sleeping together for the first time." As in, there would be more times coming (bad puns aside). Luckily, she continued and pulled me out of that train of thought. "As hard as it might be to believe, I'm really not about winning at any cost. There needs to be limits. There needs to be rules." "You lost me. You're a terrorist. Your need is to win. Period" I said. "No, I don't buy that. I disagree."

At which point Karen went into a very long, and beautiful, speech about the nature of free will. How her hatred of religion, or more specifically, how religion was used, was that it went against the idea of people being responsible for their actions. To her, saying it was God's will was a cop out. And she realized that, in spite of any practical benefits, forcing or manipulating people into things for her cause was no different.

It took ten minutes and listening to her go on and on about all sorts of grand philosophical issues. But eventually she got back to answering the question I had asked so long ago I could barely remember what it was by then. "The reason we didn't let the drug fully incubate in you, was that it was cheating. What we are asking you to do is huge. Massive. Don't think we don't realize that." "Cheating?" I said. "Yes, cheating. You need to make the decision to help us or not based on your own free will. It is very important to me that it be your choice. Not something forced upon you" she said. I understood her answer. And appreciated it. But I thought it was nuts. In my world, you got people to do what you needed them to do by using whatever means necessary. Cheating? What a silly idea. But I guess that's just the way Karen just thought about things.

We eventually reached a little house not far from Father Mike's and the converted pig pen. It hardly had any furniture in it. But it was clean. And it was away from everyone, which is what I needed most. "Is Father Mike still there?" I asked. "No, actually. He had to get back to the Mission. He should be back tomorrow though. Why?" "I just wanted to talk to him again. He's a good guy to talk to" I said. "Yeah, he is." She stood by the door as I looked around. "Do you want some company or do you want to be left alone?" she asked. As hard as it is to believe, I actually turned down her offer of companionship. She would have been a great distraction. A very fun, curvy, sexually masterful, distraction. But a distraction all the same. All she said was "Ok. I'll come back later to bring you some dinner. Unless you feel like joining us in the house, of course." "No, I won't. Thanks. See you then, then" I said. But then she didn't move. "You really don't want me to stay?" she asked. "No, I really don't." She seemed thrown off. "Huh. I don't think that's really ever happened to me before. Interesting." And then she left. What an ego. Yes she was hot and the best sex ever and willing to do all the perverse and kinky things you fantasized about. But still.

I ran after her and said I had changed my mind. She tried not to show it but she knew that I would. I mean, come on. Do you really think I would turn that down? I won't get into the vulgar details of the next several hours. I'll just say, simply, Oh, My Lord, it was mind blowing.

Karen finally excused herself for a bit of a break. I was a stud machine and I could understand her need for time to recuperate. She told me that she was going to go back to the main house for a while. She would be back later with dinner. The time apart from her gave me time to consider all the things I had been told. Or should have considered. But I was too happy and tired to think. I wondered if this was what she had done to Father Mike to make him such a convert. But, eventually, with the help of some coffee, I refocused. I was able to think about everything that had happened to get me to this point. I was able to really ponder what the Clear Thinkers were about and what they wanted to do. I was even able to reach a very, very important decision. Monumental, in fact. I finally understood what my entire purpose in life was. What it was all for. Why it had been so hard. And, most importantly, why I never really had a choice in things at all.

Karen returned that evening with a fantastic meal. She even brought me a very tasty little dessert. The next morning, I woke up in bed with Karen, naked to one side, and Isabella, naked on the other. Sandwiched between the lithe young, not so innocent, gazelle and Karen, with her porn queen looks and skills to match, I was one happy camper. The night had been one of debauchery and depravity in the most amazing of ways. I kept looking from one side to the other, admiring and remembering. Karen was completely exposed and lying on top of the sheet. A top ten sight in my life, if ever there was. However, Isabella had covered herself. I didn't approve. I carefully grabbed the sheet from under her chin and, ever so slowly, pulled it down. It was like unwrapping a gift all over again. "What are you doing?" Isabella asked. Busted. "Just admiring. You are a very beautiful girl" I said. "Whatever. I want to sleep more" she said. "Tired after last night's work out. I understand. I guess I wasn't so gross after all" I said. "No, you are. You're old." "Isabella!" Karen admonished. I hadn't noticed that she had awakened. "She's grouchy in the mornings, you should leave her alone" Karen said. "Fine" I said. What a cruel answer. I'll show her old.

Karen must have seen how hurt I was. "Say your sorry, Isabella." "Whatever." Isabella leaned up and let the sheet fall from her firm, lean body. That skin...Then she kissed me. Her eyes were mostly closed and she still looked half-asleep. But it was still quite nice. "You're not that gross" she said. "Thanks." "But you suck for scaring me like you did" she said. "Last night? You mean that thing with the butter?" "No, not that thing with the butter. When you threw me into the back of your car. You were such a dick." I remembered the incident as if it were yesterday.

Actually, it wasn't that long ago. Which was scary. So much had happened since then.

It was that morning after coming from San Sebastian's and going to Kimmel's. Isabella was such a little brat. "It seems to me you deserved a good scare for showing such disrespect. I'm sorry that dealing with someone like me is so traumatic for so many people" I said. "No, you aren't. You love it. It's an ego thing with you." "Don't make me have Karen spank you, again" I said. "Whatever, pervert. That's not why I was scared. Karen had just recruited me the day before. I was high as a kite and finally felt like my life meant something. And then you showed up like that..." Oh. That made sense. "Wait, but you were the one mouthing off. That doesn't seem very smart" I pointed out. "Whatever. You're not going to let me go back to sleep, are you?" she asked. "So, how did Karen recruit you?" I asked. Isabella looked over to Karen. "It's alright, you can tell him." Isabella sat up. "The same way she recruited you" she said. "Which was?" Isabella sat up and gestured over Karen's naked body. I wasn't getting it. She did the gesture again. "Look at her. She's gorgeous. I mean, I already had my problems with the Church and the way things were and then she threw THAT into the deal. And then the light bulb went off. The hot lesbian love scenes last night weren't just for me. Karen and Isabella really enjoyed them. It was not a first time thing for them to be together like that. Suddenly, I felt like I was an intruder.

I shouldn't have asked the question but I did. I couldn't help myself. And wondering about it was killing me. "So, are you glad I was with you last night or would you..." Isabella finished my sentence. "Preferred to have been alone. Just the two of us?" she asked. "Yes" I said. "It was fine. It makes Karen happy to mix it up now and then." I looked over to Karen. She just smirked. "Just don't make it a habit" Isabella said. "I wouldn't dream of it" I said. "But since you two lovely ladies are already here..." I leaned over and kissed Karen. Things soon heated up again. With a little persuading, eventually, Isabella even joined in.

And then fire began to rain from the skies. Black smoke blocked out the sun. Loud, thunderous, explosions were heard everywhere. The farm was under attack. As upset as I was that Isabella had stopped right in the middle of the wonderful thing she was doing to me, I slowly began to grasp what was happening. I joined Isabella at the window and saw the main house on fire. Seconds later, we saw something. Maybe. I'm not even sure we saw it, really. But it must have been a missile. The entire farmhouse went from house on fire to house no more. There was nothing left. Nothing at all.

"The shed!" Karen said. She took off out the front door without a stitch of clothing on. Isabella followed, seconds later. I stood there a second not sure what to do. My mind was made up by a thunderous blast. Everything fell from the walls. Dishes crashed down. Glass broke. It felt like the ground was opening up. I ran out after Karen and Isabella. Then I saw what the blast was. The pig pen/laboratory had been decimated. Like the farmhouse, there was nothing left of it. "Come on!"

Karen shouted back at me. "Move!" She had no need to encourage me by that point. I was already running. I waited for another blast. There wasn't any. But I kept running. I saw Karen and Isabella go over a ridge and I lost sight of them for a moment. I could have decided not to follow them, but I didn't see any better options. Waiting around for the next missile to strike didn't seem like a real good idea.

As an example of how panicked I was, let me point out some things. I was completely naked and didn't care. I didn't care in terms of modesty, obviously. Letting people check out the goods versus being dead didn't seem like much of a contest. But, more importantly, let me tell you that running through fields with gravel and high grass is not a good time without clothes on. Little cuts and bruises occurred in all sorts of places better left unscathed. But none of that even crossed my mind at the time. Only escaping. Only catching up with Isabella and Karen.

I reached the ridge and saw them again. They were running through an orchard. Two naked chicks running through an orchard and I wasn't excited by it in the least. I hope that I am making myself clear, here. There was nothing erotic about any of this. Even for me. Which is hard to do when you're talking about two beautiful women running around in front of you. But I was far too terrified to care. Especially, when bullets started to mulch the ground just feet away from me.

Dirt, grass and rocks flew into my face. I just kept running. I looked behind me expecting to see a helicopter or something. There was nothing there. It was probably a gunship of some sort, too high up to see. Or maybe a drone. I couldn't tell. I didn't matter. Nothing mattered but catching up with the girls and getting out of there.

More bullets. More dirt. I wiped it away from my eyes just in time to see that Karen and Isabella were dealing with the same thing. I could see two lines of gunfire on either side of them. A little runway of death for them to run through. They knelt down just as one of the lines moved within inches of them. I noticed that Karen held herself over Isabella. Something that would have been very touching if I hadn't been so busy trying not to get killed.

I was tired, and cut up, and bruised but somehow kept running. Another hail of gunfire from the sky. This one hit the trees beside me. As grateful as I was that it was the trees that made the ultimate sacrifice, and not me, I could have done without the apples hurling into my head. I had no idea being hit with a piece of fruit could hurt so much. But somehow, I muscled through.

I looked for Isabella and Karen and didn't see them. Had they been mulched? I scanned ahead more carefully as I subconsciously counted how long it would be until another round of bullets flew toward me. And then I saw them. The girls were entering a small building the size of a garage. Not a public, city-center garage. The kind that used to be built separate from the house with two doors you had to open by yourself without a clicker.

That fucker in the sky started up again. The bullets. Thousands of them a second. So close. So very close to cutting me in two. But I made it. I made it into the shed. Which, as it turned out, didn't matter much. The bullets ripped into the wall and tore it apart. I leapt to my right just in time to get out of their way as they cut a perfectly straight line into the roof.

I had landed badly. I landed on my right arm and hurt it somehow. Probably not broken or anything. But painful enough. As I lay on the ground inspecting the damage, I saw Isabella climbing into an old SUV parked in the middle of the garage. She started it. What Karen was doing was more of a mystery. She was crouched over a small refrigerator grabbing a beer. A cheap, nasty beer at that. As much as I liked beer, it didn't seem the time for such things. And then my brain made more sense out of what I was seeing. Karen was moving a six pack of cheap beer and pulling out a small box behind it. "Got it!" she yelled. Isabella turned the key and started the SUV. Exhaust fumes filled the room.

Karen opened the door truck door and then stared at me. She wasn't going to leave me here, was she? That just wouldn't be right after all we had been through and all the bodily fluids we had shared. "Get in, Idiot!" she yelled. As insulted as I was by the name calling, I scrambled into the back of the SUV. By the time Karen climbed into the passenger seat, Isabella was already driving off.

The truck easily plowed through the doors on the side of the structure. We were on a dirt road on the far side of the farm. Other than the noise of the speeding truck, there were no other sounds. Which was creeping me out. A lot. I had just seen two buildings and all the people inside of them turned to ash. I had just fled gunfire so powerful it changed the terrain around me. Bullets that I had never once been able to see where they were coming from. The whole thing was just not fair. If people were going to kill me, I should at least have the right to see them.

"It's fine" Karen said. She had opened the box and was looking at something in it. "The bio-agent is fine." Isabella kept speeding along. I was worried she was going to hit a curve too fast and we would flip over. Very worried. "There's some clothes behind you" Karen said. She kept looking at the test tube to make sure it hadn't cracked or the seal hadn't been broken. "Get the clothes" Karen said. It finally clicked that she was talking to me. I reached back and felt a pile of sweatshirts. No pants or anything. Just sweatshirts. I gave her one and put one on myself. Isabella was too busy trying to kill us by flipping the SUV to have her hands free. She would just have to die naked, I guess.

"Didn't they just release the bio-agent from the lab into the air? Isabella asked. "The heat destroyed it" Karen responded.

"Then lets release that one, right now, before..." Karen shook her head. "We're too far out from the city. I'm not going to risk the infection stalling out." "Clarity for all!" Isabella chanted. "That's right, clarity for all" Karen said. She leaned over and kissed Isabella on the top of the head. Isabella slowed down to a more reasonable speed. "Are you alright?" Karen asked. "Fine" I said. "I actually meant Isabella. Isabella, are you hurt at all?" Karen asked. "No, I'm fine." Everyone seemed to calm down a little. We had escaped. For now.

"Where are we going?" Isabella asked. "Drive to Bethany Way and then cut over to the Four" "Won't they find us?" Isabella answered. "No, I don't think so. But I don't know. You have any better ideas?" she asked. "Not really" Isabella replied. Apparently I wasn't worth asking. Which was a bit of a slight. But it was their show. "I'm freezing. Could you hand me a sweatshirt, Dan?" Isabella asked. I did. I grabbed her the smallest of the two left. It was still several sizes too large for her. As I turned around to hand it to her, I thought that I saw a look exchanged between Isabella and Karen. Not a "Oh, how I love you" look. A look that they had shared something they didn't want me to know about it. I told myself I was being paranoid and let it go. Which, of course, proved to be a very stupid mistake.

Isabella slowed the car down and pulled over. "I just want to put this on without killing us" she said. She took the sweatshirt from me. She held it in a way that, for a moment, I couldn't see Karen. A moment in which she seemed to have obtained a gun. Which she then pointed at me. "Don't move" she said. Isabella stopped the car. "What are you doing?" I asked. "Just shut up and keep your hands where I can see them" she said. I did as asked. Or, more accurately, I did as ordered by a super-hot woman, near my age, wearing a red, National University sweatshirt, with no pants on, who had a look in her eye that made me certain that she was nuts. Not like I hadn't already figured that out.

The car stopped. Isabella got out and walked around to the passenger side. Karen kept her finger far too tightly on the trigger. "Get out!" she said. "What's going on?" I asked. "Just get out" I did. And for some reason, I even made a ridiculous attempt to cover my privates. It's one thing sharing with a woman, or two, in the context of sex. Quite another in the context of one of them holding a gun on you. "Walk into the woods" she said. I was not liking the tone of Karen's voice. It was not reassuring to me that things were going to turn out well. Not in the least.

I walked into the woods and tip toed as best I could, so as not to cut up my feet more. What I would have given for a pair of shoes, right then. They walked me out a few hundred yards into a small clearing. The sun was shining brightly through the little gap in the trees. It would have seemed very pretty in a different context. A context that wasn't related to my last few minutes alive. Isabella stood next to Karen. She glared at me. The two of them really were a stunning couple.

"Why did you do it?" Karen asked. "Do?" I asked. "Why did you turn us into the government? They're not your friends, Dan. They're not anybody's friends." "We tried to help you and you betrayed us. Pig!" Isabella added. "Why did you do it, Dan? Why?" Karen asked. "I didn't" I said. They weren't buying it. "I left you alone for three hours. The very next morning there's a missile strike on us. How do you explain that?" she asked. "They found you. It happens. They have spy satellites and all sorts of things watching everyone. They probably saw the smoke the other day from..." "He's lying!" Isabella yelled, adamantly. She was being quite the bitch, honestly. More worrisome was that Karen seemed to concur.

I continued to protest. "I'm not. I swear. Like you said, the government wants me dead as much as you guys. I pissed off some really powerful people. You know that." Karen nodded. "He's lying! Shoot him!" Isabella yelled again. I was really beginning to hate her. Long, lean, perfectly toned legs, aside, she was really getting on my nerves. "No, I'm not lying. I'm telling you the truth. I did not report you to anyone." I said. "Prove it" Isabella said. "How do I do that?" I asked. "I don't know. But you keep claiming you're innocent. Prove it." I racked my brain for how I could do that. The fact was, I had been alone for a while. And came from a secret police background. And had the talent and experience to be a highly successful double agent. I just hadn't chosen to go that route.

"See. He can't. He's guilty. Shoot him!" Isabella said. "I'm still not sure" Karen said. "I just don't think he's capable of that." "You don't think he would turn us in if it would benefit him? Come on" Isabella scoffed. "No, I mean, I really don't think he's got the skills required. He would have had to smuggle some sort of communications device in and to have contacted somebody. I'm just not seeing it." I almost objected and laid out the case how, obviously, I could have done exactly that, if I had wanted to. However, I realized silence was the smarter course of action even though my ego was being beaten to death before my eyes. "I'm just not seeing it" Karen said again. "Then how do you explain it?" Isabella asked. "Maybe it's like he said. Maybe a satellite picked up the smoke from the burning. Maybe it was just coincidence" Karen said.

"We can't take that chance. Just shoot him, already. We have to get out of here." Oh, how I wanted to smack Isabella right then. When did she decide that she hated me so much. I thought we had been getting along, really, really well. What had I done to deserve such rage? "Just shoot him already" she said. How could she say that after all the nice things I had done for her? I had made a real effort to keep her happy. At least, in some ways. What an ungrateful brat.

Karen moved a little bit closer to me. "Dan, did you do it? Did you turn us in and give them our location?" she asked. I looked her right in those beautiful, brown eyes of hers. "No" I said, and left it at that. And then a horrible span of time passed where Karen decided what she would do. It was probably only a second or two but it felt like eternity. Innocent or guilty? It all came down to that little window of time in which she decided. She put the gun down. "Alright. I believe you." "He's lying. Shoot him. Shoot him!" Isabella yelled. And then her head exploded.

A bullet had blown her away. "They're here!" a way too well armed Anti-Terror Squad member yelled to his unseen buddies. Karen shot him. A perfectly aimed shot through his goggles. Why was he even wearing goggles? Anyway, she killed him. And the one right behind him. Man, she was good with a gun.

Karen looked down at Isabella lying on the ground. Her expression was blank. Total incomprehension. I could hear the other agents closing in. I walked over to Karen. I took the gun from her. She didn't resist. I whispered. "Karen, we have to go. You can't bring her back. Let's go." Karen was totally out of it. Losing Isabella was too much for her to make any sense out of, right then. Not that she could ever make sense out of something like that. But I held the gun in my right hand and grabbed Karen's hand with my left. I lead her deeper into the forest. "Wait" she said. She broke free and ran back to the truck. I saw more well armed men heading right toward her. She got into the passenger's side and grabbed something. The vile. She had run back to get the bio-agent. Shots pelted the truck. She managed to escape and head back toward me, vile in her hand. Still intact. Still sealed.

As we started running again, I heard a familiar voice back near Isabella's body. "Looks like we got one of them. Is that the leader?" the voice asked. The voice I had listened to almost every day for years. The voice that had both praised me and chastised me. The voice of Superintendent Kim. What happened to the middle of next month? I guess after Windsor's death, his move to Anti-Terror was more pressing. "No, that's Isabella. Not Karen" a male voice responded. "I know that voice" Karen said. I tried to figure out how she could have known Kim's voice. Maybe she had been interrogated by him at some point. "Kim's?" I said. "What? No, Dale's." Keep in mind, we were running half-naked through the woods, had armed men after us, and had just seen a young woman shot in the head. Confusion was understandable under those conditions. "It's Dale. I will never forgive him. Ever." "Who's Dale?" I repeated. "One of us. He was at the meeting and asked the question. The one about penetration rates. He betrayed us." I knew it. Anybody that used the word "penetration" in a non-sports or non-sexual context should never be trusted. Ever.

Needless to say, we got away. The woods were dense enough and lush enough that it wasn't all that hard to hide from the security forces as they searched the area. The trees were even thick enough to protect us from helicopters and spy satellites. Mosquitoes, however, were quite another thing. I would highly recommend a full set of warm clothes that covers everything to anyone planning to spend a night in the woods. It was brutal.

After one of the more miserable nights of my existence, Karen and I formed a new plan. Other than our sweatshirts, we didn't have any clothes and we didn't have any money. What we did have was a gun and a test tube, which, from all outside appearances, was completely empty. And a whole lot of scratches, bruises and bug bites in places one should never, ever, get such things. So, we decided that our first priority was getting out of the woods. Which, honestly was our second priority behind keeping the security forces, dogs, search teams, etc. from finding us. But still, we agreed that we had to get out of the forest as quickly as we could.

Secondly, we needed to get some clothes and some money. The idea was to find a convenience store or gas station and rob it. Of course, only partially dressed as we were, the media would have a field day. "BARE-ASSED BANDITS! PANTLESS PROVOCATEURS! NAKED AGGRESSION! Aside from being humiliating and to be remembered for all time as such a thing, there was another problem. Everyone in the world would watch that surveillance camera footage and see photos of us. Given the circumstances, and our remarkably good looks, we would become media sensations. All of which would make it much harder to remain unidentified. But, considering our other options, it was still the best plan we could formulate.

We found our way out of the forest sometime the next morning. Without the cover of darkness and the canopy of trees overhead, we had to be very careful not to be seen. Given that we were exhausted, cold, thirsty and hungry, not to mention, being pursued by people that wanted to kill us, it really wasn't a fun time. Luckily, however, we found a convenience store, just like we had discussed. And it was open, even on an early Sunday morning.

As Karen was looking over the gun to check how many bullets she had left (about half a clip), I spotted something else. There was a donation bin on the side of the building. A donation bin probably full of clothes. We waited a minute to make sure nobody else was around. Then we dug in. There was no underwear in the bin. But along with the old toys, broken lamps and the other crap people had tossed in there, we found what we needed. Never had putting on a pair of pants felt so good. Ever. And having shoes again...even shoes nowhere near fitting right...Oh, what a practical, wonderful thing, shoes. A life without shoes is a life of misery. I know.

As I waited for Karen to find her own new wardrobe, I noticed the writing on the side of the bin. It was St. Luke's Mission. It was one of Father Mike's competitors, if missions had such things. And it made me wonder about Father Mike and what had happened to him. Not the "losing his faith" kind of what happened to him. Just, was he safe? I assumed that he had been off of the farm still and not there during the attack. Which seemed in hindsight rather convenient. Maybe a bit too much so.

"You don't think it was Father Mike, do you?" I asked Karen. "Was what, Father Mike?" Karen asked. "The person that gave your location away." Karen thought about it a second. "You mean, along with Dale?" she asked. "Yeah." She didn't reply for a minute as she tried on a better fitting pair of pants. Finally, she answered. "No, I don't" she said. "How can you be sure? Father Mike believed in everything you want to destroy. He would do anything to protect it" I said. "But he didn't. He came around to our point of view" "How can you be so certain?" I pressed. She zipped up her pants. "Some things you just know. You know?" she said. I nodded. I didn't want to argue with her too much, given that she had used similar gut instincts to keep me from getting shot.

And then we robbed the convenience store. Thinking back, it would have made sense to get a second change of clothes out of the bin for our escape. But we were so cold and tired and so on, we really weren't thinking all that straight. We were, at least, smart enough to tie t-shirts around our faces to mask our identities. Not that Kim and his new Anti-Terror gang wouldn't put it together right away, regardless. The kid at the cash register was very co-operative. He wasn't about to risk getting shot for the eight-fifty an hour, or whatever, he was getting. It all went very smoothly. The downside was that there was only about a hundred-and-twenty dollars in cash in the register. Given that the government strongly advised, much easier to track and trace, electronic fund transfers, we were lucky to even get that.

We also got the keys to a car. The kid's. A fourteen year old beater. THAT, he was a bit upset about. But he got over it when Karen pressed the gun right up to his head. The car was filthy and had garbage all over the backseat. It also smelled moldy. Had the kid left his windows open during the rain? But it ran. Barely. So, Karen carefully drove us along back roads back toward the city. I expected to be on the road for hours but Karen had other ideas. "We can't afford to be on the road during daylight" she said. A valid enough point. So, we did something that, honestly, I thought was pretty dumb. And I said so, at the time, but lost out. We checked into a roadside motel.

"The White Dove Inn" was called "The Love Dove" by anyone who knew it. Karen explained to me that it was the sort of place that had "day use rates" by the hour and was very disinterested about who was there or why. As long as they could pony up twenty dollars an hour (three hour minimum), they were all good. So, Karen walked in, went right up to the front desk, and got us a room.

As unbelievable as it might sound, I was not remotely interested in having sex with Karen. I was exhausted and distracted by everything else happening. Karen was even worse. Isabella had died. She was not in good shape. "I have to pee" she said. I did too, which was why I was so annoyed when, instead of coming right out, Karen turned on the shower. I thought about knocking and insisting before she stepped in. But Karen was going through something I could relate to all too well. It wasn't very long ago that Anna and Boratch were taken from me. Not very long ago at all.

Karen took an annoyingly long shower. When she finally came out, in just a towel, I barely noticed how monumental her breasts were and ran into the bathroom. After relieving myself properly, I took a shower. Much like putting on pants and shoes, hot water reached a new level of appreciation for me that day. It felt so good. So amazingly good.

I put my clothes on and walked back out to the room. Karen, now dressed in a shirt and panties, was lying on the bed. She was staring at the test tube. "What are you thinking?" I asked. She smiled. Not a smile, smile. A sad smile. A horrible, she was crushed inside, kind of smile. "I can't do this" she said. She pointed to the tube. "I'm too frightened. Part of me knows how many others sacrificed themselves for this and that those sacrifices would be for nothing but..." "So, don't" I said. "Just like that? Don't?" she replied. "Yeah. If you don't want to keep to the original plan, don't. I think that's pretty understandable given what's happened. She just looked at me.

Honestly, I was shocked how this woman obsessed with "clarity" and bringing down the old way of things could give up so easily. All those speeches. All those stunts. All those people she recruited. It seemed to be what her entire life was about. Something that she would do no matter what the cost. No matter what the sacrifice. But, obviously, I was wrong. Very wrong. Karen was a big talker. But when it came to crunch time. She was a coward. A total coward that wanted to disavow all she had said and all that she claimed she was meant to do. And I hated her for it. It made me sick inside. But I couldn't let any of it show. Not then. Not yet.

I knew that Karen needed me to tell her what she wanted to hear. So, I did. Better to just be done with her than to have someone so wishy-washy involved. "You don't need to do anything. It's over. Go on with your life. Be happy. You deserve that. Nobody would resent you doing that. They would do exactly the same thing." "Sometimes I wonder if I have the right, you know?" she asked. "Of course, I know. Just think about what you're doing. Really stop for a second, and just think about the implications if your plan succeeded" I said.

And then her brain started churning out a thousand reasons why she should stop. The thousand reasons she needed before she would feel Ok aborting her plan. She started giving me explanations as to why she had to give up. All the rationalizations. "Just imagine the chaos that would ensue. Thousands of years of civilizations built around organized religions would instantly crumble. Just imagine the chaos." I didn't say anything and let her keep going. Which she did for a while before finally feeling like she had convinced herself.

"So, that's it? We just leave it here? Or destroy it or something? All that work? All those lives? For nothing?" she asked. "Yeah" I said. "What about you? Don't you care, one way or the other?" she asked. "It was never my plan" I said. Never had a truer statement been uttered from my mouth. Karen returned to looking at the tube. "I just want to be done with all this and have a normal life. That's not really asking for so much, is it?" she asked. "No, it's not. Quit beating yourself up over it. You've already made your decision and you know it." She looked back over to me. "I have, haven't I?" she said.

She put the tube aside and inched her way up the bed. I was filled with disgust and loathing for her. So weak. So very, very weak. So ugly on the inside but so very, very attractive on the outside. Those bare legs. That shirt just waiting to be ripped off...I climbed on top of her and took her. She resisted at first. Sex was the last thing she felt like doing, right then. I knew she wanted to just be left alone. But I didn't care. And, after a while, either did she. She was surprised by my aggression and determination to do as I wanted with her. So was I, actually. But, given the way she, eventually, reacted, it was exactly what she needed. A strong, determined hand to guide her. Like all of them, she wanted nothing more than to be commanded and forced to obey. It was what they craved. It was what they required. Such has been the way of things since the beginning of time. Humans were such pathetic and ridiculous creatures.

I had no difficulties with the police while walking through the heart of the city. I had robbed one of the finest tailors in the Capitol and was looking accordingly impressive. I wore a black pinstripe suit, white shirt and a silk, grey tie. However, the shoes I wore were still the ones from the charity bin. I appreciated the irony.

I had left Karen alone in the hotel room. When she asked questions, I told her that it was better, for her sake, that I didn't answer. Ignorance was my gift to her. She had, after all, been a big part of things. Not to mention, a lovely bedmate. I was almost astounded how intimately I had come to know her in the three days since we had first slept together. It felt like a lifetime. One filled with sadness and risk but one also filled with spectacular pleasure and intensity. Given the state she was in, Karen didn't press the issue of my leaving her too hard. She already had enough on her mind. I assumed she would find a way to escape and get on with her life just as she had talked about. A nice, normal, boring, everyday life. I, on the other hand, had a different fate in store.

I arrived at Cloud just in time for our late brunch reservation. The place was packed. The server was highly sympathetic when I told him my expected breakfast companion wasn't feeling well and wouldn't be making it. It wasn't a problem at all. I sat at the table feeling quite comfortable, even though I was the only one eating alone in the entire place. The table was covered in a fine white linen cloth and the plates were all white with tasteful gold trim. And the view was exceptional. Not quite as lovely as the view that morning of Isabella and Karen both in bed with me but up there. For one thing, I could practically see the entire city. I could see the office towers. I could see the apartment complexes. I could see the factories and the churches. So many churches. Many of them were far better architecture than St. Anthony's Cathedral which, by the way, was almost directly in front of me.

I ordered eggs, over-easy, with hash browns, bacon and white toast. I also ordered a side of ham. The coffee was just right. Not too bitter and burnt tasting but full of flavor and body. I understood how Cloud could get away with charging forty bucks for breakfast. Well, almost. It still seemed like a rip-off considering the meal would cost about six dollars to make at home. But whatever. The food was done to perfection.

The service was spot on. And the setting, with its vistas, spectacular.

Given what I was about to do, I wasn't the least bit nervous. Why should I have been? In fact, I took my time and indulged in the moment. I had several cups of coffee and just stared at the city below. All the people. All the commotion as the Cardinal's limo pulled up to the Cathedral. Even from up where I was, I could see the crowds gathered and treating him like a movie star. What morons.

I settled the check about forty-five minutes later using my share of the money left from the convenience store robbery. That, and a little more added from the tailor's. I had no idea those places kept so much cash on hand. I guess rich people just liked the idea of paying in cash. Better for tax time and all that. I left a generous twenty percent tip and then headed to the emergency exit. A young-looking waiter stopped me. He looked all of twenty years old. "I'm sorry, you can't go out that way. The exit is behind you" he said. I looked at him and realized that this one little punk could decide events far beyond his feeble brain's understanding. It all depended on the way he reacted next.

I flashed my People's Protection ID card. "Official Agency Business. I need to check the roof for security purposes" I said. He looked at the card very carefully. Normally people just glanced at it and assumed that it was real. But he really took his time and matched the photo to my face and everything.

"Maybe I should call the Manager" he said. "Or maybe you should quit interfering with government business and step out of my way" I replied. That got him. He moved aside and watched as I opened the door and started to make my way up the stairs. So much for saving the world, Kid.

The roof was cold and windy. But not too windy. It was just as Karen and the Clear Thinkers had said. A wind blowing directly from the tower over the cathedral and out over the rest of the city. I took the vile from my pocket and walked toward the side of the tower. The roof had no railing. Just a lot of equipment and spouts and so forth. I stood silently for a moment.

I stared out over the city once more, before it would all be changed forever. All the people. All their little lives with their petty hopes and dreams. What people wouldn't do for a little money or power. Turn against their friends. Hurt others. Lie to their loved ones. But there was beauty too. Even I could see that. The farm. Karen. The way Karen and Isabella held each other. Anna. Anna who never loved me and never would.

I held the test tube firmly as I started to open it. The seal was broken and the bio-agent was released into the wind. A thousand lives would be changed in minutes. And a thousand more after that. And so on, and so on, until the brain chemicals were inert in all. Then it would be gone. Then HE would be gone.

Unlike Karen, I had done what needed to be done, regardless of what it had cost me. And it cost me more than you could ever understand. I had gone through life exiled, first to hell and then to a place even more despairing. Earth. A place where I was further mistreated and disrespected. A place where I remained forever underappreciated and unloved. There is no greater torment than to be human. But it had to be. It always had to be. The Church had it wrong. So did the Clear Thinkers. There is a God. Or was. And I, Daniel Lucifer Hastings, had been part of his plan, all along. So, who's your Daddy now, bitches?

Kevin Leicinger is the author of BRIGHT SHADOWS, DOGS IN THE DISTANCE, CHRISTINA and several other novels. He lives in Los Angeles with his dog Winston.